U0025346

彩圖實境 旅遊英語

Traveling With English

暢銷彩圖三版

熱銷兩萬本，學校熱門指定用書

P. Walsh◎著
丁宥榆／賴祖兒◎譯
Helen Yeh◎審訂

目錄

前言

學英語最怕憑空想像。讀者一定有過這種經驗：空有一堆字彙，真正到了國外，畫面卻與字彙搭不起來，依然什麼都看不懂，什麼都說不出口。正所謂「百聞不如一見」，本書創新採用大量實景照片來介紹字彙，以視覺輔助記憶，不僅學來輕鬆，印象也特別深刻，不易遺忘。**暢銷彩圖三版**新增更多**彩圖圖解**，並因應現今旅遊趨勢補充**最新的旅遊資訊**，讓你用彩圖實境輕鬆學會旅遊英語。

在出遊前，可以先利用本書身歷其境，預習旅遊途中可能碰到的情境；出遊時，可將本書當作隨身手冊參考、隨翻隨查。本書共23個章節，涵蓋**機場**、**交通**、**住宿**、**購物**等重要旅遊主題，依照一般出國行程排列，貼近實際使用習慣。不論跟團、自助旅行，本書都是您不可或缺的好幫手。

Part ① Key Terms 關鍵詞彙

彩圖實境連結單字，加強記憶

靠「圖像」背單字，絕對比憑空死背有效。本書精選旅遊常用詞彙，依據最新旅遊趨勢新增實用必備單字，輔以大量的彩圖照片，具體呈現單字代表的意義，幫助加強吸收與記憶。

PART 1 Key Terms

① overhead compartment 頭頂置物艙
④ aisle 走道
② window seat 靠窗座位
⑤ middle seat 中間的座位
③ aisle seat 靠走道的座位
⑥ flight attendant 空服員
⑦ crew 機組人員
⑪ buckle 扣帶
⑧ captain 機長
⑨ airsickness bag 嘔吐袋
⑩ seat belt 安全帶

32

PART 2 Conversations

01 Where to, Madam? 女士，要去哪裡？

D Driver 司機　P Peggy 珮琪

D Where to, madam?
P Grand Central Station, please. I want to catch a 6 p.m. train.
D I think you'll make it if we don't get stuck in a traffic jam.
[After a while]
D Here is Grand Central Station.
P Thank you. How much is the fare?
D The meter reads $9.15.
P Here you are. Keep the change.
D Thank you.

D 女士，要去哪裡？
P 請到中央車站，我要趕晚上6點的火車。
D 如果不塞車的話，應該趕得上。
[過了一會兒]
D 中央車站到了。
P 謝謝，多少錢？
D 9.15美元
P 這裡，不用找了。
D 謝謝。

76

Part ② Conversations 會話

依情境編寫旅遊對話，現學現用

本書依據主題情境，編寫旅遊常見對話，新版並新增如行動支付、叫車APP等現今常見主題，透過簡單的會話練習，輕鬆瞭解實際旅遊情境，學會應對與表達。

Part ❸ Useful Expressions 實用句型

豐富詳盡的實用句型，隨找隨用

旅遊時可能遇到的情境非常多，僅有會話難以囊括所有的表達與應答方式，本書依主題再細分成各種情境，精編實用句型並列以關鍵字檢索，在旅遊時可輕鬆查找索引、靈活運用。

PART 3 Useful Expressions

Chap. 1 搭飛機旅行：在機場

01 Asking About Flight Schedules and Booking a Flight
詢問航班時間與訂機票

航班時間

1 Are there any planes to Boston on Sunday?
星期天有去波士頓的班機嗎？

2 Ⓐ How often is there a flight to Paris?
去巴黎的航班多久一班？
Ⓑ We have flights to Paris every hour.
我們每小時都有去巴黎的航班。

3 At what time does the next plane to London leave?
下一班去倫敦的飛機幾點起飛？

4 Ⓐ What's the next one after that? 在那之後是哪一班？
Ⓑ The next one is flight 10 at 10:45.
下一班飛機是10點45分起飛的10號航班。

飛行時間

5 Ⓐ How long is the flight from New York to Washington?
從紐約到華盛頓要飛多久？
Ⓑ Well, supposedly one hour, but it's sometimes longer.
嗯，大概需要一小時，但有時候會久一點。

訂機票

6 Ⓐ I'd like to make a reservation to Chicago for tomorrow.
我想預訂明天飛往芝加哥的機票。
Ⓑ I can give you a reservation on that.
我可以幫您訂該航班的座位。

再確認機位

7 Ⓐ Do I have to reconfirm?
我需要再確認機位嗎？
Ⓑ You must make a reconfirmation 72 hours ahead.
您必須提前72小時確認機位。

PART 3 USEFUL EXPRESSIONS

15

索引專用關鍵字

匯整同一情境句型，加上索引關鍵字更易查找。

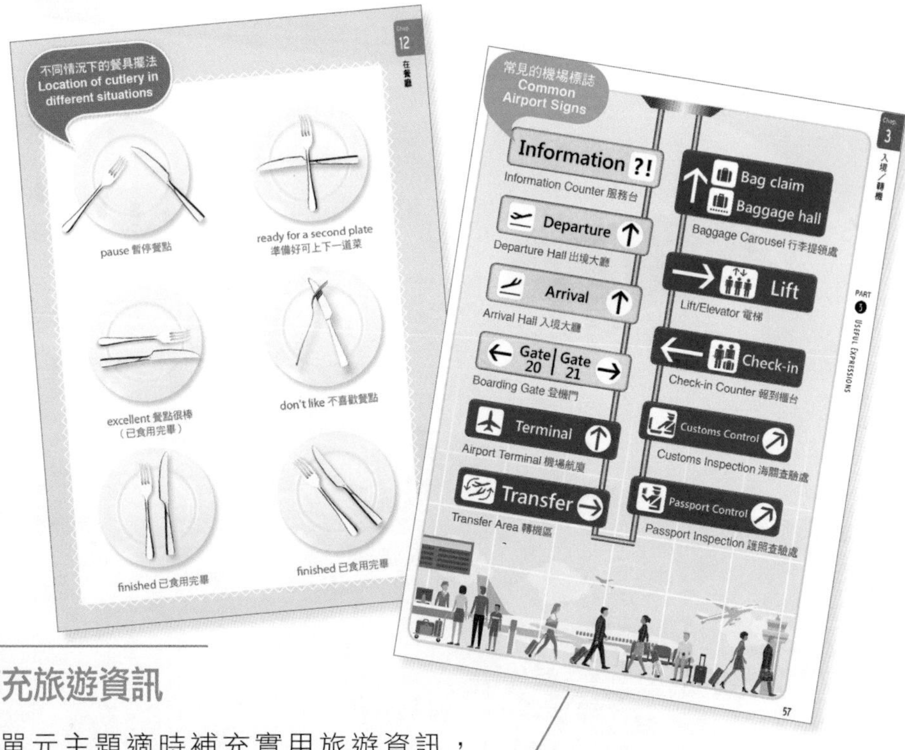

補充旅遊資訊

依單元主題適時補充實用旅遊資訊，搭配圖解，如出境流程、用餐禮儀等，各種場合都能駕輕就熟。

At the Airport

Chapter 1

搭飛機旅行：在機場

PART 1

Key Terms

① **airport** 機場

② **check-in counter** 登機櫃檯

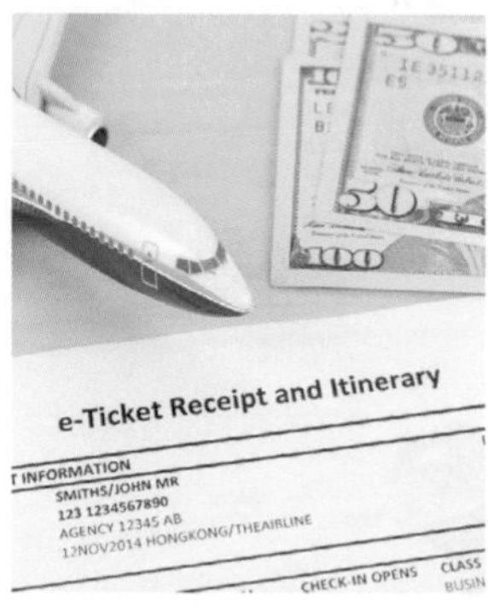

③ **e-ticket** 電子機票

④ **passport** 護照

⑤ **visa** 簽證

⑥ **boarding pass** 登機證

⑦ **luggage cart/trolley** 行李推車

002

8 **airline** 航空公司

9 **scale** 磅秤

10 **morning flight** 早班飛機

11 **night flight** 晚班飛機

DEPARTURES

Time	Destination	Flight
19:30	BEIJING	R4 4509
19:30	ATLANTA	EB 7134
19:45	LONDON	DN 0045
19:40	NEW YORK	OD 7158
19:50	FRANKFURT	NP 6890
20:05	DUBAI	UC 1207
20:10	CHICAGO	EB 3436
20:20	TOKYO	R4 4581
20:45	PARIS	NP 1976

12 **departure board**
起飛時刻表

13 **security gate** 安全門

14 **moving walkway**
電動步道

⑮ **duty free shop** 免稅商店

⑯ **(departure) gate** 登機門

⑰ **departure lounge** 候機室

⑱ **runway** 跑道

004

⑲ **fragile item** 易碎物品

⑳ **VIP lounge** 機場貴賓室

㉑ **carry-on luggage/bag** 隨身行李

㉒ **city map** 市區地圖

㉓ **book a ticket / make a reservation** 訂機票

㉔ **flight number** 航班編號

㉕ **check in** 辦理登記手續

㉖ **one-way ticket** (US) 單程票（美國）

㉗ **round-trip ticket** (US) 來回票（美國）

㉘ **single ticket** (UK) 單程票（英國）

㉙ **return ticket** (UK) 來回票（英國）

㉚ **open return (ticket)** 回程時間不定（機票）

㉛ **direct/nonstop flight** 直飛班機

㉜ **connecting flight** 轉接班機

㉝ **red-eye flight** 紅眼航班；夜間航班

㉞ **reconfirm the ticket** 再確認機位

㉟ **excess baggage** 超重行李

㊱ **baggage allowance** 行李限額

㊲ **baggage claim tag** 行李提領證

㊳ **departure** 起飛

㊴ **local time** 當地時間

㊵ **on time** 準時

㊶ **delay** 誤點

㊷ **cancel** 取消

㊸ **tourist information** 旅遊資訊

PART 2

Conversations

01 Making a Reservation 訂機票

005

R *Raymond* 雷蒙　G *Ground Staff* 地勤人員

R I'd like to make a reservation to Los Angeles for next Monday.

G Just a second and I'll check the schedule.

R I'll need an economy ticket with an open return.

G American Airlines has a flight leaving at 9:25 a.m.

R I guess that's OK. What time should I check in?

G You have to be there two hours before departure time.

R 我要預訂一張下禮拜一去洛杉磯的機票。

G 請稍等，讓我查一下時刻表。

R 我要經濟艙，回程時間不定的來回票。

G 美國航空公司有一架班機，在早上9點25分起飛。

R 這個可以，我應該什麼時候去辦理登機手續？

G 您要在飛機起飛前兩小時到達那裡。

AA AmericanAirlines

American Airlines 美國航空

02 Checking In 辦理登機手續 006

R *Raymond* 雷蒙　G *Ground Staff* 地勤人員

R I'd like to check in.

G May I have your ticket and passport, please?

R Here you are. I'd like a window seat.

G No problem. Put your baggage on the scale, please.

R All right.

G OK. Here's your ticket, boarding pass, passport and baggage claim tag. You'll be boarding at Gate 8. The boarding time is 9 a.m.

R Thank you very much.

R 我要辦理登機手續。

G 請給我您的機票和護照。

R 在這裡。我想要靠窗的座位。

G 沒問題。請把行李放在磅秤上。

R 好。

G 可以了。這是您的機票、登機證、護照和行李提領證。您的登機時間是早上9點，請由8號登機門登機。

R 非常謝謝你。

Going Through the E-gate 自動查驗通關 

H *Helen* 海倫 J *James* 詹姆斯

H Shouldn't we be going this way to passport control?

J Let's go through the e-gates.

H E-gates? I've never done that.

J Come on, I'll show you. It's easy. Lots of airports have them now.

H What do I need to do to go through an e-gate?

J Just let the machine scan your passport and then look at the monitor. At some airports, I think you need to leave your fingerprints.

H Sounds very convenient!

H 我們不是應該走這邊去護照查驗處嗎？

J 我們去走自動查驗通關吧。

H 自動查驗通關？我從來沒使用過。

J 來吧，我來教妳，這個很簡單，現在很多機場都有。

H 走自動查驗通關應該怎麼做呢？

J 只要讓機器掃描妳的護照，然後看向螢幕。
有些機場還需要留下妳的指紋紀錄。

H 聽起來好方便！

PART 3 Useful Expressions

01 Asking About Flight Schedules and Booking a Flight 詢問航班時間與訂機票 008

航班時間

1 Are there any planes to Boston on Sunday?
星期天有去波士頓的班機嗎？

2 A How often is there a flight to Paris?
去巴黎的航班多久一班？
B We have flights to Paris every hour.
我們每小時都有去巴黎的航班。

3 At what time does the next plane to London leave?
下一班去倫敦的飛機幾點起飛？

4 A What's the next one after that? 在那之後是哪一班？
B The next one is flight 10 at 10:45.
下一班飛機是10點45分起飛的10號航班。

飛行時間

5 A How long is the flight from New York to Washington?
從紐約到華盛頓要飛多久？
B Well, supposedly one hour, but it's sometimes longer.
嗯，大概需要一小時，但有時候會久一點。

訂機票

6 A I'd like to make a reservation to Chicago for tomorrow.
我想預訂明天飛往芝加哥的機票。
B I can give you a reservation on that.
我可以幫您訂該航班的座位。

再確認機位

7 A Do I have to reconfirm?
我需要再確認機位嗎？
B You must make a reconfirmation 72 hours ahead.
您必須提前72小時確認機位。

詢問票價

8 How much is the round trip? 來回票多少錢？

9 The one-way ticket from San Francisco to Boston is $500.
從舊金山到波士頓的單程票價為500美元。

直達班機

10 Ⓐ Are they non-stop flights? 它們是直達班機嗎？

Ⓑ Yes. Direct to Paris. 是的，這是直達巴黎的飛機。

11 Ⓐ Is that a direct flight? 請問是直飛的嗎？

Ⓑ That is not a direct flight. You need to transfer in Bangkok.
那不是直飛的班機，您要在曼谷轉機。

選擇艙等

12 I'd like to travel first-class, please. 我想要頭等艙。

02 Budget Airlines 廉價航空 

升級艙等

13 Ⓐ May I upgrade to first class?
我可以升等至頭等艙嗎？

Ⓑ I'm sorry. Only economy class seats are available on this flight.
很抱歉，此班班機只有經濟艙座位。

機上供餐與點心

14 Ⓐ Will you be serving a meal on this flight?
這班班機有供餐嗎？

Ⓑ As we're a budget airline, we don't serve free meals on our flights. 由於我們是廉價航空，所以機上不提供免費餐點。

15 Ⓐ Will there be complimentary drinks and snacks?
你們會提供免費的飲料和點心嗎？

Ⓑ Drinks and snacks are available, but you'll have to pay extra for them. 我們有提供飲料和點心，但需要額外付費。

03 Checking In 辦理登機手續 010

辦理登機時間

16 When am I supposed to check in?
我應該什麼時候辦理登機手續？

尋找報到櫃檯

17 Where is the check-in counter for China Airlines?
請問中華航空公司的報到櫃檯在哪裡？

18 A May I check in here for flight MU 562 to Tokyo?
飛東京的MU 562航班是在這裡辦理報到手續嗎？

B Yes, that's right. May I have your ticket and passport, please?
對，就是這裡。請出示您的機票和護照。

19 I would like to check in. 我要辦理報到。

付機場稅

20 Do I have to pay the airport tax? 我要付機場稅嗎？

選擇機上座位

21 An aisle seat, please. 我要靠走道的座位。

22 A I'd like a window seat. 我要靠窗的座位。

B I'm sorry, but there are no window seats available.
很抱歉，已經沒有靠窗的座位了。

要求坐在一起

23 Do you have any other seats open where we can sit together? 還有沒有其他連在一起的座位？

班機客滿	24 I'm afraid that all the flights are fully booked. 很抱歉，所有的班機都客滿了。
行李託運數量	25 Do you have any baggage to check in? 您有行李需要託運嗎？ 26 How many bags would you like to check in? 您有幾件行李需要託運？
行李過磅	27 Please put your bags on the scale. 請把您的行李放在秤上。
免費行李限重	28 What's the baggage allowance? 請問免費行李限額多少？
隨身行李	29 Can I carry this bag on? 我可以隨身攜帶這個包包嗎？

04 Customs Clearance and Boarding 通關安檢與登機

通過安檢門	30 Please walk through the security gate. 請通過安檢門。
要求打開包包	31 Please open your bag. We'd like to have a look. 請把您的包包打開，我們要檢查一下。
不可攜帶液體	32 Just make sure you don't have any liquid with you. 我只是要確定您沒有攜帶液體。
再次查驗行李	33 Test again. 行李再過一次X光機。
詢問登機時間	34 A When is the boarding time? 什麼時候可以登機？ B I'm afraid your flight is delayed. 您的班機可能誤點了。

開始登機廣播 35 May I have your attention, please. Thai Airlines flight TG 635 to Bangkok is now boarding. Passengers in the first class, please proceed to the boarding gate now.

各位旅客請注意，飛往曼谷的泰航TG635班機，已經開始登機，請頭等艙的旅客前往登機門。

班機延後廣播 36 Attention, please. Due to weather conditions, all flights to Taipei will be delayed. We truly regret the delay. Thank you for your cooperation and patience. We will inform you of the new departure time as soon as possible. Thank you.

各位旅客請注意，由於天候不佳，所有飛往台北的班機都將延後起飛。我們對此深表歉意，並感謝您的配合與耐心。我們將盡快通知您班機新的起飛時間，謝謝。

出境流程
Departure Procedures

第一次出國時，難免緊張興奮，甚至會不知該如何是好。
別擔心，只要跟著以下的流程走，一切簡單輕鬆！

1 櫃檯劃位 check-in counter

機場有兩個不同的大廳，分別是**出境大廳**（Departure Hall）及**入境大廳**（Arrival Hall）。出國時一定要前往出境大廳，到了那裡找到要搭乘的航空公司**劃位櫃檯**（check-in counter），即可辦理手續。有時不見得所有航空公司都有自己的劃位櫃檯，但無櫃檯的航空公司一定會委託另一家航空公司代為處理，這時只要看一下標示即可找到正確的櫃檯。一般説來，出國旅遊須在飛機起飛前兩個小時到達機場，所辦理之手續如下：

check-in counter 報到櫃檯

→ 核對證件：**機票或電子機票**（**ticket / e-ticket**）、**護照**（**passport**）、**簽證**（**visa**）

→ 託運行李：**過磅**（**weigh**）、檢查、發行李牌。行李若**超重**（**overweight**），則須支付**行李超重費**（**overweight charge; excess baggage charge**）。每家航空公司對**託運行李**（**checked baggage**）與**手提行李**（**carry-on baggage / hand baggage**）限制的件數與重量不盡相同，建議事先查好所搭乘的航空公司規定，以免在託運時才發現過重或超過件數。

weighing baggage 行李過磅

→選座位：各種座位的説法如下：

靠窗座位 **window seat**
走道座位 **aisle seat**
中間座位 **middle seat**

→領取登機證（boarding pass）：如果有託運行李，行李牌則一併交回，或是直接貼在機票上。登機證上會註明**班機號碼**（**flight number**）、**登機門**（**boarding gate**）、**座位號碼**（**seat number**），有時也會寫上**登機時間**（**boarding time**）。如果你是某航空公司的會員，或者已累積一定的哩程點數可以**升等**（**upgrade**），可於此時告知航空公司，請其查詢是否尚有機位可以升等。

boarding gate 登機門

另外，需依各機場的規定付**機場稅**（**airport tax; departure tax**）。有些國家如中國大陸及泰國等，不像國內的機場稅已於機票內含，都需要另付機場稅，請於出發前確認，否則到了當地機場時，身上沒有該國現金而付不了機場稅，這樣可是非常麻煩的喔。

departure stamp 出境章

2 查驗護照 passport inspection

將護照及登機證交付查驗，護照也會蓋上一個註明日期的**出境章**（**departure stamp**），表示已經出國囉！有時會問一兩個簡單的問題，如為何停留該國、接下來要去哪國之類的問題。

現在各國的國際機場也設置了**自動查驗通關系統**（**e-Gate**），只要事先完成自動通關申辦，以後在出入境時就能省去排隊的時間，加快通關速度。

e-Gate 自動查驗通關系統

台灣申辦自動查驗通關辦法：

■申辦資格：

1. 年滿 **14** 歲、身高 **140cm** 以上。
2. 未受禁止出國處分之有戶籍國民。

■申辦文件：護照、身分證（或駕照、健保卡）／居留證。

■申辦地點：機場、移民署服務站、外交部領事事務局（詳細地點請上網查閱）。

metal detector 金屬探測器

3 安全檢查 security inspection

在這裡又分為人走的「**金屬探測器**」（**metal detector**），及隨身行李和物品走的「**行李 X 光**」（**baggage X-ray**）兩項檢查裝置。

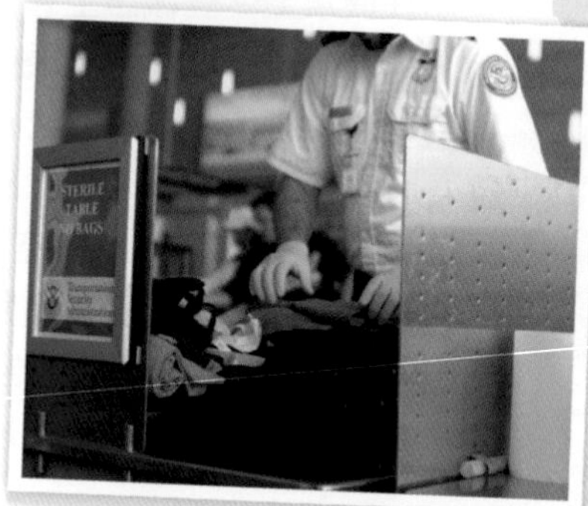
baggage X-ray 行李X光

4 進入登機門 boarding gate

憑著登機證找到正確的登機門，之後便可以在**候機室**（**lounge**）等候登機囉！這時如果時間充裕，還可以到**免稅商店**（**duty free shop**，簡稱 **DFS**）逛逛。切記！在免稅店買東西，一定要出示護照跟登機證才能購買喔！若是需要回國再提領，可以在提貨後向現場服務人員洽詢**寄物服務**（**baggage storage service**）。

lounge 候機室

5 登機 boarding

到了登機時間時，航空公司會開始廣播請大家登機；通常都是**商務艙**（**business class**）的旅客先登機，之後是老人或是有小孩的旅客，接著是**經濟艙**（**economy class**）的旅客按照機位前後，從後半段的乘客先登機。

duty free shop (DFS) 免稅商店

出境攜帶物品限制 Baggage Policy & Restrictions

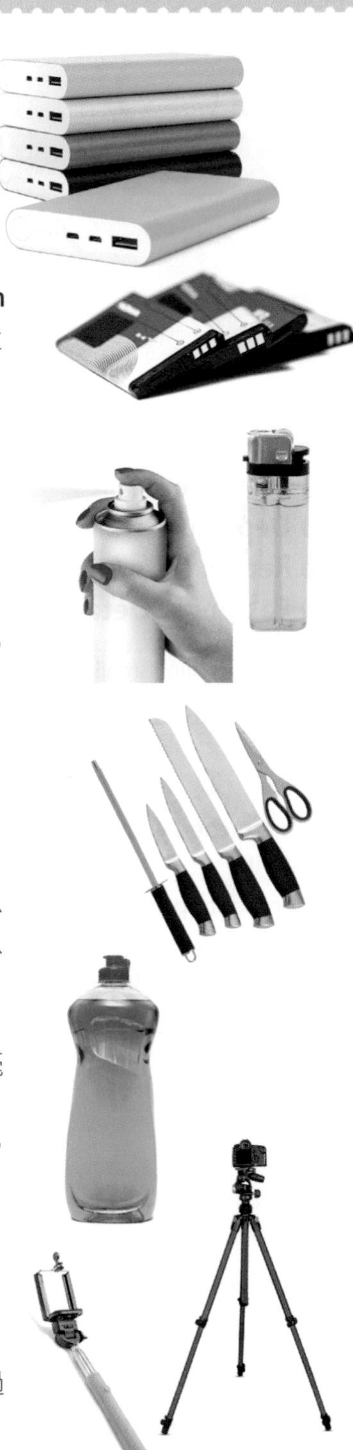

託運行李禁止品項 What NOT to pack in your checked baggage

- **行動電源（power bank）、鋰電池（lithium battery）／含有鋰電池的電子產品**：須放置隨身行李，因鋰電池在溫度與壓力變化劇烈的情況下，有膨脹甚至是起火爆炸的風險。

- **打火機（lighter）**：須隨身攜帶，且每人限帶一個傳統型打火機。

- **高壓式噴瓶（high pressure sprayer bottle）**：有些噴霧為高壓式噴瓶（如髮膠），在行李艙有爆炸的危險。

隨身行李禁止品項 What NOT to pack in your carry-on baggage

- **各式刀剪類或尖銳物品**：各種刀剪，如剪刀、美工刀、修眉刀、指甲剪等；或是如開罐器、圓規等鋒利物品，一律禁止攜帶上機。

- **超過 100 毫升的液體**：不得攜帶超過 100 毫升（100 c.c.）的液體上機（註：安全考量，因任何不超過 100 毫升的液體危害性極小），且所有裝有液體、膠狀或噴霧類的瓶罐須裝在不超過一公升（1000 c.c.）的可重複密封之透明夾鏈袋中。

- **收合後超過 60 公分的自拍桿（selfie stick）／超過 60 公分的腳架（tripod）**：管徑超過 1 公分、且長度超過 60 公分的自拍桿或腳架，因具有攻擊性也禁止攜帶上機。

線上訂機票 Booking Flight Tickets Online

1. **Leaving From** 出發地
2. **Going To** 目的地
3. **Departure Date** 出發日期
4. **Return Date** 回程日期
5. **Passenger Details** 旅客資料
6. **Class** 艙等
7. **One Way** 單程行程
8. **Round Trip** 來回行程
9. **Multi-City** 多航點行程

To: Olin@smail.com

Subject: Your booking confirmation 預訂確認

Hi Olivia, ⑩

We've attached your travel itinerary which has details of your flights, add-ons, and payment.

Remember to print a copy of the travel itinerary for your trip.

You can make changes to your booking up to 24 hours before departure. Just click on "Manage Your Booking" below to make changes.

Thanks for choosing Journey Airline.

Journey Airline

⑪ Booking Ref. M5XAAB

奧莉薇亞，您好：

隨信已附上您的行程資訊，包含了班機、附加項目以及付款細節等資料。
請記得在出發前影印一份行程資訊副本。
您最遲可在出發前 24 小時前修改您的預訂項目，只要點擊以下的「管理預訂」即可更改。
感謝您搭乘旅程航空。

旅程航空 敬上

10. **Booking Confirmation Email** 預訂確認信
11. **Booking Reference Number** 訂位代碼

電子機票1 E-ticket

Airlines

YOUR BOOKING NUMBER : WXIKXI ①

YOUR TICKET-ITINERARY

Flight ②	From ③	Time ⑦	To	Time	Aircraft ④	Class/Status ⑤ ⑥
WK 2200	Montreal-Trudeau (YUL) Thu May-04-2019	17:15	Frankfurt (FRA) Fri May-05-2019	06:30+1	333	Y Confirmed
WK 2495	Frankfurt (FRA) T1 Fri May-05-2019	07:50	Amsterdam (AMS) Fri May-05-2019	09:00	321	Y Confirmed
WK 2293	Munich (MUC) T2 Mon May-22-2019	15:30	Montreal-Trudeau (YUL) Mon May-22-2019	17:50	340	Y Confirmed

Passenger Name ⑧	Ticket Number ⑨	Frequent Flyer Number ⑩	Special Needs ⑪
(1) JONES, JOHN/MR.	012-3456-789012	000-123-456	Meal: VGML

Purchase Description ⑫	Price ⑬	
Fare (LLXSOAR, LLXGSOAR)	CAD	558.00
Canada - Airport Improvement Fee		15.00
Canada - Security Duty		17.00
Canada - GST #1234-5678		1.05
Canada - QST #12345-678-901		1.20
Germany - Airport Security Tax		18.38
Germany - Airport Service Fees		37.76
Fuel Surcharge		161.00
Total Base Fare (per passenger)		809.39
Number of Passengers		1
TOTAL FARE ⑭	CAD	809.39

Ticket is non-endorsable, non-refundable
Changes allowed, subject to availability,
no later than 2 hours before departure.
Please read carefully all fare restrictions.

Have a pleasant flight!

⑮ Paid by Credit Card XXXX-XXXX-XXXX-1234

(cc by Airodyssey)

1. **Booking Number** 預訂代碼
2. **Flight Number** 航班號碼
3. **From . . . To . . .** 出發地與目的地
4. **Aircraft Type** 班機型號
5. **Airline Class** 航班艙等
6. **Seat Status** 座位狀態
7. **Time** 出發時間
8. **Passenger Name** 旅客姓名
9. **Ticket Number** 機票號碼
10. **Frequent Flyer Number** 飛行常客號碼
11. **Special Needs** 特殊需求
12. **Purchase Description** 購買細節
13. **Price** 價格
14. **Total Fare** 總額
15. **Forms of Payment** 付款方式

電子機票2
E-Ticket

ELECTRONIC TICKET
PASSENGER ITINERARY/RECEIPT
CUSTOMER COPY

❶ Passenger:	LI, MEI-HUEI	❹ Ticket No:	0015704034215
❷ Booking Ref:	MFEGXF	❺ Issuing Airline:	AMERICAN AIRLINES, INC.
❸ Frequent Flyer No:		❻ Tour Code:	AATWAO

❼ DATE		❽ CITY/STOPOVER	❾ TIME	❿ FLY/CLS/ST	⓫ EQP/FLY TIME	⓬ FARE BASIS
15AUG	DEP	TAIPEI TAOYUAN, TPE TERMINAL 2	1000	JL802 ECONOMY (Y)	NON-STOP 788	YNE08YNO/ TW02
15AUG	ARR	TOKYO NARITA TERMINAL 2	1420	OK	03HR20MIN	
		⓭ OPERATED BY JAPAN AIRLINES/JAPAN AIRLINES INTERNATIONAL COMPANY LTD				
JAPAN AIRLINES REF:6FBQXK			SEAT:		NVA:15AUG17	BAG:2PC
15AUG	DEP	TOKYO NARITA TERMINAL 2	1830	AA60 ECONOMY (Y)	NON-STOP BOEING 777-200	YNE08YNO/ TW02
15AUG	ARR	DALLAS INTL TERMINAL D	1630	OK	12HR00MIN	
		⓮ OPERATED BY AMERICAN AIRLINES/AMERICAN AIRLINES, INC.				

❶ **Passenger Name 旅客姓名：**
拼法必須與護照姓名相同，否則無法登機，因此機票不可轉讓。

❷ **Booking Reference Number 預訂代碼**

❸ **Frequent Flyer Number 飛行常客號碼**

❹ **E-Ticket Number 電子機票號碼**

❺ **Issuing Airline 核發航空**

❻ **Tour Code 團體代號**：用於團體機票

❼ **Date 出發日期**

❽ **City/Stopover 出發與目的城市／中途停留**

❾ **Time 出發時間**

❿ **FLY (flight number) / CLS (class) / ST (status)**
航班號碼／艙等／狀態

⓫ **EQP (Equipment) / FLY Time (flying time) 班機型號／飛行時間**

⓬ **Fare Basis Code 票種代碼**

⓭ **The airline that takes passengers to the stopover**
載旅客前往中途停留點的航空公司

⓮ **The airline that takes passengers to the destination**
載旅客前往目的地的航空公司

登機證 Boarding Pass

1. **Name of Passenger** 旅客姓名
2. **From . . . to . . .** 出發地與目的地
3. **Flight Number** 班機號碼
4. **Class** 座艙等級
5. **Gate Number** 登機門號碼
6. **Boarding Time** 登機時間
7. **Seat Number** 座位號碼

班機出發時間表 Departure Board

1. **Departure Board**
   班機起飛時間表
2. **Take-Off Time** 起飛時間
3. **Destination** 目的地
4. **Airline Code** 航空代碼
5. **Flight Number** 班機號碼
6. **Boarding Gate** 登機門
7. **Remarks** 備註
8. **Departed** 已起飛
9. **Boarding** 登機中
10. **On Time** 準時
11. **Delayed** 誤點
12. **Cancelled** 取消
13. **New Departure Time**
    已更改時間

有些機場的 departure board 會標示 SCHED-TIME（scheduled-time 預訂起飛時間）和 EST-TIME（established-time 實際起飛時間）。備註欄的班機狀態還有可能出現下列訊息：

★ FINAL CALL 最後登機廣播

★ CHECK-IN NOW 辦理登機手續中

★ TIME CHANGE 時間更改

美國簽證
American VISA

1. **Issuing Post Name** 簽證核發地
2. **Control Number** 簽證號碼
3. **Surname** 姓
4. **Given Name** 名
5. **Visa Type** 簽證種類
   - Regular 一般
   - Official 公務
   - Diplomatic 外交
   - Other 其他
6. **Class** 艙等
7. **Passport Number** 護照號碼
8. **Sex** 性別
   - M (male) 男 / F (female) 女
9. **Birth Date** 生日
10. **Nationality** 國籍
11. **Entries** 入境次數
    - M (multiple) 多次入境
    - S (single) 單次入境
12. **Issue Date** 簽證核發日
13. **Expiration Date** 簽證到期日
14. **Annotation** 註解

申根簽證 Schengen VISA

1. **Valid For** 此證件適用於（申根國家）
2. **From . . . Until . . .** 簽證有效期限
3. **Type of Visa** 簽證種類
   C (short term) 短期簽證
   D (long term) 長期簽證
4. **Number of Entries** 入境次數
   mult 多次入境 / **single** 單次入境
5. **Duration of Stay** 可停留時間
6. **Issued In** 簽證辦理處
7. **On (Date)** 簽證辦理時間
8. **Number of Passport** 護照號碼
9. **Surname, Name** 申辦人姓名
10. **Remarks** 備註

On an Airplane

Chapter 2

在飛機上

PART 1

Key Terms

① overhead compartment 頭頂置物艙

④ aisle 走道

⑤ middle seat 中間的座位

② window seat 靠窗座位

③ aisle seat 靠走道的座位

⑥ flight attendant 空服員

⑦ crew 機組人員

⑧ captain 機長

⑨ airsickness bag 嘔吐袋

⑪ buckle 扣帶

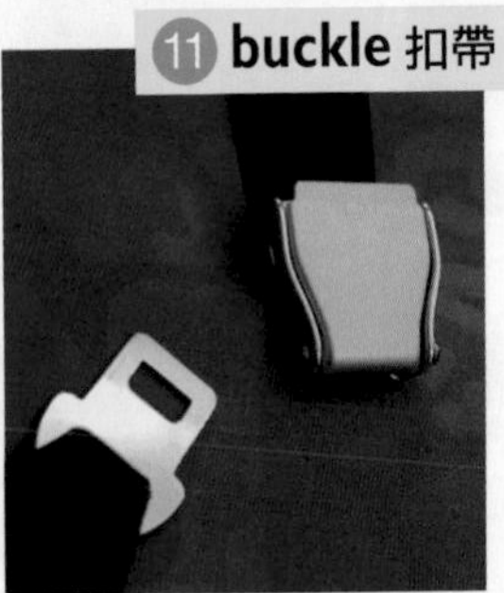

⑩ seat belt 安全帶

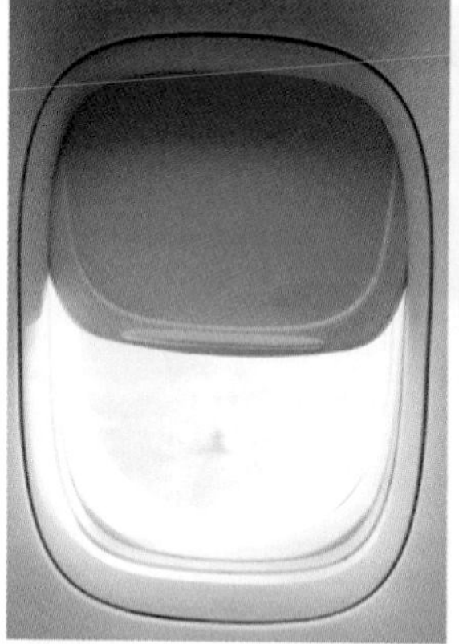

⑫ **blind** 窗戶遮陽板

⑬ **tray** 摺疊餐桌

⑭ **seat pocket** 椅背置物袋

⑮ **headphones/headset** 耳機

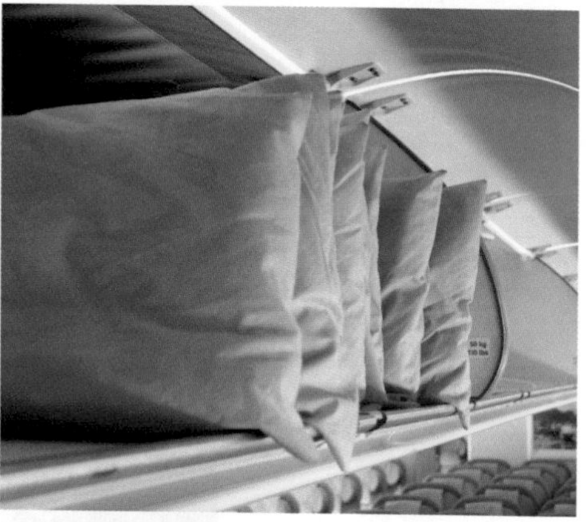

⑯ **pillow** 枕頭

⑰ **blanket** 毛毯

⑱ **console**
(電子設備或機器的)
操控臺

⑲ **touch screen** 觸控螢幕；
in-flight entertainment
機上娛樂

014

⑳ **electronic device**
電子產品

㉑ **in-flight meal**
機上餐點

㉒ **duty-free items**
免稅商品

㉓ **life jacket** 救生衣

㉔ **oxygen mask** 氧氣罩

㉕ **emergency exit** 逃生出口

㉖ **time difference** 時差

27 plane cockpit 飛機駕駛艙

28 economy class 經濟艙
29 business class 商務艙
30 first class 頭等艙
31 in-flight movie 機上電影
32 lavatory 洗手間
33 occupied（洗手間）有人使用
34 vacant（洗手間）沒人使用
35 turbulence 亂流
36 vomit / throw up 嘔吐
37 airsickness 暈機
38 ringing in the ears 耳鳴
39 jet lag 時差反應
40 vegetarian food 素食

41 beef 牛肉

42 pork 豬肉

43 fish 魚肉
44 bread; roll 麵包

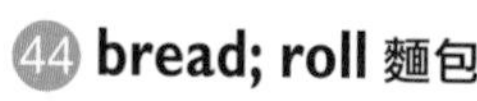
45 the international date line
國際換日線
46 altitude 高度
47 ground temperature 地面溫度
48 Centigrade 攝氏溫度（或用 Celsius）
49 Fahrenheit 華氏溫度

PART 2 Conversations

01 Having Lunch on the Plane 在機上用餐 016

D *David* 大衛 F *Flight attendant* 空服人員

D What are my choices for lunch?

F We have beef with rice and fish with noodles. Which would you like?

D Fish with noodles, please.

F Would you care for coffee or tea?

D Coffee, please.

D 午餐有什麼可以選？

F 有牛肉飯和鮮魚麵，您要哪一種？

D 我要鮮魚麵。

F 要不要喝點咖啡或茶呢？

D 請給我咖啡。

airsick 暈機

airsickness bag 嘔吐袋

02 Airsickness 暈機 017

F *Flight attendant* 空服人員　M *Monica* 摩妮卡

F　May I help you?

M　I don't feel well. I need an airsickness bag.

F　Yes, madam. There's one in the seat pocket. Here you are.

M　Thank you.

F　Should I bring you some water?

M　Yes, please.

F　請問需要什麼嗎？

M　我覺得不太舒服，麻煩給我一個嘔吐袋。

F　好的，女士，嘔吐袋就在椅背裡，來。

M　謝謝你。

F　需要喝一點水嗎？

M　好。

PART 3

Useful Expressions

01 Looking for Seats and Using the Equipment
找座位與使用設備 018

尋找座位

1 A Excuse me, could you show me where seat 18A is?
請問18A座位在哪裡？
B It's over there next to the window.
就在那裡，靠窗的那一個。

和別人換座位

2 Do you mind changing seats with me?
我可以跟你換位子嗎？

3 Can I change seats with you?
我可以跟你換位子嗎？

座位被佔

4 Excuse me. You have my seat.
不好意思，你坐到我的位子了。

座位是否有人坐

5 Excuse me. Is this seat vacant?
對不起，請問這個位子有人坐嗎？

請求幫忙放行李

6 Could you please help me put my baggage up there?
可以幫我把行李放上去嗎？

請求幫忙拿行李

7 Could you please help me get my baggage up there?
可以幫我把行李拿下來嗎？

頭頂置物箱已滿

8 A The overhead compartments are all full. Where can I put my baggage? 上面的置物箱都滿了，我的行李要放哪邊？
B You can place the baggage under the seat in front of you.
您可以將行李放在前面的座位下面。

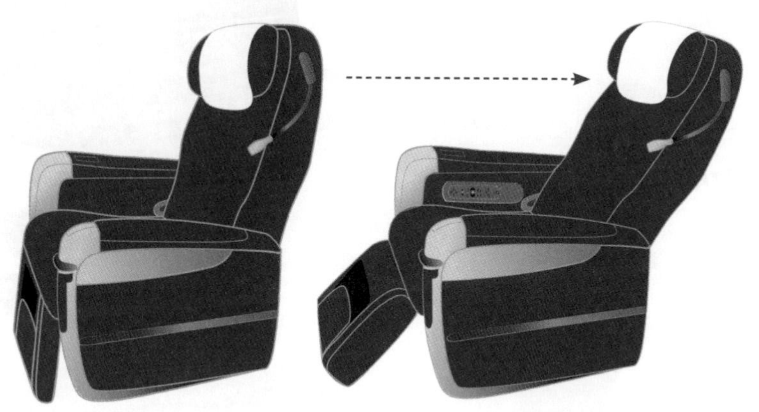

recline one's seat 將椅背放下

索取中文報紙

9 Do you have Chinese newspapers?
你們有沒有中文報紙？

繫安全帶

10 Can you tell me how to fasten the seat belt?
你可以教我怎麼繫安全帶嗎？

11 Can you tell me how to unfasten the seat belt?
請問安全帶要怎麼解開？

放下椅背

12 How do I recline my seat? 我要怎麼把椅背放下來？

豎直椅背

13 Could you put your seat up, please? 請豎直椅背好嗎？

耳機壞了

14 These headphones are not working. Can I have some new ones? 這副耳機是壞的，麻煩給我一副新的。

如何開燈

15 How do I turn on the light? 請問要怎麼開閱讀燈？

索取毯子或枕頭

16 Could you give me one more blanket?
請再給我一條毯子好嗎？

17 One extra pillow, please. 請再給我一個枕頭。

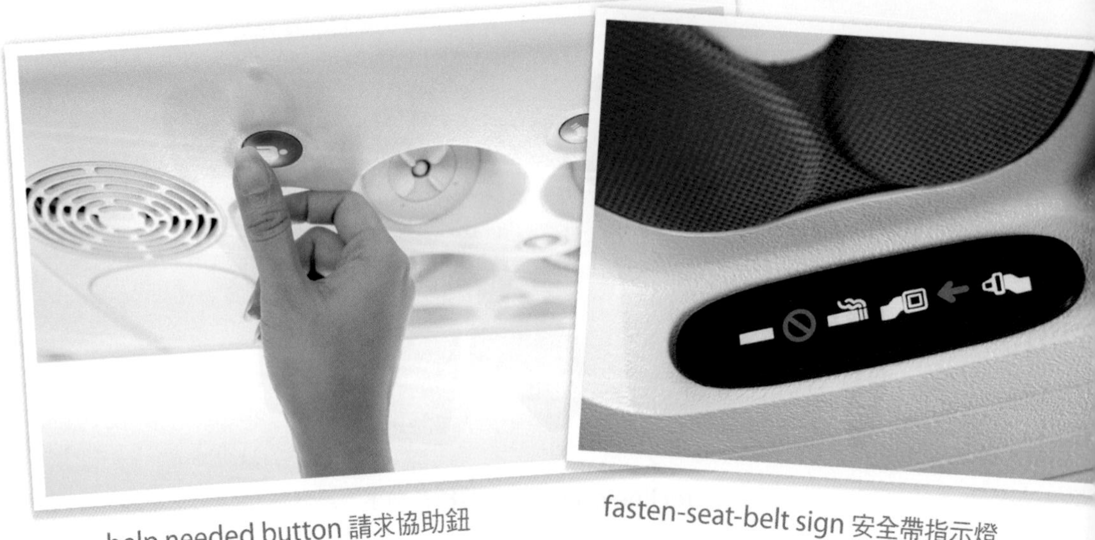

help needed button 請求協助鈕

fasten-seat-belt sign 安全帶指示燈

機上電影

18 What time does the in-flight movie start?
機上電影什麼時候開始播放？

19 Which is the movie channel?
電影頻道是哪一台？

使用電子產品

20 When can I use my electronic devices?
什麼時候可以使用電子產品？

Wi-Fi連線

21 Ⓐ Is Wi-Fi available during the flight? 機上有Wi-Fi連線嗎？

Ⓑ To use our in-flight Wi-Fi service, you'll need to buy a connectivity plan, which a member of our cabin crew can help you with.
如欲使用機上Wi-Fi，您需要購買Wi-Fi連接方案，可洽詢我們的機組人員協助您購買。

Ⓑ You can connect to the in-flight Wi-Fi service once we reach an altitude of 10,000 feet.
一旦我們抵達10,000英呎的高空，您就可以連接機上Wi-Fi。

02 Feeling Sick and Asking for Food 身體不適與飲食

尋找洗手間	22	Where is the lavatory? 請問洗手間在哪裡？
身體不適	23	I don't feel well. 我覺得不舒服。
想吐	24	I feel like vomiting. 我想吐。
索取藥品	25	Do you have anything for airsickness? 你們有暈機藥嗎？
	26	Do you have anything for a headache? 你們有頭痛藥嗎？
餐點供應時間	27	When do you start to serve dinner? 請問晚餐幾點開始供應？

airline dishes 機上餐

一般長程班機多半會印製菜單，放在座椅口袋內，或在飛機起飛後發給旅客，供旅客事先考慮想吃哪一種餐點。有些航空公司則是會在訂購機票時，詢問旅客是否要機上餐，到了機上便不再詢問乘客，而是直接依登記名冊發送餐點。

吃素的旅客，別忘了在訂機票或辦理登記時告訴航空公司人員，以便航空人員預先準備你的餐點。

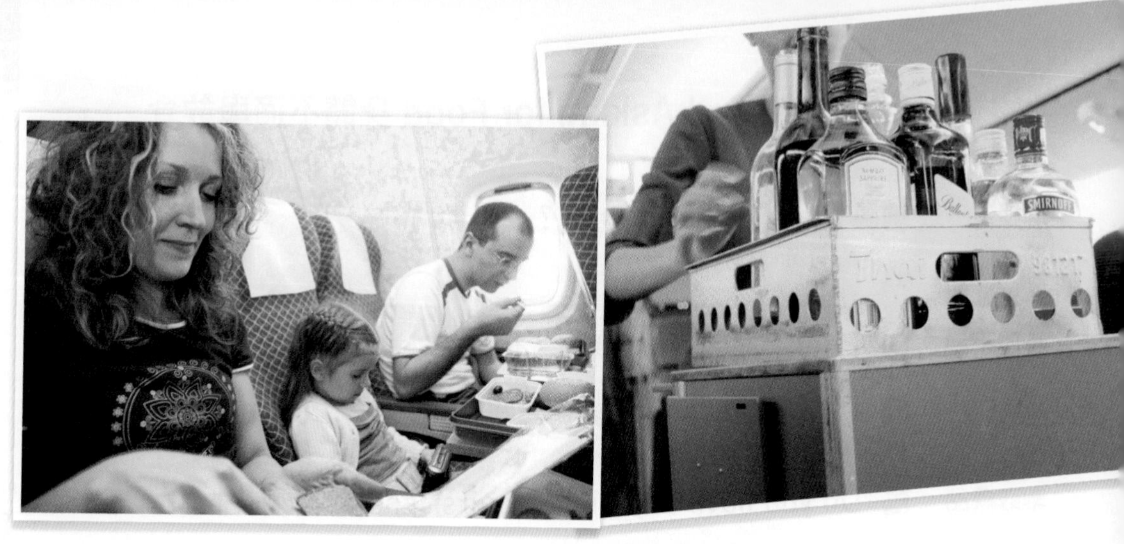

選擇餐點

28 Beef or pork? 請問您要吃牛肉還是豬肉？

29 Omelet or quiche? 請問您要吃蛋捲還是乳蛋餅？

還要麵包

30 Some more rolls? 還要再一點麵包嗎？

31 May I have some more bread?
可以再給我一些麵包嗎？

喝飲料

32 Ⓐ Would you care for something to drink?
需要喝點什麼飲料嗎？
Ⓑ Orange juice, please. 我要柳橙汁。

33 Care for some wine? 需要喝點酒嗎？

34 Some more coffee? 還要再來一點咖啡嗎？

35 Can I have a soda with lemon chips?
可以給我一杯汽水加檸檬片嗎？

吃完餐點

36 Ⓐ Are you finished? 請問您吃完了嗎？
Ⓑ Yes, I've finished. 我吃完了。
Ⓑ Not yet. 我還沒吃完。

索取泡麵

37 Do you have any instant noodles?
你們有泡麵嗎？

03 Buying Duty-free Items and Listening to the Captain's Broadcasts 購買免稅商品與機長廣播 020

購買免稅商品

38 Do you sell duty-free items on this flight?
這個班機上有賣免稅商品嗎？

39 A Which currencies do you accept, euros or US dollars?
你們收歐元還是美金？

B We accept US dollars only. 我們只收美金。

40 Can I pay by credit card? 我可以刷卡嗎？

填寫表格

41 How do I fill out this form? 請問如何填寫這份表格？

詢問當地時間

42 What is the local time now?
現在當地時間是幾點？

行經亂流

43 Ladies and gentlemen, we are approaching an area of turbulence. For your own safety, please go back to your seats and fasten the seat belts. Thank you.

各位旅客請注意，本班機即將行經亂流區，請您回到您的座位，並繫好安全帶，以求安全。謝謝您的合作。

機長廣播

44 Ladies and gentlemen, this is the Captain speaking. We will be landing at Bangkok International Airport in 20 minutes. Our flying altitude is 7000 feet. The local time is 9:45 p.m. and the ground temperature is 25 degrees Centigrade, or 77 degrees Fahrenheit. Captain Tony and all the members of his crew thank you for flying with us. We hope you enjoyed your flight.

各位旅客您好，這是機長廣播。本班機即將於20分鐘內降落曼谷國際機場。我們的飛行高度是7000英尺。當地時間為晚上9點45分，地面溫度攝氏25度，華氏77度。機長湯尼與所有組員感謝各位旅客搭乘本班機，希望各位旅客滿意這次的飛行。

I-94 表格
I-94 Form

DEPARTMENT OF HOMELAND SECURITY
U.S. Customs and Border Protection OMB No. 1651-0111

Admission Number *Welcome to the United States*

392923282 18

I-94 Arrival/Departure Record - Instructions

1 This form must be completed by all persons except U.S. Citizens, returning resident aliens, aliens with immigrant visas, and Canadian Citizens visiting or in transit.

2 Type or print legibly with pen in ALL CAPITAL LETTERS. Use English. Do not write on the back of this form.

3 This form is in two parts. Please complete both the Arrival Record (Items 1 through 13) and the Departure Record (Items 14 through 17).

4 When all items are completed, present this form to the CBP Officer.

5 Item 7 - If you are entering the United States by land, enter **LAND** in this space. If you are entering the United States by ship, enter **SEA** in this space.

CBP Form I-94 (10/04)

Admission Number OMB No. 1651-0111

392923282 18

Arrival Record

6 Family Name

7 First (Given) Name 8 Birth Date (Day/Mo/Yr) 9 10 11

12 Country of Citizenship 13 Sex (Male or Female) 14

15 Passport Number 16 Airline and Flight Number

17 Country Where You Live 18 City Where You Boarded

19 City Where Visa was Issued 20 Date Issued (Day/Mo/Yr)

21 Address While in the United States (Number and Street)

22 City and State

CBP Form I-94 (10/04)

Departure Number OMB No. 1651-0111

392923282 18

I-94
Departure Record

14. Family Name

15. First (Given) Name 16. Birth Date (Day/Mo/Yr)

17. Country of Citizenship

CBP Form I-94 (10/04)

See Other Side **STAPLE HERE**

I-94表格為出入美國時所需填寫的入境表格，現已數位化。旅客在入境美國時，只需注意更新自己的EVUS（Electronic Visa Update System 簽證更新電子系統），並在機上填寫右頁的海關申報表即可。

1 This form must be completed by all persons except U.S. citizens, returning resident aliens, aliens with immigrant visas, and Canadian Citizens visiting or in transit. 所有人都必須填寫此表格，除了美國公民、返回美國的永久居民外籍人士、持移民簽證首次入境的新移民外籍人士、入境美國的加拿大公民或是過境的外籍旅客。

2 Type or print legibly with pen in ALL CAPITAL LETTERS. Use English. Do not write on the back of this form. 請用大寫字母打字或用筆填寫清楚，使用英文填寫，不要在此表背面寫任何字。

3 This form is in two parts. Please complete both the Arrival Record (Item 1 through 13) and the Departure Record (Item 14 through 17). 此表包括兩部分，請填寫入境記錄（第1項至第13項）和離境記錄（第14項至第17項）兩部分。

4 When all items are completed, present this form to the U.S. Immigration and Naturalization Service Inspector. 填寫完畢後，請將此表交給美國移民局官員。

5 Item 7—If you are entering the United States by land, enter LAND in this space. If you are entering the United States by ship, enter SEA in this space. 第 7 項內容說明——如果您是從陸路進入美國，請在空格內填寫LAND。如果您是搭乘船隻進入美國，請在空格內填寫 SEA。

6 Family Name 姓氏

7 First (Given) Name 名字

8 Birth Date 生日

9 Day (D) 日

10 Mo (M) 月

11 Yr (Y) 年

12 Country of Citizenship 國籍

13 Sex 性別

14 Male (M) / Female (F) 男性／女性

15 Passport Number 護照號碼

16 Airline and Flight Number 航空公司與航班號碼

17 Country Where You Live 居住國家

18 City Where You Boarded 登機／登船城市

19 City Where Visa Was Issued 簽證核發城市

20 Date Issued 簽證核發時間

21 Address While in the United States (Number and Street) 在美國期間的居住地點（街道與號碼）

22 City and State 城市與州名

海關申報表
Customs Declaration Form

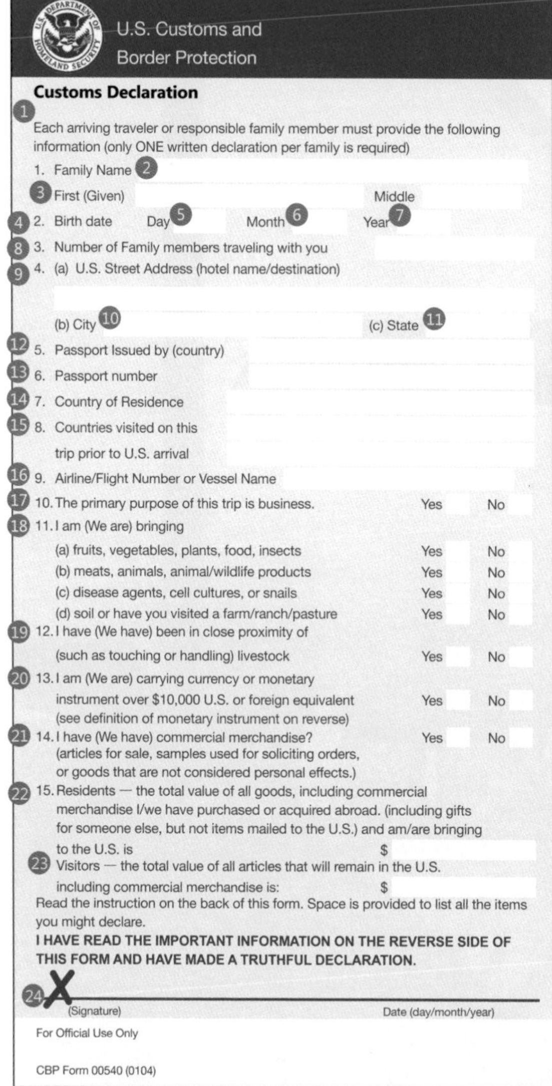
U.S. Customs and Border Protection

Customs Declaration

1 Each arriving traveler or responsible family member must provide the following information (only ONE written declaration per family is required)

1. Family Name 2
3 First (Given) Middle
4 2. Birth date Day 5 Month 6 Year 7
8 3. Number of Family members traveling with you
9 4. (a) U.S. Street Address (hotel name/destination)
(b) City 10 (c) State 11
12 5. Passport Issued by (country)
13 6. Passport number
14 7. Country of Residence
15 8. Countries visited on this trip prior to U.S. arrival
16 9. Airline/Flight Number or Vessel Name
17 10. The primary purpose of this trip is business. Yes No
18 11. I am (We are) bringing
(a) fruits, vegetables, plants, food, insects Yes No
(b) meats, animals, animal/wildlife products Yes No
(c) disease agents, cell cultures, or snails Yes No
(d) soil or have you visited a farm/ranch/pasture Yes No
19 12. I have (We have) been in close proximity of (such as touching or handling) livestock Yes No
20 13. I am (We are) carrying currency or monetary instrument over $10,000 U.S. or foreign equivalent (see definition of monetary instrument on reverse) Yes No
21 14. I have (We have) commercial merchandise? (articles for sale, samples used for soliciting orders, or goods that are not considered personal effects.) Yes No
22 15. Residents — the total value of all goods, including commercial merchandise I/we have purchased or acquired abroad. (including gifts for someone else, but not items mailed to the U.S.) and am/are bringing to the U.S. is $
23 Visitors — the total value of all articles that will remain in the U.S. including commercial merchandise is: $
Read the instruction on the back of this form. Space is provided to list all the items you might declare.
I HAVE READ THE IMPORTANT INFORMATION ON THE REVERSE SIDE OF THIS FORM AND HAVE MADE A TRUTHFUL DECLARATION.
24 X (Signature) Date (day/month/year)
For Official Use Only
CBP Form 00540 (0104)

1. Each arriving traveler or responsible family member must provide the following information (only ONE written declaration per family is required) 每位入境旅客或家庭代表均須填妥下列資料（每個家庭只需填寫一張）
2. Family Name 姓
3. First (Given) Name 名
4. Birth Date 生日
5. Day 日
6. Month 月
7. Year 年
8. Number of Family members traveling with you 同行家屬人數（不包含自己）
9. U.S. Street Address (hotel name/destination) 美國居住地址（飯店／目的地名稱）
10. City 城市名
11. State 州名
12. Passport Issued by (country) 護照發照國家
13. Passport number 護照號碼
14. Country of Residence 居住國家
15. Countries visited on this trip prior to U.S. arrival 此趟行程抵美前，還去過哪些國家
16. Airline/Flight Number or Vessel Name 航空公司／班機號碼或船艦名稱
17. The primary purpose of this trip is business. 此行主要目的為洽公
18. I am (We are) bringing 我攜帶了
    (a) fruits, vegetables, plants, food, insects 蔬果、植物、食物、昆蟲
    (b) meats, animals, animal/wildlife products 肉品、動物、動物製品
    (c) disease agents, cell cultures, or snails 病原體、細胞培養、蝸牛
    (d) soil or have you visited a farm/ranch/pasture 土壤，或您曾造訪農場
19. I have (We have) been in close proximity of (such as touching or handling) livestock 我（我們）曾經近距離接觸家畜
20. I am (We are) carrying currency or monetary instrument over $10,000 U.S. or foreign equivalent 我（我們）攜帶了超過一萬美元或等值貨幣
21. I have (We have) commercial merchandise? (articles for sale, samples used for soliciting orders, or goods that are not considered personal effects.) 我（我們）有攜帶商品？（販賣之商品、訂購之樣本等任何非屬私人之物品）
22. Residents（美國居民才須填寫）
23. Visitors — the total value of all articles that will remain in the U.S. including commercial merchandise （遊客填寫）攜帶商品總值
24. 填妥表格後，在此處簽名

Arrival & Transit

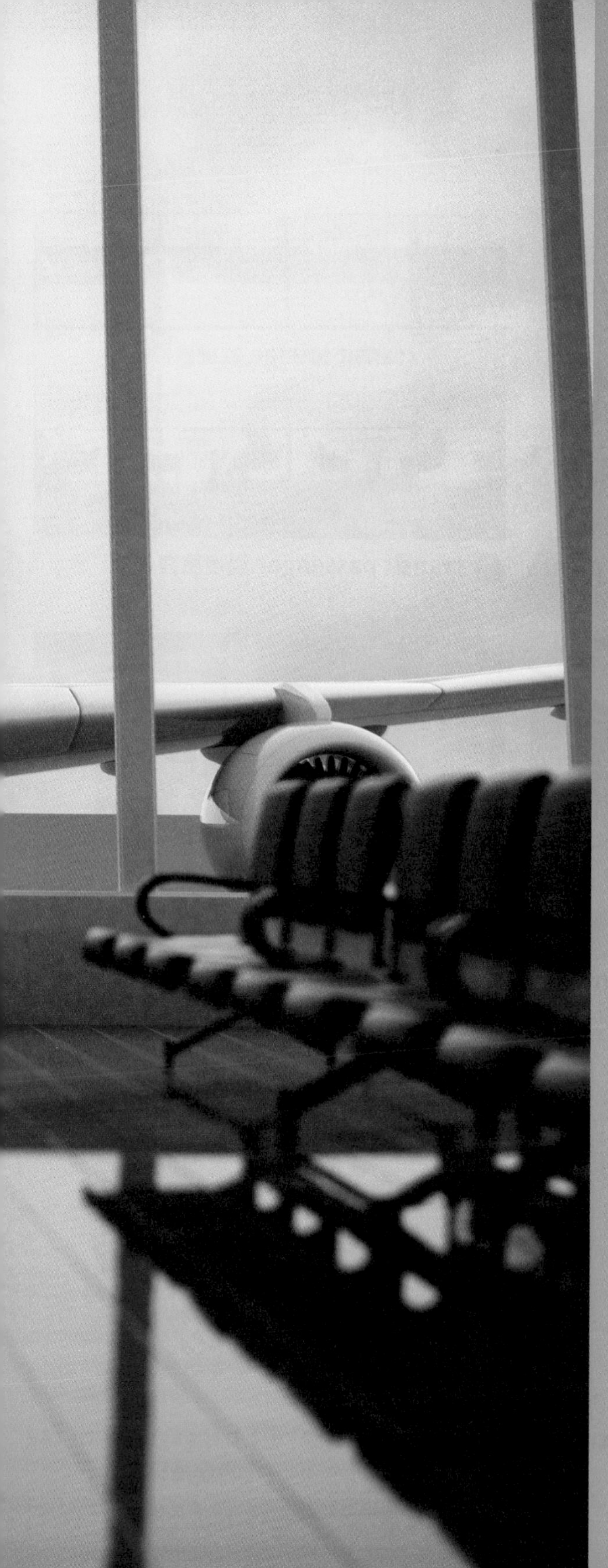

Chapter 3

入境／轉機

PART 1

Key Terms

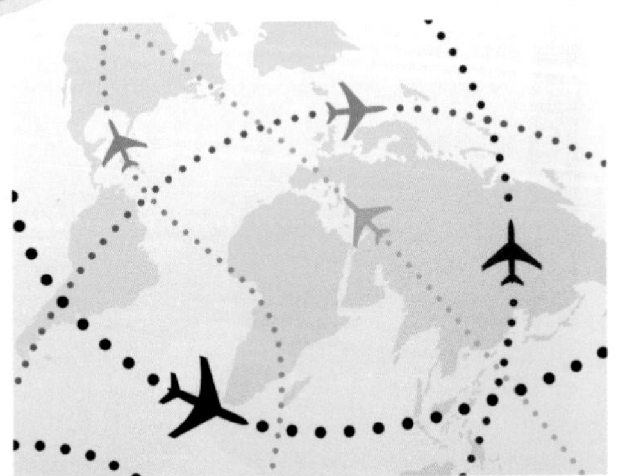

① **transit / transfer / change planes**
轉機

② **transit lounge** 轉機候機室

③ **transit passenger** 過境旅客

④ **transfer desk / transit counter**
轉機櫃檯

⑤ **immigration control/counter**
入境櫃檯

⑥ **customs declaration form**
關稅申報表

⑦ **arrival lobby** 入境大廳

⑧ **baggage claim tag**
行李提領證

022

9 liquor 酒

10 cigarette 香菸

11 airport terminal 航站大廈

12 baggage claim/carousel 行李提領處

13 sightseeing 觀光

14 on business / on a business trip
洽公／商務旅行

15 prohibited items 違禁品

16 stopover/layover 中途過境停留
17 disembarkation card 入境卡
18 customs 海關（要用複數型）
19 get through customs 通關
20 resident 居民
21 non-resident 非居民
22 foreigner 外國人
23 baggage inspection 行李查驗
24 Lost and Found Office 行李遺失招領處
25 declare 申報（納稅品等）
26 customs inspection 海關檢查
27 (customs) duty 關稅
28 duty-free 免稅的
29 duty-free allowance 免稅額
30 pay the duty for something 付……的稅
31 personal effects 私人物品
32 personal belongings 私人物品
33 for my own use 自己要用的

PART 2 Conversations

01 At the Immigration Counter 入境櫃檯 023

I *Immigration Officer* 入境櫃檯　D *David* 大衛

I　Passport and disembarkation card, please.

D　Here you are.

I　What is your purpose of visiting?

D　Sightseeing.

I　How long are you staying here?

D　Nine days.

I　All right. Thank you.

I　請出示您的護照和入境表格。

D　在這裡。

I　您此行的目的是什麼？

D　我是來觀光的。

I　您打算在這裡待幾天？

D　九天。

I　好的，謝謝您。

入境櫃檯通常分為好幾種，外籍旅客必須選擇 **Foreigner**（外國人）、**Non-Citizen**（非公民）和 **Non-Resident**（非居民）這三種窗口，並出示 **passport**（護照）、**ticket**（機票）和 **disembarkation card**（入境卡）。查驗人員通常會詢問一些旅行目的、停留時間、住宿地點等問題，一一回答後便可通過。

02 Baggage Inspection 行李檢查 024

C *Customs Officer* 海關人員　A *Amy* 艾美

C Please bring your baggage here for inspection.

A Here you are, officer.

C Is all your baggage here?

A Yes, a camera bag, a travel bag, and a suitcase.

C Have you got anything to declare?

A No. I have only personal effects.

C 請把您的行李拿過來這裡檢查。

A 好的，先生。

C 您所有的行李都在這裡了嗎？

A 是的，一個相機包、一個旅行袋和一個行李箱。

C 有什麼要申報的嗎？

A 沒有，我只有一些私人用品。

Useful Expressions

01 Transferring Flights 轉機 025

轉機廣播

1 For transit passengers, the reboarding time is 9:50 p.m.
過境旅客請於晚上9點50分重新登機。

尋找轉機櫃檯

2 Where is the CAL transfer desk?
請問華航的轉機櫃檯在哪裡？

登機時間

3 When should I reboard the plane?
請問我什麼時候要重新登機？

4 When is the boarding time?
登機時間是什麼時候？

起飛時間

5 When will the transit flight take off?
請問轉機班機什麼時候起飛？

正確候機室

6 Is this the right lounge for TG 635?
請問這是TG 635班機的候機室嗎？

機場轉機廣播

7 All connecting passengers are requested to proceed to Gate 8. 所有轉機的旅客，請前往八號登機門。

02 Conversations at the Immigration Counter 入境櫃檯對話 026

出示證件

8 A Passport, please. 請出示護照。
B Here you are. / Here is my passport. 在這裡。

9 Please give me your disembarkation card, and let me see your passport. 請給我看一下您的入境卡和護照。

旅行目的	10 A What's the purpose of your visit? 您此行的目的是什麼？ B Sightseeing. 觀光。 B I'm here on business. 我是來洽公的。
旅遊時間	11 A How long are you staying here? 您要在這裡待多久？ B A month or so. 一個月左右。
居住地點	12 A Where are you going to stay? 您會住在哪裡？ B A hotel downtown. 市中心的一家旅館。 B I will stay at a friend's place. 我會住在朋友家。
第一次造訪	13 A Have you been to Italy before? 您有來過義大利嗎？ B No, this is my first trip here. 沒有，我第一次來。
是否獨自旅遊	14 A Are you traveling alone? 您一個人來嗎？ B I'm with my husband. 我跟我先生一起來的。
在當地是否有親友	15 Any relatives here? 您在這裡有親戚嗎？ 16 Is your family going to join you in the UK? 您的家人隨後會來英國嗎？
是否跟團	17 Are you with a group? 您是跟團來的嗎？
出示回程票	18 Do you have a return ticket? 您有回程機票嗎？
詢問國籍	19 A Which country do you come from? 您從哪個國家來的？ B I'm from Taiwan. 我是臺灣人。

03 Claiming Luggage 提領行李 027

尋找行李提領處

20 Where is the baggage claim?
請問行李提領處在哪裡？

21 Which carousel is for flight TG 945?
請問TG 945班機的行李提領處在哪裡？

借過拿行李

22 Excuse me. This is my bag.
借過一下，那是我的行李。

行李遺失

23 I can't find my bag.
我的行李不見了。

行李外觀

24 Ⓐ What does your bag look like?
你的行李長什麼樣子？

Ⓑ It's a green suitcase with wheels.
我的行李是有輪子的綠色行李箱。

尋找行李推車

25 Where can I find a baggage trolley?
哪裡有行李推車？

有些機場的行李推車（baggage trolley）需要付費才能使用

04 Going Through Customs Inspection and Declaring Items at Customs 通關與申報 028

尋找通關處

26 Ⓐ Where do I go through customs inspection?
我要由哪裡通關？

Ⓐ Do you know which lines to follow?
你可以告訴我該走哪條通道嗎？

申報物品通關處

Ⓑ You can follow the red lines if you have anything to declare. 如果您有東西需要申報，請走紅色通道。

重填申報表	27 Can I fill in a new customs declaration form now? 我可以現在重新填一份海關申報單嗎？
尋找繳稅處	28 Where should I pay the tax? 我要在哪裡繳稅？
申報物品	29 Do you have anything to declare? 有什麼要申報的嗎？
攜帶菸酒	30 Ⓐ Got any tobacco? Spirits? 有帶香菸、烈酒嗎？ Ⓑ I have some cigarettes, just for my own use. 我有一些香菸，是自己要抽的。
查驗行李	31 Please bring your luggage here for inspection. 請把行李帶過來檢查。 32 Please open this baggage. 請打開這個包包。
行李不必查驗	33 Your luggage is exempted from examination. 您的行李可以不用檢查。
禮物	34 This is a gift for a friend. 這是要送給朋友的禮物。
詢問是否需繳稅	35 Must I pay duty on this? 我這個必須繳稅嗎？
出示申報單	36 Please show me your declaration form. 請給我看一下您的申報單。
私人用品	37 You have only personal effects, don't you? 您只有私人用品嗎？

05 Renting a Wi-Fi Router 租借 Wi-Fi 分享器 029

租借與歸還

38 I'd like to rent a portable Wi-Fi router for five days.
我想要租借攜帶型Wi-Fi分享器五天。

39 How do I return the router at the end of my trip?
在我旅途結束後,要怎麼歸還分享器?

帳號密碼

40 What's the ID and password for this router?
這台分享器的帳號和密碼是什麼?

41 The ID and password are on the back of the router.
帳號和密碼就在分享器背面。

附帶配備

42 Included with your router are a USB cable and an AC adaptor.
除了分享器之外,還有附帶一條USB線和電源轉接器。

常見的機場標誌 Common Airport Signs

Information ?!

Information Counter 服務台

Departure

Departure Hall 出境大廳

Arrival

Arrival Hall 入境大廳

Gate 20 | Gate 21

Boarding Gate 登機門

Terminal

Airport Terminal 機場航廈

Transfer

Transfer Area 轉機區

Bag claim
Baggage hall

Baggage Carousel 行李提領處

Lift

Lift/Elevator 電梯

Check-in

Check-in Counter 報到櫃台

Customs Control

Customs Inspection 海關查驗處

Passport Control

Passport Inspection 護照查驗處

入境常見問題句型
Common Immigration Questions

基本入境問題
Basic Immigration Questions

1 May I see your passport, please? 請出示護照好嗎？

- **Here you are.** 來。（遞出護照）
- **Here is my passport.** 這是我的護照。
- **Sure. Here are my passport and declaration form.**
  當然，這是我的護照和關稅申報表。

2 What is the purpose of your stay/visit? 您此行的目的是什麼？

- **I'm here on ________. (tour/vacation/business)**
  我是來旅遊／度假／出差的。
- **Sightseeing.** 觀光。
- **I'm visiting a friend.** 我是來探望朋友的。

3 What is your final destination? 您的目的地是哪裡？

- **I'm going to ________.** 我要去……。
- **I'm here to transfer to ________.** 我是來這要轉機去……的。

4 How long are you going to stay? 您會在這待多久？

- **I will stay here for _____ days.** 我會在這待……天。

5 Where will you stay? 您會住在哪裡？

- **I'm staying at hotels.** 我會住在飯店。
- **I will stay at a friend's place.** 我會住在朋友家。

6 How much money are you carrying? 您身上攜帶了多少現金？

- **I have ________.** 我身上有……。

個人相關問題
Personal Questions

1 Where are you from? 您來自哪裡？
- **I'm from Taiwan.** 我來自台灣。

2 What do you do? / What's your occupation? 您的職業是？
- **I'm a(n) ________.** 我是……。

3 Have you ever been here before? 您之前有來過這裡嗎？
- **Yes, I've been here ______ times.** 有的，我來過這裡……次。
- **No. This is my first time here.** 沒有，這是我第一次來。

4 Are you traveling alone? 您是一個人來的嗎？
- **Yes, I'm traveling here alone.** 是的，我一個人來。
- **No, I'm with my family/friend.** 不，我跟我家人／朋友一起。

5 Do you have any relatives or friends here?
您在本地有親戚或朋友嗎？
- **Yes. My ________ is living here.** 有的，我的……住在這裡。
- **No, I don't know anyone here.** 不，我在這裡沒有認識的人。

passport control 護照查驗處

At the immigration counter 入境櫃檯

Money Exchange

Chapter 4

兌換外幣

PART 1

Key Terms

① **currency/money exchange** 外幣兌換

② **dollar ($)** 美金

③ **1 dollar** 美金一元

④ **half dollar = 50 cents**
美金五十分

⑤ **quarter = 25 cents**
美金二十五分

⑥ **dime = 10 cents**
美金十分

⑦ **nickel = 5 cents** 美金五分

⑧ **penny = 1 cent** 美金一分

⑨ **euro (€)** 歐元

⑩ **euro cent** 歐分

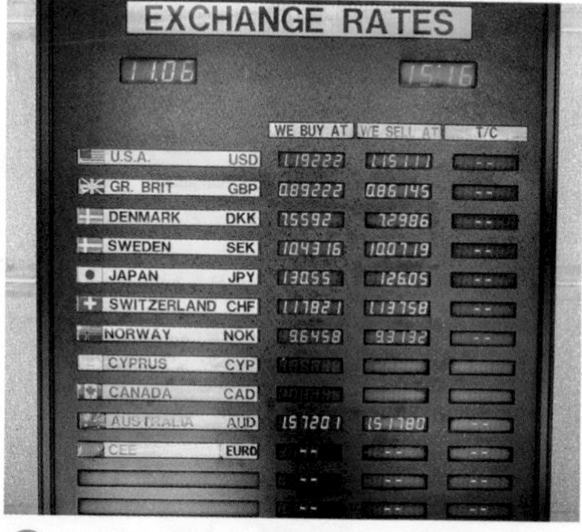

⑪ **exchange rate** 匯率

⑫ **small change** 小面額硬幣；零錢

⑬ **sign** (v.) 簽名

⑮ **bank** 銀行

⑯ **ATM**
= Automatic Teller Machine
自動提款機

⑰ **window** 辦理窗口

⑭ **traveler's check** 旅行支票

18 **withdraw** 提款

19 **receipt** 收據

20 **bill** 紙鈔

21 **coin** 硬幣

22 **banking hours** 營業時間

23 **commission / service charge** 手續費

24 **application form** 申請單

25 **New Taiwan dollar (NT$)** 新台幣

26 **pound (£)** 英鎊

27 **yen (¥)** 日圓

28 **Australian dollar ($)** 澳幣

29 **rupiah (Rp)** 印尼盧比亞

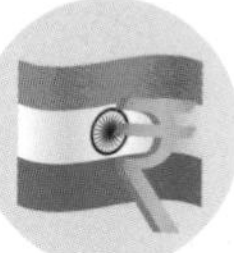

30 **rupee (Rs)** 印度盧比

31 **baht (B)** 泰銖

32 **won (₩)** 韓元

33 **ruble (RUB)** 俄羅斯盧布

34 **rand (R)** 南非蘭特

PART 2

Conversations

01 Where Can I Change Some Money?
在哪裡可以換錢？ 034

T *Timmy* 提米　A *Ann* 安　C *Clerk* 服務人員

T Could you please tell me where I can change some money?

A Over there at the bank.

T Thanks.

[At the bank]

T Excuse me, which window is the foreign exchange section?

C Please go to window 8.

T Thank you.

T 請問我可以到哪裡換錢？

A 到那邊的銀行。

T 謝謝。

〔走進銀行〕

T 請問哪一個窗口可以兌換外幣？

C 請到8號窗口辦理。

T 謝謝！

currency exchange counter 外匯兌換櫃檯

02 I'd Like to Change US Dollars Into Euros.
我想把美金換成歐元。 035

T *Timmy* 提米　C *Clerk* 櫃員

T　I'd like to change some US dollars into euros and I'd like to know today's exchange rate.

C　According to today's exchange rate, every US dollar in cash is equivalent to 0.75 euros.

T　Is there any service charge?

C　We charge a €1 commission on each deal. How much would you like to change?

T　400 US dollars. Here it is. Would you please give me small bills?

C　No problem.

T　我想把這些美金換成歐元，請問今天的匯率是多少？

C　根據外匯牌價，今天是一美元兑換0.75歐元。

T　要付手續費嗎？

C　每筆交易的手續費是一歐元。您想換多少？

T　四百美元，給妳。麻煩換小鈔給我好嗎？

C　好的。

Useful Expressions

01 Exchanging Foreign Currencies 兌換外幣 036

詢問兌幣處位置

1. Where is the Currency Exchange?
請問兌幣處在哪裡？

2. Where can I change some money?
能不能告訴我哪裡可以換錢？

無兌幣服務

3. I am sorry. We don't change foreign currency.
很抱歉，我們這裡不能換外匯。

詢問匯率

4. I want to know today's exchange rate.
我想知道今天的匯率是多少。

5. A What is the exchange rate between the US dollar and the euro today? 請問今天美元對歐元的匯率是多少？
B The current rates are on the notice board, ma'am.
女士，匯率都標示在看板上。

換錢

6. I want to change some US dollars into euros.
我想用美元換歐元。

7. I would like to exchange my NT dollars for 500 US dollars. 我想用台幣換500美金。

8. How much will that be in NT dollars? 那樣要付多少台幣？

兌換方式

9. How would you like your change? 錢您想怎麼換呢？

詢問手續費

10. What is the service charge?
手續費是多少？

11. A How much is the commission? 手續費是多少？
B We charge a $1 commission on each deal.
我們每筆交易會收1塊美金的手續費。

被要求簽名

12 Would you please sign your name at the place marked with quotation marks? 請您在引號的地方簽名，好嗎？

詢問營業時間

13 A What are your banking hours?
請問你們的營業時間是幾點到幾點？

B From 8:30 a.m. to 4:30 p.m., Monday through Friday. We are closed on Saturdays and Sundays.
星期一到星期五，上午8點半到下午4點半，星期六、日不營業。

14 Do you have 24-hour banking?
你們有24小時銀行服務業務嗎？

從提款機領錢

15 Can I withdraw money from the ATM of your bank?
我可以從你們的自動提款機提款嗎？

16 How much can I withdraw each day?
我每天可提領多少錢？

02 Changing Larger Bills Into Smaller Bills 換小鈔

換小鈔

17 Small change, please.
麻煩幫我換成零錢。

換一百元

18 I'll change one hundred and here is the money.
我想兌換一百元，錢在這裡。

錢要怎麼換

19 A How do you like your money? 您要怎麼換？

B I'd like 8 $10 bills, and the rest in small change.
我要八張10元的鈔票，其他的換零錢。

20 Could you break this into 3 twenties, 3 tens and the rest in coins, please?
請把這張（一百元鈔）換成三張20元、三張10元，其餘的換零錢。

21 Do you want 5s or 10s?
您要換五元還是十元的零錢？

美金用不完 **22** What should I do with the US dollars left with me?
如果我的美金用不完該怎麼辦？

03 Traveler's Checks 旅行支票 (038)

兌現旅行支票 **23** I'd like to cash some traveler's checks.
我想要兌現一些旅行支票。

在支票上簽名 **24** Is it necessary to sign each check?
每張支票都要簽名嗎？

索取收據 **25** May I have a receipt, please?
請給我一張收據好嗎？

旅行支票是一種預先印刷的、具固定金額的支票，持有人需預先支付給發出者（通常是銀行）相對應的金額。旅行支票如果遺失或被盜，可以補發，旅行者能夠在旅行時換取當地貨幣。

旅行者在購買旅行支票後，得先在支票上方欄位預先簽名，之後於購物或是兌換實體貨幣時，再於下方欄簽上自己的名字，收取支票者就會核對上下欄的名字是否相同，以防他人盜用。

現在，因為信用卡、ATM 已經廣泛使用，所以旅行支票的重要地位已經不如從前，接受旅行支票的店家的數量逐年遞減，支票持有者僅能到銀行兌換為當地貨幣使用。甚者，旅行支票最大的發行銀行美國運通（American Express），已經於 2007 年終止旅行支票卡的業務，並於 2020 年 6 月 30 日後停止銷售旅行支票，但若手中仍有美國運通旅行支票，之後仍可向銀行兌換。

to withdraw money 領錢

small euro change
小額歐元零錢

在國外的領錢方式&注意事項：How to Withdraw Money in a Foreign Country

1 提款卡（ATM card）

許多銀行或是郵局的提款卡，都需要事前申辦國外交易功能，才可在國外領錢；且會有跨國提款密碼，才能提領當地貨幣。（每家銀行的提領手續費與每日每筆限額不同）

2 信用卡（credit card）

若是使用信用卡在海外提款，等同於預借現金，依每家銀行可能會有不同的借貸利率與手續費，此部分宜先查明再行提領。

3 簽帳金融卡（debit card）

連結了個人銀行帳戶的金融卡，可提款也可消費。消費前需先匯款至帳戶才可進行刷卡，消費時則直接從帳戶扣除，有多少扣多少，不會產生超刷、透支或產生循環利息的款項。用簽帳金融卡在國外消費也依各家銀行而有不同的手續費金額產生。

Taking a Taxi
NEW YORK

Chapter

5

搭計程車

PART 1

Key Terms

① **call a taxi** 打電話叫車

② **catch a taxi** 攔計程車

③ **taxi stand** 計程車招呼站

④ **meter** 計費表

⑤ **safety belt** 安全帶

⑥ **vacant** 空車

⑦ **trunk** 後行李廂

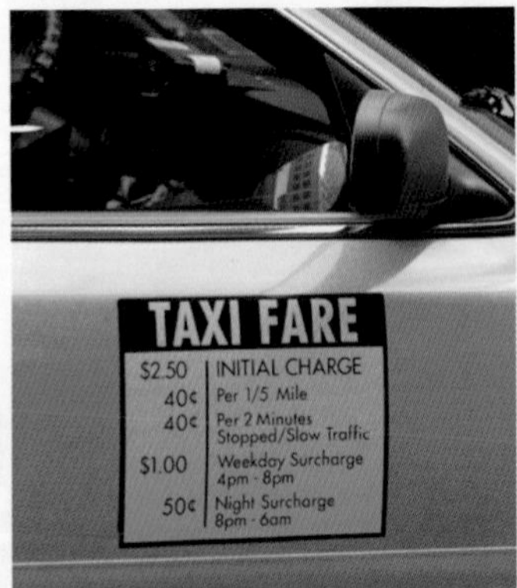

⑧ **fare** 車資
(basic fare 基本費**)**

⑨ **keep the change**
不用找錢

⑩ **traffic lights** 紅綠燈

⑪ **intersection** 十字路口

⑫ **sidewalk** 人行道

⑬ **crosswalk** 斑馬線

⑭ **taxi driver** 計程車司機

⑮ **taxi app** 叫車應用程式

⑯ **front seat** 前座

⑰ **back seat** 後座

⑱ **traffic jam** 塞車

⑲ **cab/taxi** 計程車
⑳ **pick up** 接(乘客)上車
㉑ **drop** 放(乘客)下車
㉒ **step in / get in** 上車
㉓ **get out of / get off** 下車
㉔ **destination** 目的地
㉕ **address** 地址
㉖ **slow down** 放慢速度
㉗ **speed up** 加快速度
㉘ **take a short cut** 抄捷徑
㉙ **ride** 車程
㉚ **surcharge** 加收費用

PART 2

Conversations

01 Where to, Madam? 女士，要去哪裡？ 041

D *Driver* 司機 P *Peggy* 珮琪

D Where to, madam?

P Grand Central Station, please. I want to catch a 6 p.m. train.

D I think you'll make it if we don't get stuck in a traffic jam.

[After a while]

D Here is Grand Central Station.

P Thank you. How much is the fare?

D The meter reads $9.15.

P Here you are. Keep the change.

D Thank you.

D 女士，要去哪裡？

P 請到中央車站，我要趕晚上6點的火車。

D 如果不塞車的話，應該趕得上。

〔過了一會兒〕

D 中央車站到了。

P 謝謝，多少錢？

D 9.15美元

P 這裡，不用找了。

D 謝謝。

02 To This Place, Please.
請到這裡。（指著地址說） 042

D Driver 司機　P Peter 彼得

D Where to, sir?

P To this place, please.

D Star Hotel. OK.

P How long does it take to get to the hotel?

D About 20 minutes.

[20 minutes later]

D Here's the hotel.

P How much is the fare?

D That's 10 dollars.

D 請問要到哪裡？

P 到這個地方。〔拿飯店名稱和地址給司機看〕

D 晨星飯店呀，沒問題。

P 車程大概多久？

D 大概20分鐘。

〔20分鐘後〕

D 飯店到了。

P 多少錢？

D 10美元。

taxi meter 計程車計費表／跳表機

03 Calling a Taxi With a Smartphone App
用手機叫計程車 043

G *Guest* 乘客　R *Receptionist* 總機

G Could you call me a taxi?

R Do you know about our city's taxi app?

G No, I don't. Could you tell me about it?

R It's a free app that allows you to call a taxi from anywhere in the city.

G How do I use it?

R It's very simple. Just download the app on your smartphone.

G OK. Done.

R Now you need to enter your credit card details and destination.

G And after that?

R Just tap on "Call a Taxi" and a nearby taxi will come to pick you up.

G 妳可以幫我叫一台計程車嗎？

R 您知道我們市內的計程車叫車程式嗎？

G 不，我不知道。可以跟我說更詳細嗎？

R 這是一款免費的應用程式，可以讓您在本市內任何地方叫車。

G 要怎麼使用呢？

R 非常簡單。只要在您的智慧型手機上下載程式。

G 好，下好了。

R 接著您需要輸入信用卡資訊，與您的目的地。

G 然後呢？

R 只要按下「立即叫車」的按鈕，位於附近的計程車就會前來接您。

如何使用叫車應用程式 How to Use a Taxi App

❶ open your taxi app
打開叫車應用程式

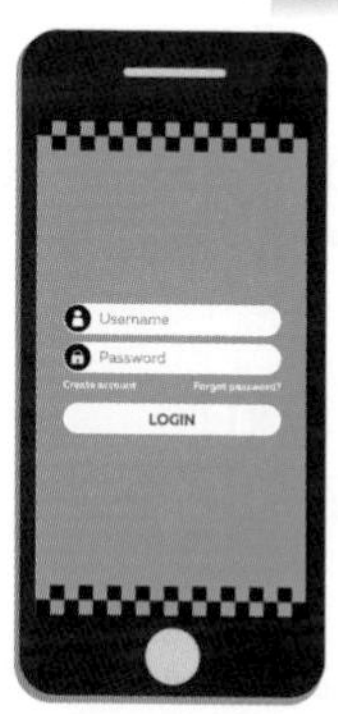

❷ enter username and password
輸入帳號和密碼

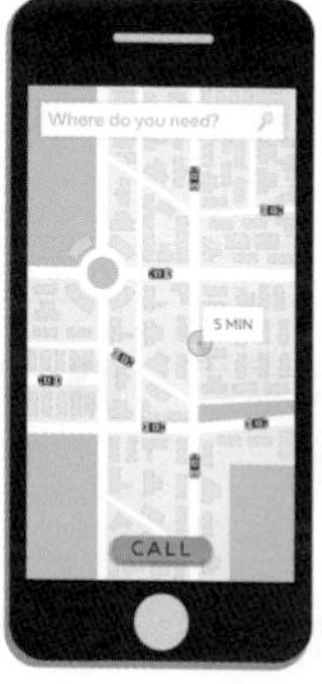

❸ type in address of destination
輸入目的地地址

❹ select a vehicle option
選擇車種

❺ tap "call" to schedule a ride
按下「叫車」預訂行程

❻ done 叫車完成

PART 3

Useful Expressions

01 Calling for and Getting in a Taxi 叫車、上車 044

打電話叫車

1 Please send a taxi to Taipei 101.
請派一輛計程車到台北101來。

2 The taxi will be there in 10 minutes.
車子會在10分鐘後到達。

3 I need a taxi tomorrow morning. Please come to pick me up at Holiday Inn at 10.
我要叫明天早上的車。麻煩早上10點到假日酒店接我。

確認乘客叫車

4 Did you call a taxi?
您有叫計程車嗎？

詢問招車地點

5 Where can I catch a taxi?
我可以在哪裡招計程車？

尋找計程車招呼站

6 Where is the taxi stand? I'm a stranger here.
計程車招呼站在哪裡？我對這裡不熟。

7 Is there a taxi stand nearby? 這附近有計程車招呼站嗎？

攔計程車

8 Taxi! 計程車！

詢問車資
照表收費

9 A How much is the fare to the airport? 到機場要多少錢？
B It depends on the meter reading. 我們是照表收費的。
B It's flat rate of $40 from downtown to the airport.
從市區到機場的表定價是40美元。

請乘客上車

10 OK. Step in, please.
好的，請上車。

招到計程車後，可先詢問司機是否知道你的目的地要怎麼去。一旦確認司機知道地址，可以請他估價(**to estimate the fare**)。最好在出發前先了解大略的車資，啟程時也要確認計程車司機有按跳表機(**taxi meter**)，抵達目的地時才不會被高昂車資嚇到，或是被司機漫天喊價。

有些國家需要給司機小費，例如在紐約，不成文的規定是要付 15% 到 20% 的小費；在其他國家，像是英國，給小費的方式則是請司機不用找零即可。

要求打開後行李箱

⑪ **Could you please open the trunk?**
麻煩打開後行李廂好嗎？

請乘客繫安全帶

⑫ **Now the driver and the passenger are required to wear safety belts.** 現在司機和乘客都必須繫上安全帶。

問目的地

⑬ **Where to, sir?** 先生，請問要到哪裡？

⑭ **Where do you want to go?** 您要去哪裡？

詢問車程

⑮ **I'm staying at the Grand Hyatt Hotel. How long is the ride from here?**
我現在住在凱悅大飯店。從這裡出發坐車要多久？

說明目的地

⑯ **Can you take us to the National Museum of History?**
可以送我們去國立歷史博物館嗎？

⑰ **Drive me to Central Park, please.** 請載我到中央公園。

⑱ **Please take me to this address.**
請送我去這個地址。(拿出地址給司機看。)

⑲ **To this place, please.** 請到這個地方。(拿出地址給司機看。)

02 During the Ride and Getting out of the Taxi
行車中、下車 045

趕時間	20 A I've got to be at the airport before noon. Can we make it? 我必須在中午之前趕到機場。你可以趕到嗎？ B We should make it if the lights are with us. 如果一路綠燈的話，我們可以及時趕到。
不趕時間	21 Don't drive too fast, please. 請不要開太快。
要求轉彎	22 Turn right at the next corner. 前面路口右轉。
請乘客不要吸菸	23 I'm sorry, sir, but no smoking is allowed here in the car. 先生，對不起，車內禁止吸菸。
塞車	24 Oh, we're in a traffic jam. 噢，我們塞在車陣裡了。
要求走捷徑	25 I'm in a hurry. Please take a shortcut. 我趕時間，請抄捷徑。
單行道	26 This is one-way traffic. 這是單行道。
到目的地	27 Here's the hotel. 旅館到了。
要求停車	28 Please stop here. 請在這裡停車。 29 Just drop me here. I'll walk over to the park. 在這裡讓我下車就好。我自己走去公園。 30 I'd like to get off at the next intersection. 我要在下個十字路口下車。 31 A Please stop in front of the exhibition center. 麻煩停在展覽中心前面。 B Sorry, I can't stop here. No parking is allowed here in front of the exhibition center. 對不起，我不能在這裡停車。展覽中心門前不准停車。

要求司機等待

32 **Can you wait for a while?**
你可以等我一下嗎？

下車時詢問車資

33 **How much do I owe you?**
我該付你多少錢？

34 Ⓐ **How much is the fare?** 請問多少錢？
Ⓑ **It's there on the meter.** （車費）顯示在計費表上。

夜間加成

35 **There's a 10 percent surcharge on night rides.**
夜間搭載要加一成。

不用找錢

36 **Keep the change, please.** 不用找了。

Giving Directions 引導方向

across 穿越

go straight ahead
直走

go down/along
繼續直行

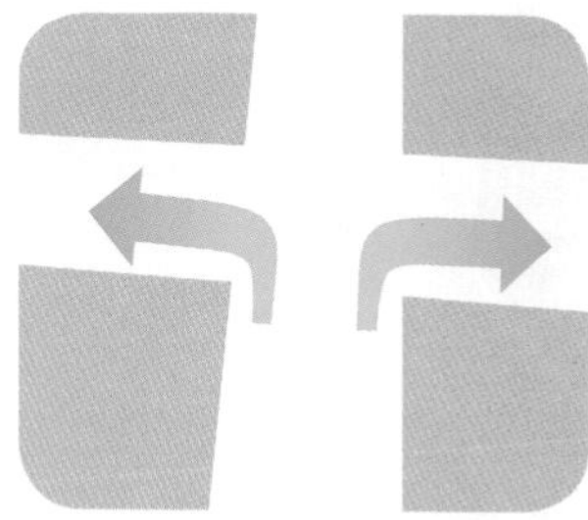

turn left
左轉

turn right
右轉

opposite from
在……對面

towards
朝著……

go past
穿過……

Traveling by Train
D

Chapter 6

搭乘火車或地鐵

PART 1

Key Terms

① **railroad station** 火車站

② **platform** 月台

③ **track** 鐵軌

④ **route map** 路線圖

Liverpool – Nottingham – Norwich

Service operated by	*CT*	*CT*	*CT*	*CT*	*CT*	*CT*	*CT*	*CT*	*CT*
	◇	◇	◇	◇	◇	◇	◇	◇	◇
Liverpool Lime Street				12.50	13.52	14.52	15.52	16.52	17.52
Warrington Central				13.16	14.18	15.18	16.18	17.18	18.18
Manchester Piccadilly			12.44	13.43	14.44	15.43	16.43	17.43	18.43
Stockport			12.54	13.54	14.54	15.54	16.55	17.54	18.56
Sheffield		12.52	13.58	14.41	15.39	16.39	17.39	18.40	19.37
Chesterfield		13.06	14.13	14.56	15.54	16.53	17.53	18.54	19.53
Nottingham	12.32	13.44	14.54	15.48	16.40	17.38	18.46	19.34	20.35
Grantham	13.14	14.20		16.24	17.24	18.18	19.22		21.19
Peterborough	13.43	14.56	16.05	17.00	17.53	18.55	19.55		21.55
Ely	14.28	15.38	16.41	17.39	18.35	19.32	20.31		22.31
Thetford	14.49	15.59	17.02	18.00	18.56	19.55	20.52		22.52
Norwich	15.28	16.37	17.35	18.35	19.29	20.28	21.25		23.35

⑤ **timetable** 火車時刻表

⑥ **ticket window** 售票口

⑦ **ticket** 車票

⑧ **ticket stub** 票根

⑨ **express** 快車

⑩ **ticket machine** 自動售票機

⑪ **gate** 剪票口

⑫ **locker** 寄物櫃

⑬ **train car** 車廂

⑭ **conductor** 列車掌

⑮ **dining car** 餐車

⑯ **first-class** 頭等車廂

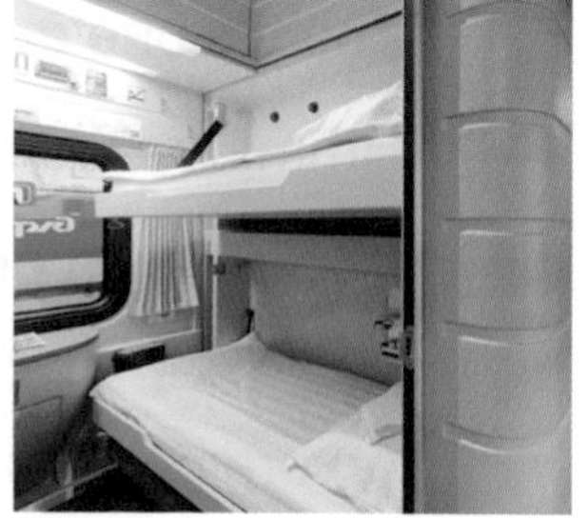

⑰ **sleeper** 臥舖車

⑱ **catch the train** 趕火車

⑲ **ticket office** 售票處

⑳ **reserve a seat** 劃位

㉑ **fare** 票價

㉒ **one-way ticket** (US) 單程票（美國）

㉓ **round-trip ticket** (US) 來回票（美國）

㉔ **single ticket** (UK) 單程票（英國）

㉕ **return ticket** (UK) 來回票（英國）

㉖ **refund the ticket** 退票

㉗ **change trains** 換車

㉘ **train type** 車種

㉙ **through/nonstop train** 直達車

㉚ **stopping/local train** 慢車（每站停的車）

㉛ **full** 客滿

㉜ **line** 鐵路線

㉝ **car** (US) / **coach** (UK) 普通車廂（美國／英國）

㉞ **aisle seat** 靠走道的座位

㉟ **window seat** 靠窗的座位

㊱ **excursion** 短程旅行

PART 2 Conversations

01 Traveling by Train in England 在英國搭火車 048

P *Peter* 彼得　B *Booking clerk* 售票員

P Good morning. Could you tell me the times of trains to London, please?

B Yes. There are trains at 7:59, 9:18, and 10:32.

P What time does the 7:59 train get to London?

B At 9:36.

P What about coming back? I'd like to come back at about 7 p.m.

B There's one at 7:10 p.m. and the next one is at 7:40 p.m.

P Hmm, how much is a return ticket?

B If you get on before 4 p.m. or after 6 p.m., there is a saver return which is £9. An ordinary return is £16.

P An ordinary return, please.

P 早安。可以告訴我去倫敦的火車發車時間嗎？

B 好的。7點59分、9點18分和10點32分各有一班。

P 7點59分的火車幾點到達倫敦？

B 9點36分。

P 回程的時間呢？我想在晚上7點左右回來。

B 晚上7點10分有一班，再下一班是7點40分。

P 嗯，來回票多少錢？

B 如果您在下午4點之前或6點之後上車，有優惠票價9英鎊的當天來回票。普通來回票是16英鎊。

P 請給我一張普通來回票。

02 Traveling by Train in America 在美國搭火車 049

A *Adam* 亞當　B *Booking clerk* 售票員

A What time does the train for Boston leave?

B 9:25 on Platform 12, Track B.

A When does it arrive?

B It should be there at 11:45, but it may be a little late.

A How much is a one-way ticket?

B It's $32.00.

A 去波士頓的火車什麼時候開？

B 9點25分，在12月台，軌道B。

A 什麼時候抵達波士頓？

B 應該是11點45分到，不過有時候會誤點。

A 單程車票一張多少錢？

B 32美元。

如果你打算在美國做短途旅行，建議你可以搭乘火車。坐火車可以避免繁瑣的安檢，另一方面空間也比較大，並且可以使用手機和筆記本電腦，有些車廂甚至安裝有電源插頭。而且，坐火車還可能比搭乘飛機便宜而且省時。

Amtrak 是美國國家鐵路客運公司，是十分穩靠的交通工具，提供相當完善的服務。可以在行程前先上 Amtrak 網站（www.amtrak.com）查看時刻表。

Amtrak 美國國鐵

03 Ordering Train Tickets Online 線上訂火車票

T *Tourist* 旅客　I *Information Desk Clerk* 服務櫃檯人員

T I'd like to visit Bath for a day. Is there a train from here?

I Yes. There's frequent train service from here to Bath.

T Do I just buy my tickets at the station?

I You can, but it will be cheaper if you book an advance ticket online.

T How do I do that?

I Just visit the National Rail website. You can pay online with your credit card.

T How do I get my tickets? Are they mailed to me?

I You pick up your pre-booked tickets at the station from one of the ticket machines.

T 我想要去巴斯一天，這裡有火車會到嗎？

I 有的，這裡到巴斯有固定的火車往返。

T 我只要在車站買票就好了嗎？

I 您可以這麼做，但若您預先在網路上訂票會更便宜。

T 要怎麼訂？

I 只要上國家鐵路局網站就好，您可以用信用卡付款。

T 那我要怎麼拿票？會寄給我嗎？

I 只要在車站的售票機台領取您預訂的票即可。

01 Looking for the Train Station and Asking for the Train Schedule 尋找火車站和詢問火車時刻

尋找火車站

1. Where is the nearest railroad station?
請問離這裡最近的火車站在哪裡？

尋找地鐵站

2. Where is the nearest subway station?
請問離這裡最近的地鐵站在哪裡？

購票地點

3. Where is the ticket window? 請問售票處在哪裡？

4. Can I buy a ticket here? 我可以在這裡買票嗎？

售票機是否找零

5. Can I get change from the ticket machine?
自動售票機會找零嗎？

詢問訂位

6. A Can I reserve seats on the train? 我可以訂位嗎？
B You needn't reserve seats on that train. It's never full.
那班車不必訂位，因為從來就坐不滿。

該搭哪一班車

7. Which train do I take to Seattle?
去西雅圖應該搭哪一班車？

8. Can I take this train to London?
去倫敦可以坐這班車嗎？

該搭哪一條路線

轉車

9. A Which line goes to Chinatown?
請問到中國城要搭哪一條線？
B Take the Blue Line to Seventh Street Station, and then change to the Red Line.
先搭藍線到第七街，再轉紅線。

schedule board 時刻表

問停靠站

⑩ Does this train stop at Union Square?
這班車會停聯合廣場嗎？

進站時間

⑪ When does it get in? 火車何時進站？

發車時間

⑫ Ⓐ When is the next train to Los Angeles?
下一班到洛杉磯的車幾點開？

Ⓐ What time does the next train leave? 下一班火車幾點開？

Ⓑ The next one leaves at 6:30 on Platform 20.
下一班車6點30分從第20月台開出。

Ⓑ There's one at 8:30 and one at 9:40.
有一班車8點30分開，還有一班9點40分開。

Ⓑ One just left about 5 minutes ago, and there's another one at 10:30. 有一班車五分鐘前剛開走；下一班車10點30分開。

抵達時間

⑬ Ⓐ What time does it reach Washington?
火車什麼時候到華盛頓？

Ⓐ When does it get there? 幾點會到那裡？

Ⓑ It's scheduled to arrive at 11:50.
按照列車時刻表是11點50分到。

Ⓑ It's due in at noon. 中午會到。

火車時刻表

⑭ Can I have a look at the timetable?
我可以看一下時刻表嗎？

⑮ Excuse me. I'd like to find out about trains to Cambridge.
不好意思，我想請問一下去劍橋的火車時刻。

02 Buying Tickets and Choosing Train Types
購票、選擇車種 052

買票

16 I want a first-class single to London.
我想買一張到倫敦的頭等單程車票。

17 I'd like to buy a ticket to San Francisco.
我想買一張到舊金山的火車票。

18 Two round-trip tickets for tomorrow, non-smoking.
兩張明天的來回車票，非吸菸車廂的。

快慢車

19 A Is it an express train? 這班是快車嗎？
B It's a local train. 這班是慢車。

20 I want to take an express train, not a local train.
我要搭快車，不要慢車。

臥鋪車

21 One sleeper to Milan, please. 一張到米蘭的臥鋪票。

22 Please give me one ticket to Seattle for the sleeping car.
我要一張到西雅圖的臥鋪票。

23 Can I have an upper berth? 我可以選上鋪嗎？

24 I'd like the lower berth. 我想要睡下鋪。

問路程遠近

25 Is it a long ride?
路程遠不遠？

詢問票價

26 A What's the fare? 票價多少？
A How much is the fare to Los Angeles?
去洛杉磯的火車票一張多少錢？
B It's $30.00 one way or $55.00 round trip.
單程票價30美元，來回票價55美元。

27 What's the round-trip fare? 來回票多少錢？

是否要換車

28 A Do I have to change trains? 我需要換車嗎？
B You needn't change trains. It's a through train.
您不必轉車，這一班是直達快車。

歐美許多國家在通過驗票口時，乘客通常只需將票卡插入驗票機，機器會自動驗票。搭乘火車途中，則會有車掌一一驗票，請務必將票根保留。

03 Heading to the Platform to Catch the Train
前往月台搭車 053

搭車月台

29 A Which platform is for the train to Oxford?
去牛津的火車是在哪個月台搭車？
A What platform does the train leave from?
這班火車由第幾月台開出？
B Please go to Platform 7. 請前往七號月台。

30 A How can I get to Platform 4? 我要怎麼到四號月台？
B Go through that door on your left and down the stairs. There is Platform 4.
穿過您左手邊的那道門，再走下樓梯，那裡就是四號月台。

確認火車

31 Does this train go to Berlin? 這班車是到柏林的嗎？

32 Is this the train to Milan? 這是往米蘭的車嗎？

錯過火車

33 I missed the train. 我錯過火車了。

搭錯火車

34 I took the wrong train. 我搭錯車了。

退票

35 I'd like to get a refund on this ticket. 我想退票。

如果你要搭乘地鐵或捷運，所需的會話基本上和火車一樣。❶ 在美國及澳洲，地鐵稱為 subway（洛杉磯稱 Metro），❷ 在英國稱為 underground 或 tube，❸ 在法國稱為 Metro（上車時必須自己拉桿或按鈕才會開門）。

有些地方的地鐵會發行一日票、週票或月票，長時間待在某地的旅客也可以購買這類車票。

04 On the Train 在火車上 (054)

尋找座位

36 In which car can I find seat 35W?
請問座位35W是在哪一節車廂？

找洗手間

37 Where is the lavatory (restroom/toilet)? 請問洗手間在哪裡？

驗票

38 May I see your ticket, please? 請出示車票好嗎？

補票

39 Do I have to pay an extra charge? 我需要補票嗎？

詢問剩餘站數

40 How many more stops are there before we get to Seattle?
請問到西雅圖還有幾站？

尋找餐車

41 Ⓐ Is there a dining car on this train? 這班車上有餐車嗎？
Ⓑ The dining car is in the seventh carriage.
餐車在第七車廂。

預訂餐車座位

42 Do I need to reserve a table for the dining car?
我需要預約餐車的座位嗎？

43 I'd like to make a reservation for two at 6:30 tonight.
我想預約今晚6點半，兩個人的位子。

下車尋找出口

44 Which is the exit for Chinatown?
請問往中國城的出口是哪一個？

dining car 餐車

Renting a Car

Chapter 7

租車

PART 1

Key Terms

① **rent a car** 租車

② **international driver's license / international driving permit** 國際駕照

③ **rate** 費用

④ **try (it)** 試車

⑤ **check in / return** 歸還車子
⟷ **check out** 租走車子

⑥ **compact** 小型車

⑦ **SUV = sport utility vehicle** 休旅車

⑧ **van** 箱型車

⑨ **speed limit** 速限

⑩ **police officer** 警察

⑪ **parking space** 停車位

⑫ **parking lot** 停車場

⑬ **parking meter** 停車計費表

⑭ **one-way** 單行道的；單向的

⑮ **No U-turn** 禁止迴轉

⑯ **road map** 地圖

⑰ **scrape/scratch** 刮痕

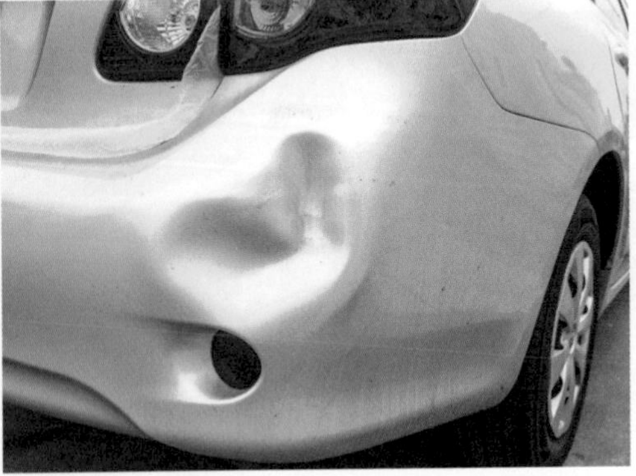

⑱ **dent** 凹痕

⑲ **automatic car** 自排車

⑳ **manual car** 手排車

㉑ **start a car** 發動車子

㉒ **mileage** 哩程數

㉓ **under construction** 道路施工

㉔ **be broken down** 拋錨

㉕ **flat tire** 爆胎

㉖ **deposit / security hold** 押金
㉗ **rental agreement** 租車合約
㉘ **insurance** 保險
㉙ **full insurance/coverage** 全險
㉚ **Personal Accident Insurance** (PAI) 個人意外險
㉛ **Personal Effects Protection** (PEP) 攜帶物品險
㉜ **Low Protection** (LP) 強制險
㉝ **Theft Protection** (TP) 竊盜險
㉞ **Loss Damage Waiver** (LDW) = **Collision Damage Waiver** (CDW) 碰撞險（發生車禍導致汽車毀損時，可免除負擔賠償金）
㉟ **walk-through** 檢視車子是否有毀損
㊱ **dead end** 此路不通

PART 2 Conversations

01 I'd Like to Rent a Car. 我想租車 059

V *Victor* 維多　C *Car Rental Clerk* 租車行

V I'd like to rent a car.

C May I see your driver's license, please?

V Here is my international driver's license. What kinds of cars do you have?

C We have Honda, Citroen, and Toyota. Which make and model do you prefer?

V I'll take the Citroen DS 5. What is the rate for the car per day?

C The price is €60 per day. Do you want insurance?

V Full coverage, please.

C That's an extra €10 a day.

V Do I have to fill up when I check in?

C Yes.

V 我想要租車。

C 請出示您的駕照好嗎？

V 這是我的國際駕照。你們有什麼車？

C 我們有本田、雪鐵龍和豐田的車，您想要哪一種？

V 那我要租雪鐵龍的DS 5。租金一天多少？

C 一天60歐元。您要保險嗎？

V 我要加全險。

C 那一天要多加10歐元。

V 我還車的時候需要把油加滿嗎？

C 要的。

02 Booking a Car Rental Online 線上預訂租車 060

M Is it possible to book a car online next time, to save time?

C Yes, just visit our website. You can book your car there.

M What's the booking process?

C Just choose your model and the date and location of your pick-up. We'll have the car ready for you when you arrive.

M Is it cheaper to book a car online than in person?

C We often have Internet-only deals. So yes, it can be cheaper to rent online.

M 為了節省時間，下次我可以線上預訂租車嗎？

C 可以的，只要上我們的網站，就可以預訂租車。

M 預訂流程是什麼呢？

C 只要選擇您要預訂的車種，然後選定您的取車日期和地點。我們就會在您抵達時將車準備好。

M 線上預訂租車會比親自來租還便宜嗎？

C 我們通常會有線上專屬優惠價，所以線上預訂是有可能比較便宜。

03 The Car Isn't Running Smoothly. 車子開起來不太順。 061

A *Anna* 安娜　V *Victor* 維多

A The car isn't running smoothly. I'd like to have a look at it.

V What's the matter with it?

A I'm not sure. It could be the tires. Let's stop here.

V How about the tires?

A Nothing serious. The right one needs some air.

A 車子開起來不大對勁，我想檢查一下。

V 出了什麼毛病？

A 不清楚。有可能是輪胎出問題，我們先在這裡停一下。

V 輪胎怎麼了？

A 沒什麼大問題，右邊輪胎需要充氣。

PART 3

Useful Expressions

01 Renting a Car 租車 062

找租車處

1. Where can I rent a car? 哪裡可以租車？

租車

2. I'd like to rent a car. 我想要租車。
3. I'd like to rent a compact car. 我要租一台小型車。

租用時間

4. Ⓐ For how long? 您要租多久？
   Ⓑ Four days. 四天。

詢問車種

5. Which make and model would you like to rent? 您要租哪一種車款？
6. What kinds of cars do you have? 你們有哪些車？
7. Do you have a Peugeot 206 here? 你們有標緻206的車嗎？

自排或手排

8. Manual or automatic? 您要手排車還是自排車？

Let's find your ideal car

Pick-up Location ❶
city, airport, station, region, district
☐ Drop car off at a different location ❷

Pick-up Date: ❸ Jul 25 2019 | 10 | 00
Drop-off Date: ❹ Jul 28 2019 | 10 | 00

☑ Driver aged between 30–65?

❺ Purpose of rental (optional) ○ Business ○ Leisure

✓ No credit card fees ❻
✓ No amendment fees ❼
✓ 24/7 phone support ❽

Search

❶ Pick-up Location 取車地點
❷ Drop car off at a different location 甲地租乙地還
❸ Pick-up Date 取車日期
❹ Drop-off Date 還車日期
❺ Purpose of rental (optional) Business / Leisure 租車用途（選填）出差／出遊
❻ No credit card fees 無信用卡衍生費用
❼ No amendment fees 無改單費用
❽ 24/7 phone support 24小時電話支援

Types of Cars 車子種類

sedan car 轎車

van 箱型車

compact car 小型車

SUV 休旅車

limousine 豪華轎車

hybrid car 油電混合車

出示駕照

9 May I see your international driving permit?
請出示您的國際駕照好嗎？

詢問租金

10 What is the rate for the car per day? 一天的租金是多少？

11 How much is the daily rental? 一天的租金是多少？

12 Could you show me the rate list? 有沒有價目表可以看？

押金

13 A How much is the deposit? 押金要多少？
B There is a $500 deposit. 需要500美元的押金。

保險費

14 Does this include insurance? 這個價錢有含保險費嗎？

全險

15 Full coverage, please. 我要保全險。

意外險

16 I would like the accident insurance. 我要保意外險。

加滿油

17 Do I have to fill up when I check in?
我還車時需要把油加滿嗎？

哩程數限制

18 Is the mileage free? 開車哩程數不計費嗎？

19 Is there any mileage limit? 開車哩程數有限制嗎？

20 What is the charge per mile? 哩程數怎麼收費？

路標 Road Signs

STOP 停車再開

DO NOT ENTER 禁止進入

YIELD 讓道

DETOUR 繞道

RAILROAD CROSSING 鐵路平交道

DEAD END 此路不通

ONE WAY 單行道

INTERSTATE ROUTE 州際公路

U.S. ROUTE 美國國道

MINIMUM SPEED 最低速限

SPEED LIMIT 最高速限

DO NOT PASS 禁止通行

NO U-TURN 禁止迴轉

NO LEFT TURN 禁止左轉

NO RIGHT TURN 禁止右轉

NO MOTOR VEHICLES 禁止汽機車通行

還車地點

21 Ⓐ Where should I return the car? 我要在哪裡還車？

Ⓑ You need to return the car here. 你必須把車開回這裡。

22 Can I return the car at any of your branches?
我可以到你們任何一家分店還車嗎？

23 I'd like to return the car at the airport. 我想在機場還車。

要求看車

24 May I see the car first? 我可以先看車嗎？

要求試車

25 I'd like to try the car before I rent it. 我想先試車再租。

要求換車

26 I don't think this car is in very good condition. Can I see another? 我覺得這部車不太好，我可以看別部嗎？

如果要租車，建議在出發前先上網或是打電話訂車，車商就會在約定的時間，將車子送到指定地點或機場。

需特別注意，在英、紐澳等國開車是右座駕駛（right-hand drive），不同於國內的左駕（left-hand drive），開車時要特別小心。租車前建議先試車，並檢查車子本身是否有刮痕或受損，這些都須在事前先跟車行人員說清楚。若真的發生事故，該由哪一方承擔責任，也都必須先當面談清，以免事後衍生更多問題。

還車	27 I want to return this car. Here's the rental agreement. 我要還車，這是租車合約。
車子有刮痕	28 Ⓐ There is a scrape on the door. 車門上有一道刮痕。 Ⓑ It was there when I rented this car. 我租車的時候就有了。

02 On the Road 開車上路 063

尋找停車場	29 Is there a parking lot nearby? 附近有停車場嗎？ 30 Can I park here? 我可以把車停在這裡嗎？
靠右行駛	31 We'll have to keep to the right. 我們必須靠右行駛。
詢問速限	32 What's the speed limit in the city? 市區限速是多少？
確認路線	33 Are you sure we're on the right route? 你確定我們沒走錯路？ 34 Can we take any other route? 還有別的路可以走嗎？
單行道	35 This is one-way traffic. 這是單行道。

03 Car Malfunction 汽車故障 064

覺得倒霉	36 What bad luck! 真倒楣！
車有問題	37 Ⓐ What's wrong with the car? 車子怎麼了？
車子發出怪聲	Ⓑ The car makes strange noises. 車子發出奇怪的聲音。
煞車失靈	38 The brakes cannot hold well. 剎車不靈。
	39 There is something wrong with the brakes. 煞車有點問題。
輪胎沒氣	40 I've got a flat tire. 輪胎沒氣了。／輪胎爆胎了。
電瓶沒電	41 The battery is dead. 電瓶沒電了。
無法發動	42 The car is hard to start. 車子不好發動。
引擎問題	43 It might be the engine. 可能是引擎（出問題）。
車子拋錨	44 My car is broken down. 我的車拋錨了。
請求拖吊	45 Can you send somebody to tow it away? 請派人來拖吊好嗎？

國際駕照（International Driving Permit）申辦

(cc by Ywang.tw)

若要出國自駕，務必要在出國前先辦好國際駕照，申辦方式如下：

★ 換國際駕照所需證件：

① 身分證或居留證正本
（若為代委託辦理，則請代辦人攜帶雙證件）

② 原駕照正本

③ 2 吋半身照片 2 張

④ 護照影本（用以查核英文姓名及出生地）

★ 申辦費用：250 元

★ 申辦地點：監理站的「駕照綜合窗口」

汽車構造 Car Parts

windshield 擋風玻璃

side/wing mirror 後照鏡

windshield wiper 雨刷

trunk 後行李箱

hood 車蓋

headlight 車燈

tire 輪胎

signal light 方向燈

license plate 車牌

bumper 保險桿

steering wheel 方向盤

emergency brake 手煞車

gauge 儀表

dashboard 儀錶板

horn 喇叭

gear 排檔桿

driver's seat 駕駛座

passenger seat 副駕駛座

back seat 後座

child safety seat
兒童安全座椅

rear-view mirror 後視鏡

GPS (global positioning system) 導航系統

exhaust pipe 排氣管

engine 引擎

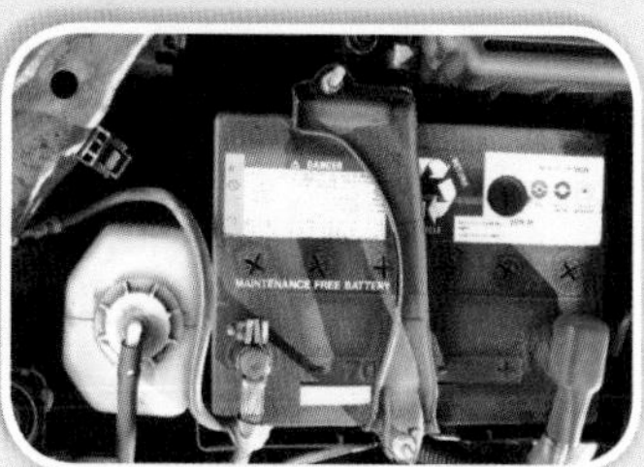
battery 電瓶

jumper cables 救車線

emergency warning triangle 三角警示牌

traffic cone 交通錐

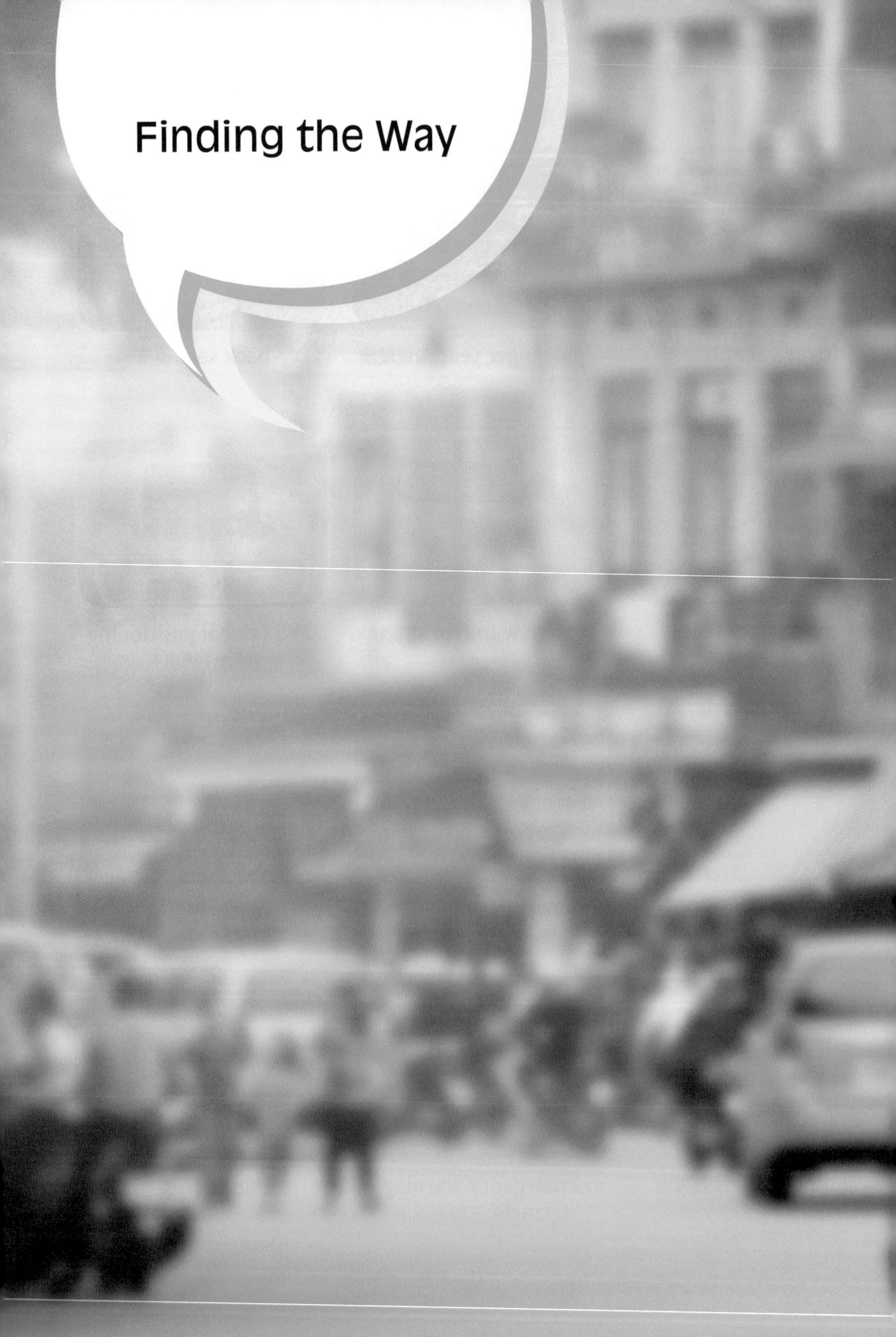

Finding the Way

Chapter 8

問路

PART 1

Key Terms

① **landmark** 地標

② **lose one's way** 迷路

③ **direction** 方向

④ **ask for directions** 問路

⑤ **city map** 市區地圖

⑥ **traffic lights** 紅綠燈

⑦ **block** 街區

⑧ **at the corner** 在轉角

⑨ **cross the street** 過馬路

⑩ **public restroom/toilet** 公共廁所

⑭ **navigation app** 導航應用程式

⑮ **sign** (n.) 標牌；標誌

⑯ **address** 地址

⑰ **road** 道路

⑱ **area** 地區

⑲ **location** 位置

⑳ **mark** 標誌

㉑ **look for** 尋找

㉒ **miss** 錯過

㉓ **building** 建築物

㉔ **across/opposite** 在……對面

㉕ **head** (v.) 前往

㉖ **on foot** 步行

PART 2

Conversations

01 Could You Tell Me the Way to . . . ?
請問去……怎麼走？ 067

V *Vicky* 薇琪　P *Peter* 彼得

V Excuse me. Could you tell me the way to the Star Hotel?

P Yes. Go down the main road. You can't miss it.

V How long will it take me to get there?

P It's only about a five-minute walk.

V Thank you very much.

P You're welcome.

V 不好意思，可以請問你晨星飯店怎麼走嗎？

P 可以，沿著大路往前走，就可以找到了。

V 到那裡大概要多久？

P 只要走五分鐘左右。

V 非常感謝你。

P 不用客氣。

02 I Think I'm Lost Here. 我想我迷路了。 

V *Vincent* 文森 A *Annie* 安妮

V Good morning, madam. I think I'm lost here.
The place I want to go to is a hotel called the Hilton.

A Do you know in which area?

V No, I am sorry I have no idea. I am a stranger here.

A I see. Well, do you know anything near the hotel?

V Oh, yes. My friend told me the hotel was near the Central Railway Station.

A Then you'll have to take a bus and get off at the Central Railway Station.

V Can you show me where the Central Railway Station is on this map?

A OK.

V 女士，早安。我想我迷路了，我要去希爾頓大飯店。

A 你知道是在哪一個地區嗎？

V 對不起，我不知道，我對這裡不熟。

A 這樣啊。那你知道飯店附近有什麼地標嗎？

V 知道，我朋友說是在中央火車站附近。

A 那麼你就坐公車到中央火車站下車。

V 妳可以指給我看中央火車站在這張地圖上哪裡嗎？

A 可以啊。

PART 3

Useful Expressions

01 Asking for Directions and Giving Directions 問路與報路 069

請求幫助	**1** Excuse me. I wonder if you can help me. 不好意思，可不可以請你幫個忙？
迷路	**2** I lost my way. 我迷路了。 **3** I'm lost. 我迷路了。
詢問目前所在位置	**4** What is this street? 這是哪一條街？ **5** Where are we on this map? 我們在地圖上的哪個位置？
問路	**6** Where can I find the railway station? 請問火車站在哪裡？ **7** I'm looking for the Hilton Hotel. 我想找希爾頓飯店。 **8** Could you tell me the way to the City Zoo? 請問去市立動物園怎麼走？ **9** How can I get there? 怎樣才可以到那裡？ **10** Excuse me. I'm looking for a supermarket. Is there one near here? 不好意思，我在找超市，請問這附近有嗎？
對方不知道路	**11** I'm afraid I don't know. 我也不知道。 **12** I'm a stranger here myself. 我對這裡也不熟。
過馬路就找得到	**13** Cross the street, and you will find the school. 穿過馬路，你就會看到學校。 **14** It's across the street from here. 從這裡過馬路過去就是了。

city map 市區地圖

沿著路走

15 Go straight back down this street for about three minutes and you'll find yourself at the park.
你沿這條路往回走大約三分鐘，就可以找到公園。

16 Just go down this street, and you'll find the hotel.
沿這條路往前走，你就可以找到那間旅館。

17 Take the second road on the left and go straight.
從左邊第二條馬路一直往前走。

走到路底

18 Keep going until you come to an end. 一直走到底。

19 Please go to the end of this road.
請走到這條馬路的盡頭。

轉彎

20 Turn left at the first corner, and it's the second building on your left. 在第一個路口左轉，左邊第二棟大樓就是了。

走過街區

21 Go that way for three blocks, then turn right.
往那裡走經過三條街，然後向右轉。

22 Yes. It's two blocks straight ahead. You can't miss it.
是的，過了前面兩條街就可以看到了。

在轉角處

23 Well, let me see. Oh, yes, it's just around the corner.
我想想看。喔，對，就在轉角的地方。

02 Finding the Address on a Map and Explaining the Bus Routes 看地圖、地址／說明公車路線 070

畫地圖

24 Could you draw a map, please? 你能畫張地圖給我嗎？

25 Could you mark it here? 你幫我標明一下好嗎？

尋找地標

26 Are there any signs along the way? 一路上有什麼標示嗎？

27 Are there any landmarks? 有什麼顯著的地標嗎？

對方幫忙看地址

28 Can I check the address you have?
地址給我看一下好嗎？

帶路

29 Let me take you there. 讓我帶你去吧。

30 I'm going that way. I'll show you. 我正好要去那裡，我幫你帶路。

詢問路程

31 Can we get there in about ten minutes?
我們十分鐘內到得了那裡嗎？

32 How far is it to the post office? 這裡離郵局多遠？

33 How long will it take me to get there? 我到那裡要多久？

走路是否能到

34 **Can I get to the hotel on foot?**
走路到得了飯店嗎？

詢問方向

35 **Which direction is it to the hospital?**
去醫院要往哪個方向走？

36 **Is this the correct direction?** 這個方向對嗎？

確認路線

37 **Is this the right way to the Hilton Hotel?**
這是去希爾頓飯店的路嗎？

38 **Should I go this way or that way?**
我應該走這條路，還是那條路？

詢問公車路線

39 Ⓐ **Does this bus go to Green Lake?**
這輛公車有到碧潭嗎？

Ⓐ **Can I travel from here to the Star Hotel by this bus?**
這輛公車有到晨星飯店嗎？

Ⓑ **It's going as far as the railway station.**
這輛車只到火車站為止。

該坐哪一路公車

40 Ⓐ **I'm going to the National Palace Museum. Which bus should I take?** 我想要去故宮博物院，應該坐哪一路的公車？

Ⓑ **Take a number 37 or 49 bus.** 坐37路或49路公車。

帶路去坐公車

41 **Walk with me. I'm heading in the direction where you'll be catching the bus you want.**
跟著我走，我要去的正好和你要搭公車的地方是同一個方向。

尋找公廁

42 **Is there a public restroom near here?**
這附近有公共廁所嗎？

navigation app 導航程式

At the Gas Station

Chapter 9

加油站

PART 1

Key Terms

① **gas station** (US) / **petrol station** (UK) 加油站（美／英）

② **gas gauge** 油錶

③ **run out of gas** 沒油了

④ **regular** 普通汽油

⑤ **unleaded** 無鉛汽油

⑥ **premium** 高級汽油

⑦ **diesel** 柴油

⑧ **insert** 插入

⑨ **gas pump** 加油機

⑩ **gas pump nozzle** 油槍

⑪ **gas/fuel tank** 油箱

⑫ **gas tank door** 油箱門

⑬ **gas tank cap** 油箱蓋

⑭ **self-service gas station** 自助式加油站

⑮ **full-service gas station** 有站務員服務的加油站

⑯ **oil** 機油

⑰ **gallon** 加侖（**liter** 公升）

⑱ **press the button** 按按鈕

074

㉖ **fill up something** 將……加滿；填滿

㉗ **select the gas** 選擇汽油

㉘ **release** 釋放

㉙ **nearby** 附近

㉚ **come to (the total amount of money)** 共……元

PART 2 Conversations

01 At the Full-Service Gas Station 請站務員加油 075

V *Victor* 維多　M *Mandy* 曼迪　A *Attendant* 站務員

V We're running out of gas. How far is the nearest gas station?

M It's only a few kilometers to the nearest gas station.

[Five minutes later]

V Fill it up, please.

A What kind of gas would you like?

V Regular, please.

A OK.

V How much is that?

A It comes to $50.

V 我們快沒油了，最近的加油站還有多遠？

M 再開幾公里就到了。

〔五分鐘後〕

V 請加滿。

A 要加哪一種油？

V 普通汽油。

A 好的。

V 多少錢？

A 總共50美元。

gas station attendant 加油站站務員

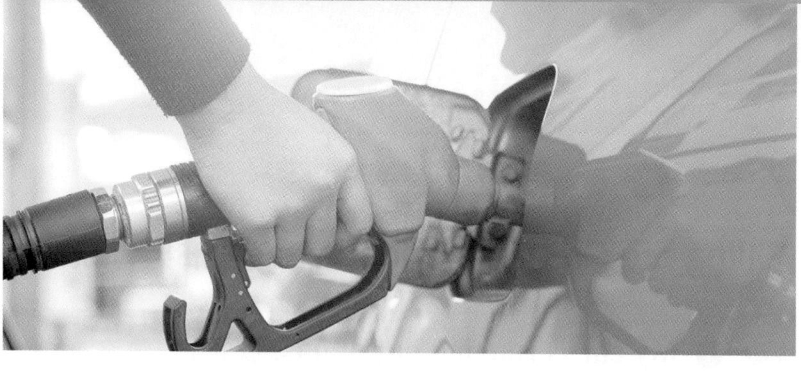

02 At the Self-Service Gas Station 在自助加油站 

P *Phoebe* 菲碧　H *Harry* 哈利

P Excuse me. Can you tell me how to fill up the tank?

H Of course. First, run the credit card through the machine, and select the gas you'd like.

P What should I do after that?

H Insert the nozzle into the tank of your car. Be careful, the gas hose is very heavy. Now press the button on the pump to allow the gas to flow, and pull up on the trigger in the handle of the gas hose. The gas will be released into the tank of your car. When the tank is full, the fuel will stop pumping.

P That's easy! Thank you.

P 不好意思，你可不可以教我怎麼加油？

H 可以啊。先刷卡，並選擇你要哪一種油。

P 然後呢？

H 然後將油槍嘴插入車子的油箱，小心點，管子很重的。好，現在按下加油機上的按鈕，油會開始流出來，把油槍握把上面的板機壓住，就可以加油了。油一加滿，機器會自動停止加油。

P 滿簡單的耶，謝謝！

PART 3

Useful Expressions

01 Filling the Gas Tank and Paying 加油與付款 077

車子快沒油

1 My car is running out of gas. 我的車子快沒油了。

2 There isn't any gas in the tank. 油箱裡沒油了。

詢問加油站地點

3 Is there a gas station nearby?
這附近有加油站嗎？

4 How far is the nearest gas station?
離這裡最近的加油站有多遠？

要加哪種油

5 A What kind of gas do you want? 您要哪一種汽油？
B Regular, please. 普通汽油。
B Unleaded, please. 無鉛汽油。

要加多少油

6 A How much gas do you want? 要加多少汽油？
B Ten gallons of regular gas, please.
請加十加侖的普通汽油。

加滿

7 Fill it up with regular, please. 請加滿普通汽油。

8 Could you fill it up, please? 請你把油加滿好嗎？

加機油

9 Fill it up with unleaded and check the oil, please.
請加滿無鉛汽油，還有檢查一下機油。

10 Do you want any oil? 要加機油嗎？

水箱加水

11 I've got enough oil, but I haven't got much water.
我有足夠的機油，但水不夠。

檢查胎壓

12 Please check the tire pressure for me. 請幫我檢查一下胎壓。

check the tire pressure 檢查胎壓

gas/fuel gauge 油錶

self-service gas station 自助加油站

詢問油價	⓭ How much for one gallon? 一加侖多少錢？ ⓮ What is the price per liter? 一公升多少錢？ ⓯ What does it come to? 一共多少錢？
如何付款	⓰ Do I have to pay first or later? 我要先付錢還是後付錢？
自助式加油	⓱ Ten dollars for No.3, please. 三號機請加10美元。
詢問如何自助加油	⓲ How do I use the pump? 請問要怎麼加油？ ⓳ Could you show me how to fill up the tank? 可以告訴我怎麼加油嗎？
何處付款	⓴ Where do I pay? 我要到哪裡付錢？

At the Hotel:
Checking In
203

Chapter 10

旅館登記住宿

PART 1

Key Terms

① **reception** 接待櫃檯

② **lobby** 大廳

③ **service bell** 服務鈴

④ **check in** 辦理住宿登記 ⟷ ⑤ **check out** 退房

⑥ **single room** 單人房

⑦ **double room** 雙人房（一張大床）

⑧ **twin room** 雙人房（兩張單人床）

⑨ **triple room** 三人房

⑩ **suite** 套房

⑪ **bath** 衛浴設備

⑫ **elevator** 電梯

⑬ **key** 鑰匙

⑭ **key card** 鑰匙卡

⑮ **breakfast** 早餐

⑯ **shuttle bus** 接駁車

⑰ **swimming pool** 游泳池

⑱ **buffet restaurant** 自助餐廳

⑲ **gymnasium (gym)** 健身房

⑳ **sauna** 三溫暖

㉑ **bar** 酒吧

㉒ **tennis court** 網球場

23 **coffee shop** 咖啡廳

24 **conference room** 會議廳

25 **emergency exit** 逃生門

26 **bellboy** 大廳服務員（負責提行李、開房門）

27 **doorman** 門房（負責開關飯店門和計程車門）

28 **room maid** 房間打掃人員

29 **reservation** 預約

30 **vacancy** 空房

31 **registration form/card** 登記住宿卡

32 **rate** 住宿費

33 **deposit** 訂金

34 **discount** 折扣

35 **tip/gratuity** 小費

36 **valuables** 貴重物品

37 **wake-up call / morning call** 晨喚服務

PART 2 Conversations

01 I'd Like to Check In.
我要辦住宿登記。（已預約住宿） 082

R *Receptionist* 接待櫃檯　S *Steve* 史提夫

R Good afternoon. May I help you?

S Yes. I made a reservation and I'd like to check in.

R Your name, please?

S Steve Johnson.

R Oh, yes. A double room for two nights. Is that correct?

S Yes, it is.

R Would you please fill out this registration card?

S No problem.

R 午安。我能為您效勞嗎？

S 是的。我訂了房間，現在想辦理住宿登記。

R 請問貴姓大名？

S 史提夫‧強森。

R 喔，有的。一間雙人房兩晚，對嗎？

S 對。

R 請您幫我填寫這份登記表格好嗎？

S 沒問題。

Fill out the registration card 填寫登記表格

02 Do You Have Any Vacancies Now? 請問目前有空房嗎？（臨時住宿） 083

S *Sandy* 珊蒂　R *Receptionist* 接待櫃檯

S Do you have any vacancies now?

R Certainly, madam. What kind of room would you like to have?

S A single.

R We have a room commanding a good view of the sea.

S What's your rate?

R One hundred dollars a night, madam.

S That's fine. I'll take it.

S 請問目前有空房間嗎？

R 當然有，女士。您想要什麼樣的客房？

S 單人房。

R 我們有一間可以俯瞰海景的房間。

S 價錢多少？

R 一晚一百美元，女士。

S 好，我要那一間。

a room with sea view 海景房

03 Checking In With an Online Reservation 以網路預約辦理住宿登記 084

R *Receptionist* 接待櫃檯　G *Guest* 顧客

R Good afternoon, sir. Are you checking in?

G Yes. I've booked a single room for two nights.

R May I ask how you made the reservation?

G I did it online through a hotel-booking service.

R OK. I'll need your last name and your booking confirmation code.

G My last name is Peters, and the confirmation code is CY4587GB.

R Thank you, Mr. Peters.

[searches for the booking]

Yes, your room is ready for you now.

R 先生，午安。請問您要辦理住宿登記嗎？

G 是的，我有預訂兩晚的單人房。

R 請問您是透過哪裡預訂的呢？

G 我是在一個訂飯店的網站線上預訂的。

R 好的，請告訴我您的姓氏以及訂房確認代碼。

G 我姓彼得斯，我的確認代碼是 CY4587GB。

R 謝謝您，彼得斯先生。

〔尋找預訂資訊〕

有了，您的房間已經準備好了。

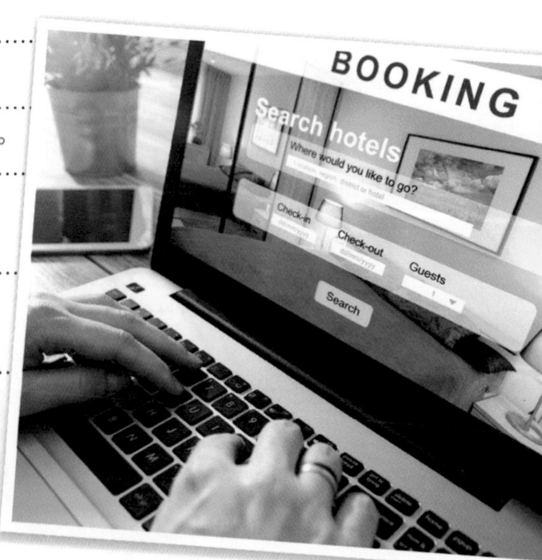

01 Booking a Room (Without a Reservation)
訂房（未預約）085

未先訂房

1. I don't have a reservation. 我沒有預約。

預訂旅館

2. Do you have any vacancies for tonight? 今晚還有空房嗎？
3. I'd like to make a reservation for tomorrow.
我要預訂明天的房間。
4. Can I book a double room? 我可以訂一間雙人房嗎？

訂雙人房

5. Do you have a double room for tonight? 今晚還有雙人房嗎？

訂單人房

6. I'd like to reserve a room with a single bed.
我想預訂一間單人房。

有浴室的房間

7. I can let you have a room with a bath.
我可以給您一間附有浴室的房間。

有景觀的房間

8. I'd like a room with a view. 我想要景觀好的房間。
9. It has a wonderful view of the sea.
在那裡可以看到美麗的海景。

房間升等

10. We will put you in a deluxe room at no extra charge.
我們會給您一間豪華套房，不額外收費。

旅館客滿

11. I'm afraid not, sir. We're booked solid right now.
先生，抱歉沒有，現在都客滿了。
12. I'm sorry, but we're fully booked up.
對不起，我們這裡已經客滿了。

住宿費用	13 How much is it per night? 住一晚多少錢？ 14 What is the rate? 住宿費用是多少？ 15 How much is a twin room? 雙人房要多少錢？
是否含稅	16 Does it include tax and service charge? 這個價錢有含稅和服務費嗎？
住宿時間	17 When would you like to stay here? 您預計什麼時候來住？ 18 How long do you plan to stay here? 您打算在這裡住多久？
便宜房間	19 Do you have less expensive rooms? 有沒有便宜一點的房間？
要求折扣	20 Could you give me a discount if I stay for three nights? 住三晚的話有沒有折扣？
要求看房間	21 May I see the room, please? 我可以先看看房間嗎？
決定房間	22 I'll take the room. 我要訂這間房。

02 Checking In (With a Reservation) 登記住宿（已預約） 086

已先訂房	23 I have a reservation. 我有預約住宿。
辦理住宿登記	24 Check in, please. 我要辦理住宿登記。 25 I made a reservation and I'd like to check in. 我有預約，想辦理住宿登記。

door hanger 門口掛牌

詢問資料

26 **May I have your name, please?** 您的大名是？

27 **Could you spell out your name?** 請問您的姓名怎麼拼？

填寫表格

28 **Will you fill in this registration form, please?**
請幫我填寫這張登記表好嗎？

飯店早餐

29 **Is breakfast included?** 有附早餐嗎？

30 **What time is breakfast served?** 早餐幾點供應？

31 **Where is the restaurant for breakfast?** 早餐要在哪裡吃？

使用保險箱

32 **Could you keep my valuables in the safe?**
幫我把貴重物品放在保險箱好嗎？

退房時間

33 **When should I check out?** 什麼時候要退房？

房間鑰匙

34 **Here is your room key.** 這是您的房間鑰匙。

房間樓層

35 **Which floor is it?** 房間在幾樓？

36 **Is the room on the third floor?** 房間在三樓嗎？

大廳服務員提行李

37 Ⓐ The bellboy will take your bags and show you to your room. 服務員會來幫您提行李袋，並帶您去房間。

Ⓑ Don't bother. I'll take care of them myself. 不用麻煩了，我自己拿就好了。

電梯位置

38 Excuse me. Where is the elevator? 請問電梯在哪裡？

外出回來索取鑰匙

39 May I have the key for room 704? 請給我704號房的鑰匙。

minibar 迷你吧台

03 Checking Out 退房 087

退房

40 Check out, please. 我要退房。

41 I want to check out. 我要退房。

42 I'm checking out this morning. 我今天早上辦理退房。

hotel 飯店；酒店；旅館

inn/tavern 小旅館

B&B (bed and breakfast) 民宿

(youth) hostel 青年旅館

capsule hotel 膠囊旅館

延遲退房 43 My plane leaves in the evening. Can I check out later?
我是搭傍晚的飛機，我可以晚一點退房嗎？

是否使用迷你吧台 44 Ⓐ Did you use the minibar? 您有使用迷你吧台嗎？
Ⓑ No, I didn't. 我沒有使用。

付款方式 45 How are you going to settle your account? 您打算如何付款？
46 And your method of payment? 您的付款方式是什麼？

要求查看帳單 47 Could I have my bill? 我可以看一下帳單嗎？
48 What is this for? 這筆費用是什麼？

領取貴重物品 49 I'd like to get my valuables.
我要領取我寄放的貴重物品。

請求保管行李 50 Can you keep my baggage until three p.m.?
你能幫我保管行李到下午3點嗎？

apartment hotel 公寓式飯店；短／日租公寓

villa 別墅

motel 汽車旅館（俗稱摩鐵）

casino hotel 賭場酒店

resort hotel 度假勝地的旅館

At the Hotel Room

Chapter 11

旅館客房服務

PART 1

Key Terms

3 **light bulb** 燈泡

4 **safe** 保險箱

5 **fridge/minibar** 冰箱；迷你飲料吧台

6 **lock** 門鎖

8 **kettle** 水壺

9 **remote control** 遙控器

089

⑩ **hair dryer** 吹風機

⑪ **blanket** 毛毯

⑫ **outlet/socket** 插座

⑬ **towel** 毛巾

⑭ **toilet paper** 衛生紙

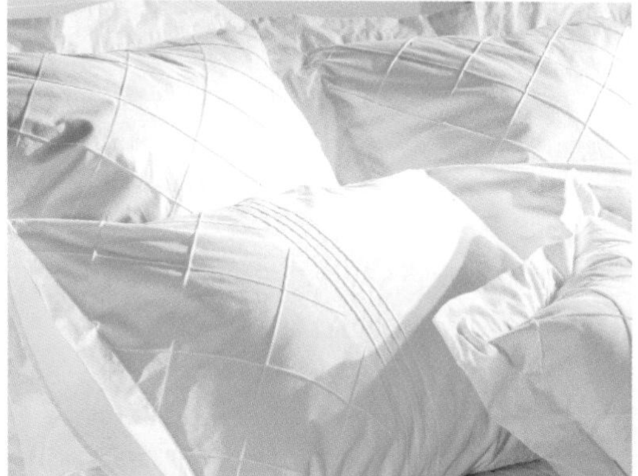

⑮ **pillow** 枕頭

⑯ **sheet** 床單

090

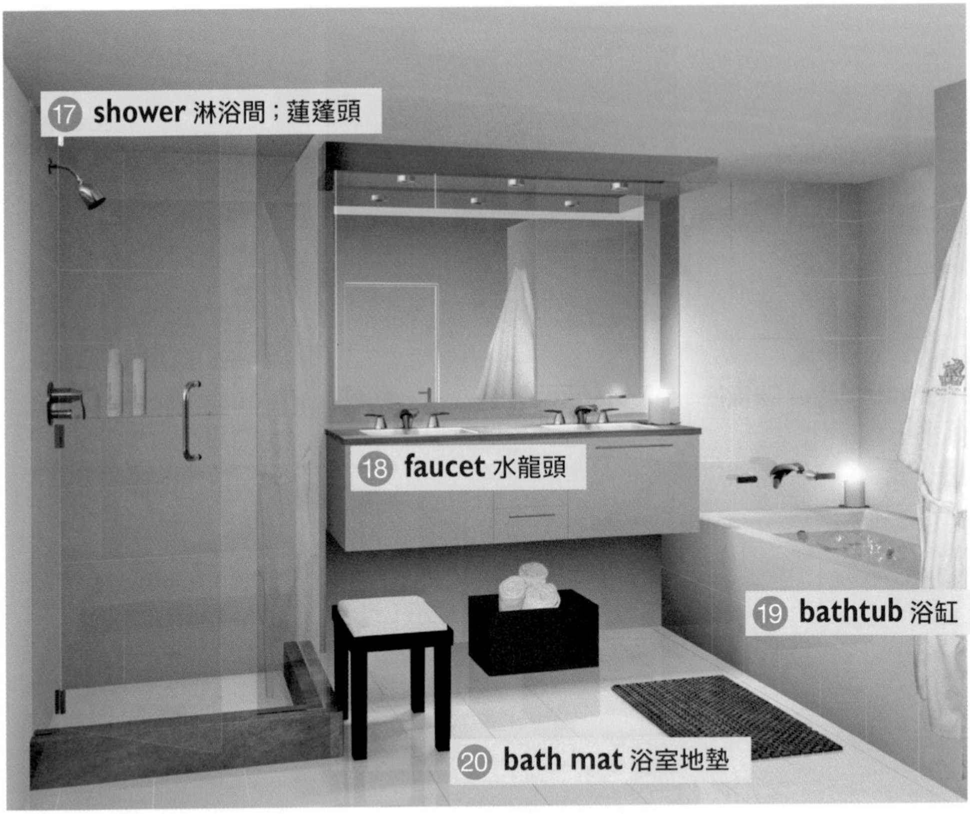
17 shower 淋浴間；蓮蓬頭
18 faucet 水龍頭
19 bathtub 浴缸
20 bath mat 浴室地墊

21 toilet 馬桶

23 shampoo 洗髮精
24 body lotion 身體乳液
SHAMPOO
BODY LOTION
22 soap 肥皂
25 shower gel 沐浴精
26 comb 梳子

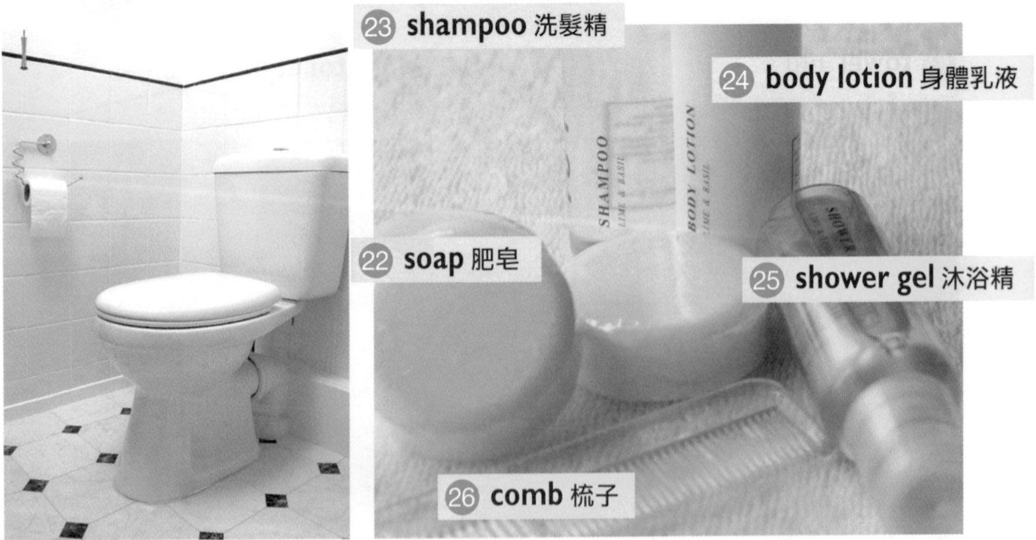

27 **Jacuzzi** 按摩浴缸

28 **bath plug** 浴缸塞子

29 **room service** 客房服務

30 **DO NOT DISTURB**
「請勿打擾」告示牌

31 **PLEASE MAKE UP ROOM NOW**「請打掃房間」告示牌

32 **alarm clock** 鬧鐘

33 **heater** 暖氣

34 **battery** 電池

35 **pay movie** 付費電影
36 **laundry** 送洗衣物
37 **internal call** 內線電話
38 **external call** 外線電話
39 **long-distance call** 長途電話
40 **international call** 國際電話

01 The . . . in My Room Doesn't Work.
我房間裡的……壞了。 092

S *Steven* 史蒂芬　F *Front Desk Clerk* 櫃檯人員

S Is this the front desk?

F Yes, sir. What can I do for you?

S This is Room 705. The air conditioner in my room doesn't work.

F I'll have that taken care of immediately.

S And may I have two more towels, please?

F No problem. We'll bring you the towels in just a minute.

S Thanks.

S 請問是櫃檯嗎？

F 是的，先生。請問有什麼需要嗎？

S 這裡是705號房，我房間的空調壞了。

F 我馬上派人過去處理。

S 還有，可以再給我兩條毛巾嗎？

F 沒問題，我們一會兒就幫您送去。

S 謝謝。

02 A Morning Call 晨喚服務 093

F *Front Desk Clerk* 櫃檯人員　A *Angela* 安琪拉

F Front Desk. What can I do for you?

A This is Room 320. Can I have a morning call tomorrow?

F What time do you want us to wake you up?

A Seven, please.

F OK. I've set it up for you.

A Thank you.

F 櫃檯您好，很高興為您服務。

A 我的房間號碼是320。明天早上可以叫我起床嗎？

F 請問您希望幾點起床？

A 7點。

F 好的，已經幫您設定好了。

A 謝謝。

01 Requesting Things and Equipment Repairs 索取物品及設備維修 094

客房服務	❶ This is Room Service. 這裡是客房服務部。
告知房號	❷ This is Room 608. 這裡是608號房。 ❸ My room number is 512. 我的房間號碼是512。
遇到問題	❹ I have a problem. 我遇到一點問題。 ❺ I have a complaint to make. 我有一個問題需要解決。
索取毛巾	❻ May I have two more towels, please? 請問可以再給我兩條毛巾嗎？
索取毛毯	❼ May I have an extra blanket? 可以再給我一件毛毯嗎？
索取礦泉水	❽ Do you provide drinking water in the room? 你們房間裡有沒有提供飲用水？
索取吹風機	❾ Do you provide a hair dryer? 你們有提供吹風機嗎？
衛生紙用完	❿ There is no toilet paper in the bathroom. 浴室裡沒有衛生紙了。
缺肥皂	⓫ There is no soap in the bathroom. 浴室裡沒有肥皂。
缺洗髮精	⓬ There is no shampoo in the bathroom. 浴室裡沒有洗髮精。

hotel maid 房務服務生

housekeeping cart 房務推車

沒有毛巾	13 There are no towels in my room. 我房裡沒有毛巾。
請人送物品過來	14 Could you bring it to me? 你可以幫我送過來嗎？
沒有熱水	15 There is no hot water in my room. 我的房間裡沒熱水。 16 The hot water is not hot enough. 水不夠熱。
空調壞了	17 The heater in my room doesn't work. 我房間裡的暖氣壞了。 18 The air conditioner is not working. 空調不能用。
中央空調太冷	19 It's too cold. 房間太冷了。
門不能鎖	20 I can't lock the door. 我的門鎖不起來。
電燈壞了	21 The light in my room is not working. 我房間的燈壞掉了。 22 The light bulb has burned out. 燈泡燒掉了。

馬桶壞掉 23 The toilet does not flush. 馬桶不能沖。

電話不通 24 The telephone doesn't work. 電話不能用。

請人修理 25 A Could you check it out, please? 麻煩你們來看一下好嗎？

A Could you fix it? 你能修好嗎？

B I'll have that taken care of immediately.
我馬上處理這件事。

02 Using Facilities and Dealing with Room Problems 使用設施與其他客房問題

095

保險箱如何使用 26 How do I use the safe in my room?
房間裡的保險箱要怎麼用？

房間太吵 27 The room is too noisy for me to sleep. May I change to a quieter room?
這個房間太吵了，我睡不著。可以幫我換到安靜一點的房間嗎？

打電話 28 How do I make internal calls? 請問內線要怎麼打？

29 How do I make external calls? 請問外線要怎麼打？

30 I'd like to make an international call to Taiwan.
我想打國際電話回台灣。

使用網路 31 A Can I get online in my room? 房間裡可以上網嗎？

B You can go to the Entertainment Center on the third floor for Internet service. 您可以到三樓的娛樂中心上網。

忘了帶鑰匙 32 I left the key in my room. Could you open the door for me?
我把鑰匙留在房間裡了，你能不能幫我開門？

晨喚服務 33 I need a morning call at seven tomorrow morning.
請在明天早上7點叫我起床。

房裡用餐	34 We would like to have our meals in our room. 我們想在房裡用餐。
	35 What would you like to order? 請問您要點些什麼？
	36 This is Room 615. Could you please send up a continental breakfast for two people? 請送兩份歐式早餐到615號房。
衣物送洗	37 Do you have a laundry service? 你們有衣物送洗的服務嗎？
	38 Could you come to pick up my laundry? 能請你們來收我的送洗衣物嗎？
	39 When can I get it back? 我什麼時候可以拿回來？
代收傳真	40 Can you receive a fax for me? 你們可以幫我收傳真嗎？
	41 Can I ask them to fax it to the hotel? 我可以請他們傳真到飯店來嗎？
代寄信件	42 Can you mail this letter for me? 你可以幫我寄這封信嗎？
使用游泳池	43 Is the pool free for guests? 游泳池是免費供房客使用的嗎？
各種服務費用	44 How much is the charge? 要多少錢？
	45 Charge it to my room, please. 請把費用算在我的住宿費裡。

當飯店服務人員幫你提行李或送餐點到房間時，你可以先在門邊問「Who is it?」（哪一位？），確認之後再開門。服務人員離開時，你應該禮貌性地遞上小費，並說聲「Thank you. (This is for you.)」。

小費約為1塊美金或80歐分。如果是請服務生送毛巾、毛毯或吹風機之類的東西到房間，則不需給小費。每天早上外出時，也可留下同樣的金額在床頭，給整理房間的服務人員。

In the Restaurant

Chapter

12

在餐廳

PART 1

Key Terms

1 **restaurant** 餐廳

2 **waiter** 服務生
waitress 女服務生

3 **menu** 菜單

4 **order** 點餐

5 **appetizer** 開胃菜

6 **soup** 湯

7 **salad** 沙拉

8 **main dish / entrée** 主菜

9 **side dish** 附餐

⑩ **set meal** 套餐

⑪ **specialty / local food** 當地特產

⑫ **dessert** 甜點

⑬ **beverage** 飲料

⑭ **steak** 牛排

⑮ **dressing** 沙拉醬

⑯ **spaghetti** 義大利麵

⑰ **red wine** 紅酒

⑱ **white wine** 白酒

⑲ **borsch** 羅宋湯

⑳ **Caesar salad** 凱薩沙拉

㉑ **seafood** 海鮮

098

22 **beef** 牛肉

23 **pork** 豬肉

24 **lamb** 羊肉

25 **fish fillet** 魚排

26 **shrimp** 蝦子

27 **octopus** 章魚

28 **lobster** 龍蝦

29 **crab** 螃蟹

30 **rib** 肋排

31 **pizza** 披薩

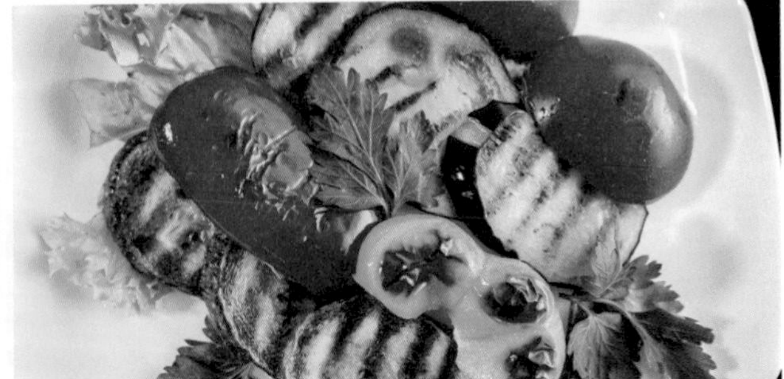

32 **vegetarian dish** 素食

099

33 **spoon** 湯匙

34 **knife** 刀子

35 **fork** 叉子

36 **napkin** 餐巾

37 **grill**
（在烤架上）燒烤

38 **roast**
（用烤箱）烘烤

39 **stew** 燜；燉

40 **boil** 水煮

41 **fry** 油炸

42 **spicy** 辣的
43 **salty** 鹹的
44 **greasy** 油的
45 **tasteless** 沒味道的
46 **raw** 生的
47 **rare** 三分熟的
48 **medium** 五分熟的
49 **medium-well** 七分熟的
50 **well-done** 全熟的
51 **dress code** 服裝規定
52 **check** 帳單

PART 2

Conversations

01 I'd Like to Reserve a Table for Two.
我想預訂一張雙人桌。 100

A *Anthony* 安東尼　R *Receptionist* 櫃檯人員

A I'd like to reserve a table for two, please.

R For what time, sir?

A Around 8:30 p.m.

R May I have your name please, sir?

A Yes, Anthony Fox.

R Mr. Fox, we'll hold the table for you for ten minutes. Please be sure to arrive before 8:40.

A 我想訂一張雙人桌，麻煩了。

R 您想訂幾點的，先生？

A 晚上8點30分左右。

R 請問您貴姓大名？

A 安東尼・福克斯。

R 福克斯先生，我們會幫您保留座位10分鐘，請在8點40分前到達。

02 I'll Have a Steak. 請給我來一份牛排。 101

W *Waitress* 服務生　J *Jason* 傑森

W Are you ready to order now, sir?

J Yes, I'll have a steak, please.

W How would you like the steak, rare, medium, or well-done?

J Rare, please.

W Would you like something to drink?

J Coffee, please.

W 先生，請問您準備好點餐了嗎？

J 可以了，請給我一客牛排。

W 牛排要幾分熟呢？三分熟、五分熟，還是全熟？

J 我要三分熟。

W 您要喝點什麼嗎？

J 我要咖啡，謝謝。

How Would You Like to Pay?
您想用什麼方式付款？ 102

A *Anthony* 安東尼　S *Server* 服務生

A Excuse me, can I have the bill, please?

S Of course. How would you like to pay, sir?

A What forms of payment do you accept?

S We accept payment by cash, credit card, and several digital wallet services.

A In that case, I'll pay with my phone. Do you accept Apple Pay?

S We do. Wait a moment, please. I'll be right back.

A 不好意思，我要買單。

S 好的，先生，您想用什麼方式付款？

A 你們接受什麼付款方式？

S 我們接受現金、刷卡，還有幾家數位支付服務。

A 這樣的話，我要用手機付款。你們接受Apple Pay嗎？

S 有的，請稍等一下，我隨即回來。

pay with your phone
手機付款

如何使用行動支付 How to pay with your mobile phone

① Add your credit card to your payment-enabled mobile phone or device.
在你的手機或行動裝置綁定信用卡。

② Look for the contactless symbol on the terminal at checkout.
在結帳櫃檯尋找感應圖示。

③ Hold your phone or device over the symbol to pay.
將手機或裝置放置於圖示上方感應付款。

註：此種感應支付之手機需支援 NFC 功能，透過 NFC 感應支付的有 Apple Pay、Samsung Pay 與 Android Pay。

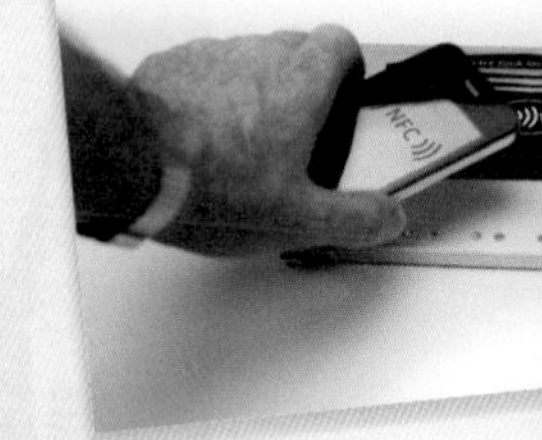

01 Looking for a Restaurant and Making a Reservation 尋找餐廳與預約訂位 103

推薦好吃的餐廳	1 Is there a nice restaurant near the hotel? 請問飯店附近有沒有不錯的餐廳？
推薦中式餐廳	2 Are there any good Chinese restaurants in this area? 這附近有沒有好吃的中式餐廳？
推薦便宜餐廳	3 Any cheaper restaurants here? 這附近有便宜一點的餐廳嗎？
是否要預約	4 Do I need a reservation? 我需要預約嗎？
請別人幫忙預約	5 Could you please phone the restaurant and reserve a table for me? 你可以幫我打電話到那家餐廳訂位嗎？
詢問是否接受電話訂位	6 Do you take telephone reservations? 你們接受電話訂位嗎？
自己預約 詢問人數	7 A Hello. I'd like to book a table. 喂，我想訂一張桌位。 B For how many guests, please? 請問有幾位客人？
自己預約 客滿	8 A I'd like to reserve a table for six at 7 p.m. tomorrow. 我想訂一張六人桌，明天晚上7點鐘。 B I'm afraid we don't have any tables open at that time. 很抱歉，那個時段已經客滿了。
服裝規定	9 Do you have a dress code? 你們有服裝規定嗎？

dress code 服裝規定

02 Entering the Restaurant 進入餐廳 104

是否有訂位 **10** Ⓐ Have you made a reservation? 請問您有訂位嗎？

告知已訂位 Ⓑ I'm Julie White. I reserved a table for two at 8.
我叫茱莉·懷特。我預訂了一張八點鐘的雙人桌。

沒有訂位 Ⓑ I don't have a reservation. 我沒有訂位。

說明人數 **11** A table for three, please. 我要一張三人桌。

12 Have you got a table for eight? 你們有八人桌嗎？

靠角落的座位 **13** Do you have a corner table for two?
請問靠角落有兩個人的位子嗎？

直接找位子 **14** Is this place vacant? 這個座位有人嗎？

靠窗的座位 **15** Ⓐ Can we take the small table by the window?
我們可以坐靠窗的那張小桌子嗎？

Ⓑ Sorry, madam, the one by the window has been booked by others.
對不起，女士，靠窗的那張桌子已經有人預訂了。

服務生帶位（有預約）

16 I'll show you to your table.
讓我帶您到預訂的桌子。

17 Your table is ready now, sir. Come this way.
先生，您的餐桌已經準備好了，請往這邊走。

18 Here is your table. Is it all right?
這是您的餐桌，請問還可以嗎？

服務生帶位（無預約）

19 Will this table be all right? 請問坐這裡可以嗎？

20 What about that one? 坐那裡好嗎？

21 Would you like to sit over there near the door?
您願意坐在靠近門的地方嗎？

決定座位

22 This one is very good. We'll take it.
這個位子不錯，我們就坐這裡了。

要求換位

23 Can we change tables?
我們可以換桌嗎？

換禁菸區的座位

24 Can we change to the non-smoking area?
我們能換到禁菸區嗎？

餐廳客滿

25 A Sorry, all our tables are full now.
很抱歉，我們現在客滿。

問等候時間

B How long do we have to wait? 我們需要等多久？
B Do we have to wait for a long time? 我們需要等很久嗎？

03 Asking for a Menu and Asking for Recommendations 要求點餐並詢問菜色

105

索取菜單

26 May I see the menu, please? 請給我看一下菜單好嗎？

27 Do you have a Chinese menu? 你們有中文菜單嗎？

索取酒單	28 Can we have the wine list? 我們可以看一下酒單嗎？
餐前飲料	29 I want to have a drink before the meal. 飯前我想先喝點飲料。
詢問是否要點餐	30 May I take your order now? 請問您準備好點菜了嗎？ 31 Are you ready to order, sir? 先生，您要點菜了嗎？
要求點餐	32 We would like to order now. 我們要點餐。
還沒決定點餐	33 Not ready yet. 我們還沒好。 34 We need a little more time to think about it. 我們還需要考慮一下。
請服務生推薦餐點	35 What do you recommend? 你推薦什麼？ 36 Which would you say is the best? 你覺得哪一個最好？ 37 Can you tell me their different features? 你可以告訴我每樣菜的特色嗎？
詢問顧客口味	38 Which do you prefer, Chinese food or Western food? 您喜歡中餐還是西餐？
服務生的推薦	39 I would recommend lamb chops. 我推薦羊小排。 40 The fish here is very delicious. 這裡的魚非常可口。 41 These are the best of our restaurant. 這些是我們餐廳的招牌菜。
當地特產	42 A What's the specialty of this place? 這裡的招牌菜是什麼？ B This place is noted for steaks. 這裡以牛排聞名。 43 I'd like to have some local specialties. 我想吃一些有地方特色的菜。

一般正式的西餐廳，套餐的程序大約是：

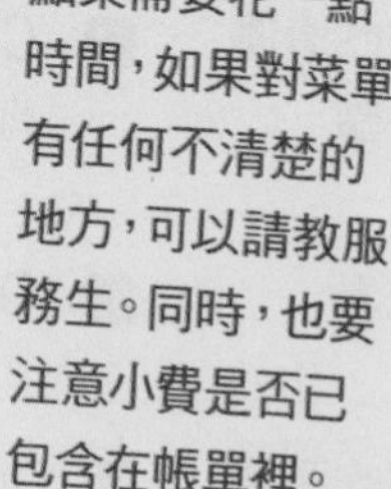

詢問今日特餐

44 What's today's special? 今天的特餐是什麼？

45 A What do you have today for supper?
今天晚餐你們供應什麼菜色？

B We have all kinds of Western food at your choice.
我們有各式西餐供您挑選。

上菜快的餐點

46 What can be served very quickly? I have only 30 minutes.
哪一種餐點可以比較快上菜？我只有三十分鐘。

不吃的料理

47 A Are there any foods you don't like to eat?
有沒有您不吃的食物？

B I'm allergic to seafood. 我對海鮮過敏。

想吃中國菜

48 Do you have typical Chinese food? 你們有道地的中國菜嗎？

49 What kind of Chinese food do you serve?
你們供應哪些中國菜？

想吃法國菜	50 **Will you recommend some French dishes?** 請幫我們介紹幾樣法國菜好嗎？
想吃清淡一點	51 **Could you fix me something light?** 你可以幫我準備清淡一點的菜嗎？
吃素	52 **Do you have vegetarian dishes?** 你們有沒有素食餐點？
想吃套餐	53 **Do you have set meals?** 你們有沒有套餐？
詢問餐點的差別	54 **What is the difference between this and this?** 這個和這個有什麼不同？（指著菜單說）

04 Ordering Food 開始點餐 106

點跟別桌一樣的菜	55 **What did they order? I would like to order the same thing.** 請問他們點的是什麼？我要點一樣的。
指著菜單點菜	56 **I'll have this and this.** 我要這個和這個。（指著菜單說）
開胃菜	57 **Would you like an appetizer?** 您要不要來點開胃菜？
湯	58 **What's the soup of the day?** 今天有什麼湯？ 59 **I'd like a bowl of tomato soup, please.** 請給我來碗番茄湯。
沙拉	60 A **I think I'll have a vegetable salad.** 我要一份蔬菜沙拉。 B **What kind of dressing do you want on your salad?** 您的沙拉要配什麼醬？

主菜

61 Ⓐ What would you recommend for a main dish?
你推薦什麼主菜 ？

說明供應的料理

Ⓑ We have ham, steak, roast beef, and fried chicken today. 我們今天供應火腿、牛排、烤牛肉和炸雞。

Ⓑ Lobster, crab, and prawns are being served today.
今天有龍蝦、螃蟹和明蝦。

海鮮

62 Do you have lobster? 你們有龍蝦嗎？

牛排

63 Ⓐ How do you like your steak? 請問您的牛排要幾分熟？

Ⓑ Medium-well, please. 七分熟。

Ⓑ I prefer it well-done, please. 我喜歡吃全熟的。

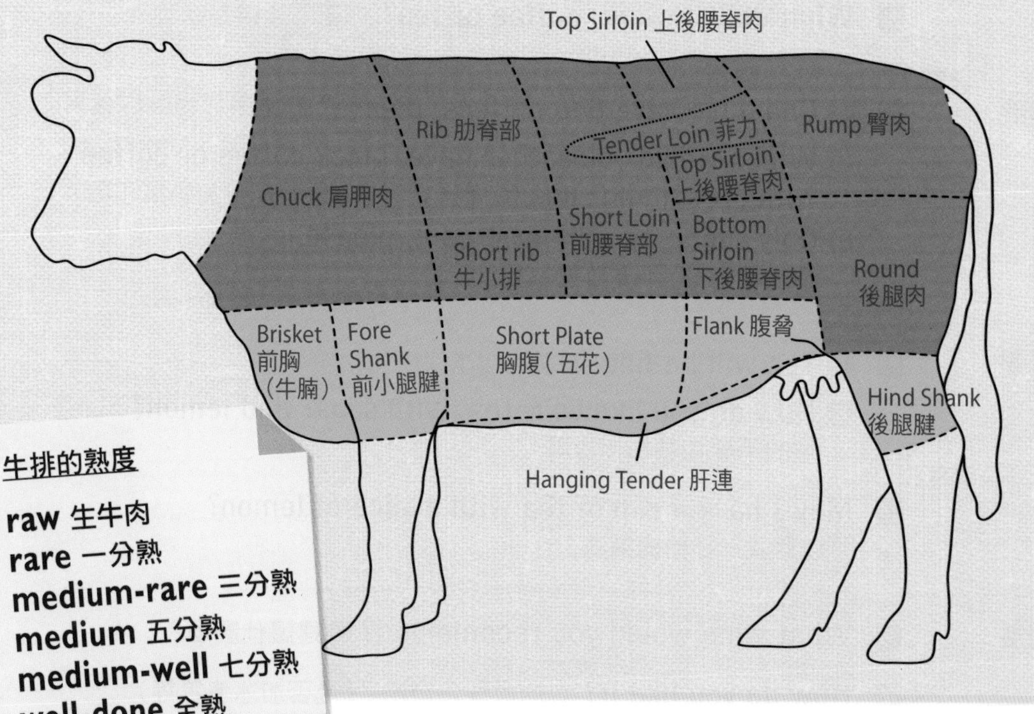

牛排的熟度

raw 生牛肉
rare 一分熟
medium-rare 三分熟
medium 五分熟
medium-well 七分熟
well-done 全熟

附餐	64	Would you like more side dishes? 您要再來一點附餐嗎？
	65	What comes with the steak? 牛排的附餐是什麼？
炸馬鈴薯片	66	I'd like to have crisps. 我想要一些炸馬鈴薯片。
要白飯	67	I wonder if I can have some rice. 我可以要一些白飯嗎？
辣不辣	68	Is this dish very spicy? 這道菜會很辣嗎？
甜點	69	Ⓐ Would you like to order a dessert? 您要來份甜點嗎？ Ⓑ I'll have some ice cream for dessert. 我想要冰淇淋當甜點。 Ⓐ What flavor would you like? 您要什麼口味的？
點飲料	70	Would you like something to drink? 您想喝點什麼嗎？
	71	What do you want, coffee or tea? 你要喝茶還是咖啡？
咖啡	72	Ⓐ Could we have two coffees, please? 請來兩杯咖啡好嗎？ Ⓑ Which would you rather have, black coffee or coffee with cream and sugar? 您喜歡黑咖啡，還是要加奶精和糖？ Ⓐ Only sugar, no milk or cream, please. 請加糖就好，不要鮮奶或奶油。
喝茶	73	Ⓐ Tea will be fine. 茶就可以了。 Ⓑ How do you like your tea, with sugar and lemon? 您的茶要加糖和檸檬嗎？
	74	May I have a cup of tea with a slice of lemon? 可以給我一杯檸檬茶嗎？
喝酒	75	What wine would you recommend? 你建議什麼酒？
	76	How do you like it? 您的酒要怎麼喝？（是否加冰塊等等）

fruit juice 果汁

soft drinks 碳酸飲料

tea 茶

coffee 咖啡

alcohol 酒類

換飲料

77 Please switch that to Budweiser. 請把它換成百威啤酒。

78 Can I have coffee instead? 我可以換咖啡嗎？

決定點某道菜

79 I'll take it anyway.
我就點這道菜。

點一樣的餐點

80 Make it two, please. 請來兩份。

81 The same for me, please. 我也點一樣的菜。

是否加點其他的

82 Ⓐ Is there anything else you would like to have?
您還要點什麼嗎？

Ⓐ Anything else? 還要點什麼嗎？

結束點餐

Ⓑ I think that's enough. 我想這些就夠了。

05 Starting the Meal 開始用餐 107

餐具掉了	83 I dropped my fork. Could you bring me another one, please? 我的叉子掉了，可以再給我一支嗎？
餐點遲遲未到	84 My order hasn't come out yet? 我點的菜還沒來嗎？ 85 We ordered a half hour ago. 我們已經點了半個小時了。
沒有點某樣菜	86 I didn't order this. 我沒有點這個。
餐點沒熟	87 This meat is still raw. 這個肉還是生的。
湯裡有異物	88 There is something in my soup. 我的湯裡有怪東西。
餐點太鹹	89 This dish is too salty. 這道菜太鹹了。
餐點太油	90 This dish is too greasy. 這道菜太油了。
餐點太辣	91 This dish is too spicy. 這道菜太辣了。
餐點沒味道	92 This dish is tasteless. 這道菜沒味道。
取消餐點	93 May I cancel my order? 我可以取消餐點嗎？
加水	94 Could you bring me some more water, please? 請幫我加點水好嗎？
詢問是否吃完	95 A Have you finished? 請問您吃完了嗎？ B Not yet. 還沒。
請服務生清理桌面	96 Could you clean the table, please? 請幫我們收一下桌子。

打包
97 Please pack the leftovers for me.
請幫我把剩下的打包。

詢問打烊時間
98 When do you close?
你們幾點打烊？

06 Paying the Bill 結帳 

買單
99 Check, please. 麻煩幫我買單。

核對帳單
100 Can we get the check/bill? 可以給我們帳單嗎？

詢問費用
101 How much is that, please? 請問那個多少錢？

102 What's this for? 這筆費用是什麼？

付款方式
103 Can I pay by cash? 可以付現嗎？

104 Can I pay by credit card? 可以刷卡嗎？

105 Ⓐ Do you accept Apple Pay? 你們接受Apple Pay嗎？
Ⓑ Yes, we accept all digital wallet services.
有的，我們支援所有電子支付的付費方式。

分開付
106 We are splitting the check. 我們要分開付。

107 Let's use LINE Pay to split the bill.
我們用LINE Pay來分開付吧。

服務費
108 Is service included? 服務費有包含在內嗎？

小費
109 How much should we tip? 應該要付多少小費？

西餐用餐禮儀 Table Etiquette

1 左叉右刀：

應以左手持叉、右手持刀，將餐巾放在大腿上。

2 刀叉擺放方式：

- 中途若要放下刀叉，應擺放成八字形，代表尚未食用完畢。
- 若是食用完畢，可將刀叉合併擺在一起，則代表已可將餐盤收走。

3 使用順序：

一般來說，會從離餐盤最遠的刀叉開始使用，按每道菜的順序依序使用一種餐具。

4 拿不到遠方的菜餚或調味料時：

若是需要遠方的菜餚或調味料，不應越過他人拿取，可禮貌地向他人詢問，如：「可以遞給我鹽巴嗎？」（**Would you pass the salt, please?**）

不同情況下的餐具擺法
Location of cutlery in different situations

pause 暫停餐點

ready for a second plate
準備好可上下一道菜

excellent 餐點很棒
（已食用完畢）

don't like 不喜歡餐點

finished 已食用完畢

finished 已食用完畢

Fast Food
Le INSALATE
GRAN Chicago CLASSIC
È ARRIVATA LA COLAZIONE CHE NON C'ERA..
CBO

Chapter 13

速食店

PART 1

Key Terms

⑤ **onion rings** 洋蔥圈

⑥ **chicken nuggets** 雞塊

⑦ **fried chicken** 炸雞

⑧ **chicken tender** 雞柳條

⑨ **apple pie** 蘋果派

110

⑩ **ketchup** 番茄醬

⑪ **mustard sauce** 芥末醬

⑫ **barbecue sauce** 烤肉醬

⑬ **sweet and sour sauce** 糖醋醬

⑭ **pepper** 胡椒粉

⑮ **tacos** 墨西哥玉米捲

⑯ **chicken burger** 雞堡

⑰ **fish burger** 魚堡

⑱ **French fries** 薯條

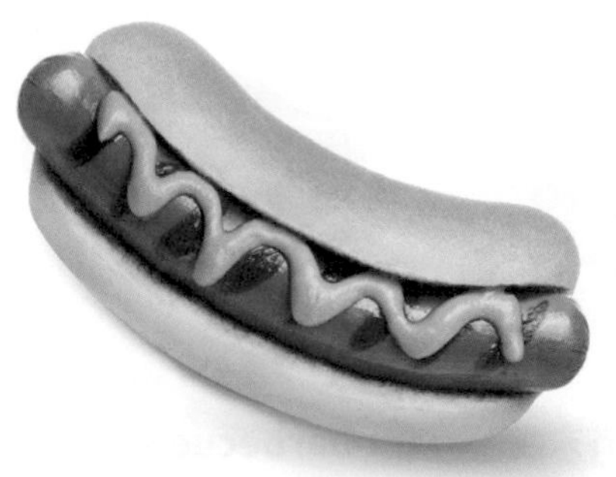

⑲ **hot dog** 熱狗堡

⑳ **bacon** 培根

㉑ **Coke** 可樂

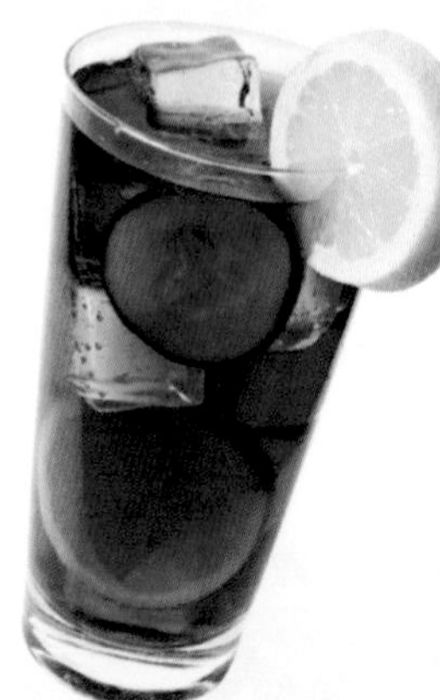

㉒ **iced tea** 冰茶

㉓ **milkshake** 奶昔

㉔ **coffee** 咖啡

㉕ **cream** 奶油

26 **sugar** 糖

27 **hot chocolate** 熱巧克力

28 **orange juice** 柳橙汁

29 **sundae** 聖代

30 **ice cream** 冰淇淋

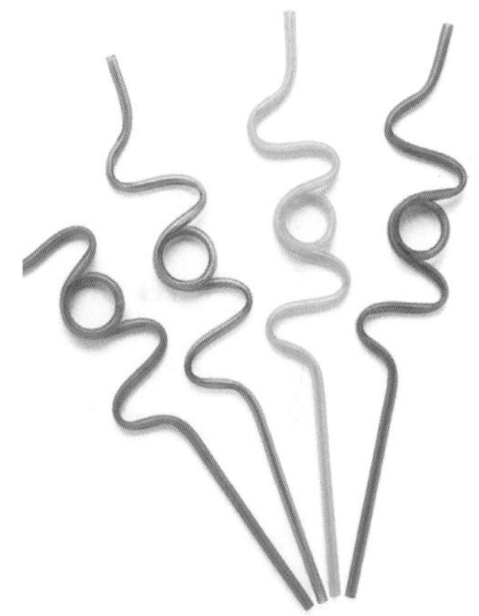

31 **straw** 吸管

32 **napkin** 餐巾紙

33 **small** 小的
34 **medium** 中的
35 **large** 大的
36 **refill** 續杯
37 **without ice** 去冰

38 **flavor** 口味
39 **strawberry** 草莓
40 **chocolate** 巧克力
41 **vanilla** 香草

01 Two Number 3s, Please. 我要兩份三號餐。 113

S *Steven* 史蒂芬　C *Clerk* 店員

S Two number 3s, please.

C All right. What would you like to drink?

S Diet Coke.

C Regular or large?

S Regular, please.

C OK. Anything else?

S No, thanks.

C For here or to go?

S For here.

S 我要兩份三號餐。

C 好的，請問您要喝什麼？

S 健怡可樂。

C 普通杯還是大杯的？

S 普通杯。

C 好的，還需要什麼嗎？

S 這樣就好，謝謝。

C 內用還是外帶呢？

S 內用。

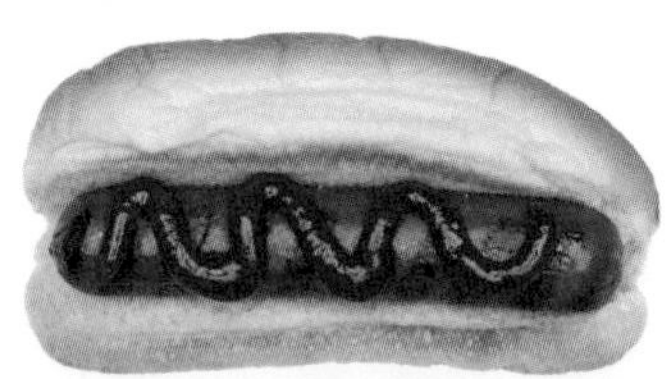

hot dog with ketchup 淋番茄醬的熱狗

hot dog with ketchup and mustard
淋番茄醬和芥末醬的熱狗

hot dog with ketchup, mustard, and onions
淋番茄醬和芥末醬、加洋蔥的熱狗

hot dog with ketchup, mustard, and onions, and relish
淋番茄醬和芥末醬、加洋蔥和佐料的熱狗

02 What Flavor Would You Prefer?
您要什麼口味？ 114

C *Clerk* 店員　S *Steven* 史蒂芬

C Good afternoon, sir. Can I help you?

S I'd like a beef burger, French fries, and a milkshake, please.

C What flavor would you prefer, sir?

S I'm not quite sure. What do you have?

C We have strawberry, chocolate, vanilla, and banana.

S Very well. I'll try the banana flavor.

C Anything else, sir?

S No, thanks. That will be all.

C 午安，先生。您要點什麼？

S 我想要一個牛肉漢堡、一份薯條和一杯奶昔。

C 請問您要什麼口味的？

S 我也不知道，你們有哪幾種口味？

C 有草莓、巧克力、香草和香蕉口味。

S 好，我要香蕉口味的。

C 還要什麼嗎，先生？

S 不用了，謝謝。這樣就好。

奶昔主要由牛奶和冰淇淋混合而成，以水果口味為多，例如草莓、香蕉、芒果或巧克力等。

01 Ordering Fast Food at the Counter and Finding a Table 在速食餐廳點餐和找座位 115

點漢堡

1. I'd like a beef burger, please. 我要一個牛肉漢堡。
2. Two cheeseburgers, please. 我要兩個吉士漢堡。

點薯條

3. I'd like large French fries. 我要一份大薯。
4. A cheeseburger and French fries.
   我要一個吉士漢堡和一份薯條。

點奶昔

5. Ⓐ I'd like a milk shake, please. 我要一杯奶昔。
   Ⓑ What flavor would you prefer, ma'am?
   您要什麼口味的奶昔？

點可樂

6. Ⓐ A diet Coke to go, please. 一杯健怡可樂外帶。
   Ⓑ Large or regular? 大杯的還是普通杯？

點套餐

7. Two number 4s, please. 我要兩份四號餐。

選擇醬汁

8. Ⓐ What sauces would you like? 您要什麼醬汁？
   Ⓑ Sweet and sour sauce, please. 糖醋醬。

點炸雞

9. Two orders of fried chicken, please. 我要兩份炸雞。

選擇雞肉部位

10. I'd like a chicken breast instead of a leg.
    我要雞胸肉，不要雞腿。

不要加配料

11. Please don't put any pickles on my hamburger.
    我的漢堡裡不要加醃黃瓜。
12. No onions on my hamburger, please. 我的漢堡不要加洋蔥。

對於炸雞部位有特別喜好的人，不妨在點餐時詢問服務生能否更換部位。

chicken drumstick 雞腿

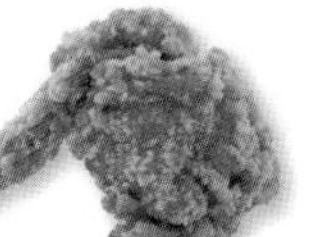

chicken wing 雞翅

chicken breast 雞胸肉

餐點要等	**13** The fries will be up in about two minutes. Do you mind waiting? 薯條還要等兩分鐘，您要等嗎？
是否還要點別的	**14** Ⓐ Anything else, ma'am? 還需要點些什麼嗎，女士？ Ⓑ No, thanks. That will be all. 不了，謝謝，這樣就好。
內用或外帶	**15** Ⓐ Is it for here or to go? 請問內用或外帶？ Ⓑ For here. 我要內用。 Ⓑ To go, please. 我要外帶。 **16** Large French fries and one Coke to go, please. 我要外帶一份大薯和一杯大杯可樂。
要番茄醬	**17** Could I have an extra ketchup? 可以再給我一包番茄醬嗎？
給錯餐點	**18** I ordered the cheeseburger, not the fish burger. 我點的是吉士漢堡，不是魚堡。
索取吸管	**19** Do you have any straws? 有沒有吸管？
要餐巾紙	**20** I need some napkins. 我需要一些餐巾紙。 **21** Where can I get some napkins and straws? 哪裡有餐巾紙和吸管？
咖啡續杯	**22** Can I refill my coffee? 請問咖啡可以續杯嗎？ **23** Are refills free? 可以免費續杯嗎？
與人共用桌子	**24** Is this seat vacant? 這個座位有人嗎？ **25** Can I sit here? 我可以坐這裡嗎？ **26** Do you mind if I share the table with you? 可以跟你們共用一張桌子嗎？

Shopping
Information

Chapter

14

購物：一般用語

PART 1

Key Terms

① **shopping center** 購物中心

② **department** 百貨部門

③ **window** 櫥窗

④ **on sale** 特價中

⑤ **elevator** 電梯

⑥ **escalator** 電扶梯

⑦ **size** 尺寸

⑧ **color** 顏色

⑨ **style/design** 款式

⑩ **specialty** 具有當地特色的產品

⑪ **sold out** 已售完

⑫ **try on** 試穿；試

⑬ **mirror** 鏡子

⑭ **home appliance** 家電用品

⑮ **sporting equipment** 運動用品

⑯ **black** 黑色的

⑰ **white** 白色的

⑱ **red** 紅色的

⑲ **pink** 粉紅色的

⑳ **blue** 藍色的

㉑ **yellow** 黃色的

㉒ **green** 綠色的

㉓ **brown** 咖啡色的

㉔ **gray** 灰色的

㉕ **orange** 橘色的

㉖ **purple** 紫色的

㉗ **beige** 米色的

㉘ **counter** 櫃檯

㉙ **item** 物品

㉚ **out of stock** 缺貨

㉛ **in stock** 有庫存

㉜ **recommend** 推薦

㉝ **business hours** 營業時間

01 Is This the Right Counter for . . . ?
這櫃位是賣……的嗎？ 118

S *Salesclerk* 店員　J *Jennifer* 珍妮佛

S May I help you?

J Is this the right counter for gloves?

S Yes, madam. What sort of gloves do you want?

J Well, let me see some of each.

S Certainly. What size do you take?

J Six and a quarter, I believe, but you'd better measure my hand to make sure.

S I think a six is your size. How do you like these? I can recommend them; they're very reliable.

J Very well, I'll take these.

S 我能為您效勞嗎？

J 這櫃位是賣手套的嗎？

S 是的，女士，您要哪種手套？

J 嗯，每種都讓我看看。

S 好的。您戴什麼尺寸的？

J 我想應該是6吋25的吧，不過你還是先量一下我的手吧，以免出錯。

S 我看6吋的就夠了。這些您喜歡嗎？我推薦您買這幾種，它們的品質很有保障。

J 還不錯，我要買這雙。

02 Asking Where Things Are in a Department Store 在百貨公司裡找東西 119

C *Customer* 顧客 I *Information Desk Clerk* 服務台人員

C Excuse me. On which floor can I find toasters?

I All of our home appliances are on the fifth floor.

C Thank you. Is there an elevator?

I Yes, it's just over there.

C Ah, I see it. I'm also looking for a tennis racket.

I Sporting equipment is on this floor, down at the far end.

C Great. Thank you for your help.

I You're welcome. Happy shopping!

C 不好意思，請問烤土司機在幾樓？

I 家電用品都在五樓。

C 謝謝你。請問有電梯嗎？

I 有的，就在那裡。

C 喔，我看到了。我同時也在找羽球拍在哪裡。

I 運動用品就在這層樓，在這條路盡頭那裡。

C 太好了，謝謝你的協助。

I 不客氣，祝您購物愉快！

PART 3

Useful Expressions

01 Looking for a Shopping Mall and a Specific Store 尋找購物中心和特定專櫃 120

詢問購物地點

1 Is there a shopping center around here?
這附近有購物中心嗎？

詢問營業時間

2 Is that store open on Sundays? 那家店星期天有開嗎？

3 What are their business hours?
請問那家店的營業時間是幾點到幾點？

店家上前詢問

4 A May I help you, ma'am? 有什麼需要我幫忙的嗎，女士？
A What can I do for you? 我可以幫您什麼忙嗎？

尋找電梯

B Where can I find the elevator? 請問電梯在哪裡？

只是隨便看看

5 I just want to look around. 我只是看看。

6 I'm just looking. 我只是隨便看看。

詢問專櫃販售商品

7 Do you carry cashmere sweaters here?
你們有賣喀什米爾毛衣嗎？

8 Is this the right counter for gloves?
請問這裡是賣手套的櫃位嗎？

詢問顧客想買什麼

9 A Are you looking for something special?
您在找（要買）什麼特定的東西嗎？

說明想要的樣式

B I want something like this.
我在找像這樣的東西。

商品齊全

10 We have the very thing you want. 我們剛好有您想要的東西。

11 We have many styles and shades for you to choose from.
我們的商品種類很多、花色齊全，可供您選擇。

12 We have various goods in different sizes.
我們的貨品種類多、尺寸齊全。

02 Choosing Products 選擇產品 121

觸摸產品

13 May I touch this? 這個可以摸嗎？

請店員拿架上產品

14 May I take a look at the handbag right there in the second row on the second shelf?
我可以看看放在第二個架子上第二排的那個手提包嗎？

15 Ⓐ Show me that necklace, please.
請讓我看看那條項鏈。
Ⓑ Is this the one you want? 您要的是這個嗎？
Ⓐ No, not that one. The gray one.
不對，不是那個，是灰色的那個。

推薦產品

16 How would you like this one? 您覺得這個怎麼樣？

souvenir 紀念品

推薦新品

17 Have you seen our new hats?
您看過我們的新帽子了嗎？

想買當地特產

18 Are they specialties of Greece?
這些是希臘的特產嗎？

19 I'm looking for something special made in this country.
我想買本地特有的商品。

20 What do you recommend as a souvenir from this country?
你可以推薦一些本國的紀念品嗎？

詢問產地

21 Where is this made? 它們產自哪裡？

產品暢銷

22 It's one of our best-selling items.
這是我們店裡的搶手貨之一。

特賣

23 This is the special season for bargain sales.
現在是大減價的特賣季節。

手工製品

24 It's entirely hand-made with wonderful workmanship.
這是道地手工製作，工藝精湛。

看樣品

25 Here are some samples, sir.
先生，這裡有一些樣品。

非賣品	26 It's not for sale. 這是非賣品。 27 They're on exhibit. 這些是展示品。

03 Out of Stock and Requesting Items 商品缺貨與進貨 

產品缺貨	28 I'm sorry, but I'm afraid they're out of stock right now. 很抱歉，現在可能沒有貨了。 29 Sorry, we've sold out, sir. 先生，對不起，我們全賣完了。 30 Sorry, but we don't have it in stock. 對不起，我們沒貨了。
到倉庫找貨	31 I'll have a look in our store warehouse. Please wait a moment. 請稍等一下，我去倉庫看看。
調貨	32 We haven't got any, but we can order it for you. 我們倉庫裡已經沒貨了，不過可以幫您訂購。

是否會進貨 33 A Are you likely to get more in?
你們還會進貨嗎？

進貨時間 B That will be ready by this Saturday.
這個星期六就會有了。

B We get a fresh stock every morning.
我們每天上午會進新貨。

B Perhaps in 2 or 3 weeks we'll have some.
可能要兩三個星期我們才會有貨。

04 Making the Purchase Decision 決定是否購買 

購買數量 34 A How many would you like? 您要買幾個？

B One will be enough. 一個就好了。

B I'll take two of this. 我要買兩個。

拿不定主意

35 I have no idea. Which one would you recommend?
我拿不定主意，你會推薦哪一種？

36 Can you give me some suggestions? 可以給我一些建議嗎？

無購買意願

37 I don't think I'll take any today. 我今天先不買了。

38 I'll think about it. Thank you. 我再考慮看看，謝謝。

對產品不滿意

39 None of these fit me. 這些沒有一個適合我。

40 That isn't quite what I want. 那不是我想要的那種。

41 I don't think the scarf matches my coat.
我覺得這條圍巾和我的外套不搭。

42 I look awful in the blue hat. 我戴這頂藍色的帽子不好看。

決定購買

43 **You're right. This one will do.** 你說的對，就買這個。

44 **It's the thing for me.** 這正是我想要的。

45 **All right, I'll take this one.** 好吧，我就買這個。

還要不要買別的

46 **What else are you going to buy?** 您還要買點別的嗎？

47 **Is that all, sir?** 先生，您還要買點別的嗎？

48 **Can you think of anything else you need?**
您還需要些什麼嗎？

49 **Are you sure one will be enough?** 您確定一個就夠了嗎？

請商家送貨

50 **Could you send it to Taiwan?**
你能幫我寄去台灣嗎？

Outlet 暢貨中心

起源於美國與歐洲等地，近幾年台灣也越來越興盛。暢貨中心即為各家名牌將過季商品，以較低的價格展出販售的商場。

Shopping for Clothes, Bags, and Shoes

Chapter 15

購物：服飾、鞋包配件

PART 1

Key Terms

124

① **sunglasses** 太陽眼鏡

② **umbrella** 雨傘

③ **scarf** 圍巾

④ **glove** 手套

⑤ **hat** 帽子

⑥ **necktie** 領帶

125

⑦ **swimming suit** 泳衣

⑧ **swimming trunks** 泳褲

⑨ **spaghetti-strapped shirt** 細肩帶上衣

⑩ **tank top** 背心

⑪ **T-shirt** T恤

⑫ **long sleeve** 長袖

⑬ **short sleeve** 短袖

⑭ **shirt** 襯衫

⑮ **blouse** 女性上衣

⑯ **sweater** 毛衣

⑰ **turtleneck** 高領上衣

⑱ **suit** 套裝；西裝

⑲ **dress** 洋裝

127

20 **skirt** 裙子

21 **jacket** 夾克

22 **overcoat** 大衣

23 **jeans** 牛仔褲

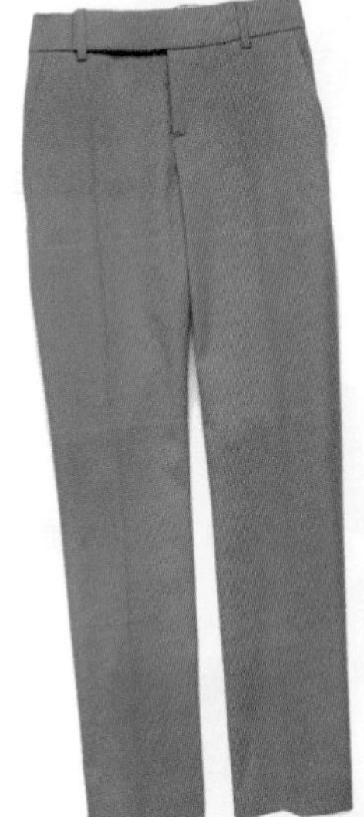

24 **pants** (US) 長褲（美式）
trousers (UK) 長褲（英式）

25 **shorts** 短褲

128

26 **sandals** 涼鞋

27 **boots** 靴子

28 **flip-flops** 人字拖

29 **high heels** 高跟鞋

30 **leather shoes** 皮鞋

31 **sneakers** 運動鞋

32 **shoelace** 鞋帶

33 **shoe polish** 鞋油

34 **socks** 襪子

129

35 **shoulder bag** 側背包

36 **handbag** 手提包

37 **wallet** 皮夾

38 **briefcase** 公事包

39 **button** 鈕釦

40 **pocket** 口袋

41 **cotton** 棉

42 **wool** 羊毛

43 **silk** 絲

44 **leather** 皮革

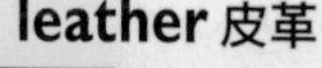

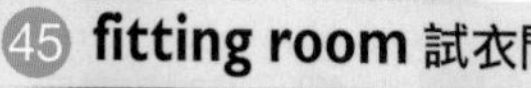

45 **fitting room** 試衣間

46 **measure** 測量

47 **tight** 緊的

48 **loose** 鬆的

49 **fit** 合適；合身

50 **fashionable** 時髦的；流行的

51 **old-fashioned** 過時的；老派的

PART 2

Conversations

01 May I Try On This Pair of Shoes?
我能試穿這雙鞋嗎？ 130

Y *Yvonne* 怡芳 S *Salesclerk* 店員

Y May I try on this pair of shoes?

S Of course. What is your size?

Y I think it's 35.

S OK. I'll get it for you.

Y Hmm, I don't feel very comfortable.

S Try this one, please. This is made of real leather and is very soft. How is it?

Y This is just right for me. I'll take this one.

Y 我可以試穿這雙鞋嗎？

S 當然可以。您穿幾號？

Y 我穿35號吧。

S 好的，我去拿。

Y 嗯，穿起來不太舒服。

S 那試試這一款真皮的比較軟。怎麼樣？

Y 這雙很舒服，我就買這雙。

02 I'd Like to Buy a Shirt. 我想買一件襯衫。 131

S *Salesclerk* 店員 J *Jason* 傑森

S May I help you, sir?

J I'd like to buy a shirt.

S What color do you want?

J I prefer the blue one.

S What size are you?

J I'm not sure. Could you measure me, please?

S No problem. I think 40 will be fine for you.

J Can I try it on?

S Of course. The fitting room is this way, please.

S 先生，您要買什麼嗎？

J 我想買一件襯衫。

S 您要什麼顏色的？

J 我要藍色的。

S 請問您穿幾號？

J 我不太確定。你可以幫我量一下嗎？

S 沒問題。您應該可以穿40號。

J 我可以試穿嗎？

S 當然可以，試衣間在這邊。

PART 3

Useful Expressions

01 Choosing the Size and the Style of Clothes and Accessories 選擇服飾或配件的尺寸與樣式 132

告知店員想買什麼

1. I'd like to buy a white shirt. 我想買一件白襯衫。
2. I'd like to look at your sweaters. 我想看一下毛衣。
3. I'm looking for a cotton skirt. 我想買一條棉布裙。
4. Bring me a pair of woolen gloves, please.
   請給我拿副羊皮手套。
5. Would you mind showing me some scarves?
   拿幾條圍巾給我看一下好嗎?

詢問顧客想買什麼

6. What sort of shirt are you interested in?
   您比較喜歡哪一種襯衫?
7. Do you need socks or gloves?
   您需要襪子或手套嗎?
8. What kind of coat would you like to see?
   您想看哪種外套?

買名牌包

9. Do you carry Burberry handbags?
   你們有賣Burberry的手提包嗎?

買鞋子

10. I need a pair of shoes. 我想買一雙鞋子。
11. Are there any proper shoes for making a trip?
    有適合旅行穿的鞋子嗎?

clothes shopping 購買衣物

try on high heel shoes 試穿高跟鞋

選擇款式

12 **Any particular style?** 有要什麼特別的樣式嗎？

13 **Any other styles?** 有沒有其他款式？

14 **Do you have any other designs?** 你們還有其他款式嗎？

15 **Can you show me something similar?**
可以讓我看看其他類似的款式嗎？

詢問顧客喜好

16 **Which one do you like?** 您喜歡哪一種？

17 **Do you like this one?** 這個您喜歡嗎？

選擇顏色

18 A **What color do you want?** 您想要什麼顏色的？
B **White or some light color, I think.** 白的或淺色的。
B **Black, please.** 請給我黑色的。

19 A **The color favors you.** 這個顏色很適合您。
B **It's a little too showy.** 這個有點太顯眼了。

有沒有別的顏色

20 **Do you have any other colors?** 還有沒有別的顏色？

21 **Do you have the same pattern in other colors?**
這種圖案有別的顏色嗎？

22 **Do you have brown ones in the same style?**
這種樣式有咖啡色的嗎？

選擇尺寸

23 Ⓐ What size, please? 您想要什麼尺寸的？

Ⓐ What is your size? 您穿幾號的？

Ⓑ I don't know my size. 我不知道尺寸。

Ⓑ I think it's 36. 我應該是穿36號的。

24 Here's one in your size. 這一件是您要的尺寸。

measure 丈量

請店員量尺寸

25 Can you measure my size?
你可以幫我量一下我的尺寸嗎？

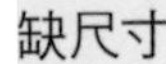

缺尺寸

26 Sorry, we don't have any one in your size.
抱歉，我們沒有您要的尺寸。

選擇品牌

27 Is there any special brand you'd like?
您有什麼特別喜歡的牌子嗎？

28 What's the trade mark?
這是什麼牌子的？

02 Asking About the Products' Material and Quality 詢問商品材質與品質 133

zipper 拉鍊

詢問材質

29 What kind of material is this?
這是什麼質料？

30 Is it made of silk? 這是絲製的嗎？

31 Ⓐ What is this made of?
它是用什麼做的？

Ⓑ It's made of leather with a zipper.
是皮製的，還有拉鍊。

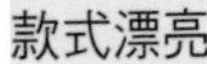

款式漂亮

32 This is extremely beautiful. 這個的確非常漂亮。

款式太素

33 That looks a bit too plain. 那個看起來太素了。

款式不時髦

34 This looks to me a little old-fashioned.
這個款式看起來舊了一點。

款式太時髦

35 I'd like something not too fashionable.
我想買不要太時髦的。

最新樣式

36 Could I see some of the new styles, please?
可以看一下新的款式嗎？

37 It's the very latest fashion.
這是最新的樣式。

38 It's the prevailing fashion.
這是最時髦的樣式。

品質好

39 It's of good quality. 這個品質很好。

40 It's the best quality hat, and our own make.
這頂帽子的布料是最好的，而且是本店自製的。

會不會褪色

41 Will it wear well, and won't the color fade?
這耐穿嗎？不會褪色嗎？

42 Is the color fast? 會褪色嗎？

會不會縮水

43 Will it shrink?
會不會縮水？

耐不耐洗

44 Is it washable? 耐洗嗎？

是否能用洗衣機洗

45 A Can I wash it in a washing machine?
這可以用洗衣機洗嗎？

手洗

B It needs to be hand-washed.
必須要手洗。

套裝不分售

46 A Could you break up the suit? I only want to buy the coat. 這套衣服可以分開賣嗎？我只想買外套。

B We can't break up the set.
這是一套的，我們不分開賣。

03 Trying On Clothes and Shoes 試穿衣服或鞋子 134

衣服穿法

47 How to wear it? 這件衣服要怎麼穿？

試穿

48 Can I try it on? 我可以試穿一下嗎？

49 May I try on this pair of shoes?
我可以試穿一下這雙鞋子嗎？

50 I'd better try on both feet and see whether the shoes are comfortable to wear. 我最好兩腳都試穿一下，看穿起來舒不舒服。

51 May I try both styles? 我可以兩種樣式都試試看嗎？

52 Try this one, please. 請試試這件／雙。

找試衣間

53 Where may I try it on? 我可以在哪裡試穿？

54 Where are your fitting rooms? 請問試衣間在哪裡？

55 The fitting room is this way, please. 試衣間在這邊。

照鏡子

56 Where is the mirror? 哪裡有鏡子？

57 How do I look? 好看嗎？

合身

58 Ⓐ Does it fit? 還合適嗎？
Ⓐ How is it? 怎麼樣？
Ⓑ It seems to be a perfect fit. 好像很合適。
Ⓑ This is just my size. 這剛好是我的尺寸。

59 Ⓐ Do you think they are all right? 您覺得合適嗎？
Ⓑ It seems to be all right. 好像不錯。
Ⓑ It suits me. 這個適合我。

不合身

60 It doesn't fit me. 這不合身。

fitting rooms 試衣間

衣服太緊 61 It's a little tight around the waist. 腰部有點緊。

衣服太鬆／太長／太短 62 This is too loose/long/short. 這件太鬆了／太長了／太短了。

鞋子太大 63 They are too big for me. 這雙鞋太大了。

鞋子太緊 64 The shoes are too tight in the front. 這雙鞋的前面太緊了。

不舒服 65 I don't feel very comfortable. 我覺得穿起來不太舒服。

換尺寸 66 Do you have any larger ones in the same color? 你有沒有同樣顏色大一點的？

67 It's too tight. Don't you have anything a little bit larger? 太緊了。有沒有大一點的？

68 Show me a smaller size, please. 請拿小一點的給我。

換低跟的鞋子 69 Do you have other shoes with lower heels? 有沒有跟比較低的鞋子？

Shopping for Jewelry and Watches

Chapter 16

購物：首飾及手錶

PART 1

Key Terms

135

① **necklace** 項鍊

② **earring** 耳環

③ **bracelet** 手鐲

④ **ring** 戒指

⑤ **brooch** 胸針

⑥ **pearl** 珍珠

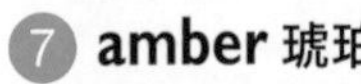

⑦ **amber** 琥珀

⑧ **jade** 玉

⑨ **ruby** 紅寶石

⑩ **sapphire** 藍寶石

⑪ **emerald** 翡翠

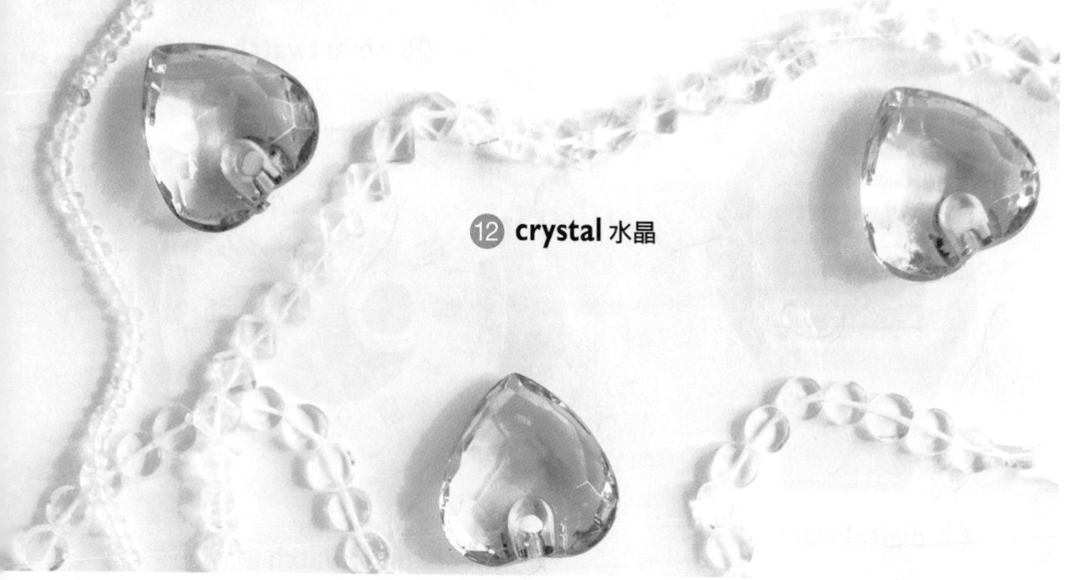

⑫ **crystal** 水晶

137

⑬ **silver** 銀

⑭ **gold** 金

⑮ **stainless steel** 不鏽鋼

⑯ **copper** 銅

⑰ **diamond** 鑽石

⑱ **smartwatch** 智慧型手錶

⑲ **digital watch** 電子錶

⑳ **mechanical watch** 機械錶

138

㉑ **pocket watch** 懷錶

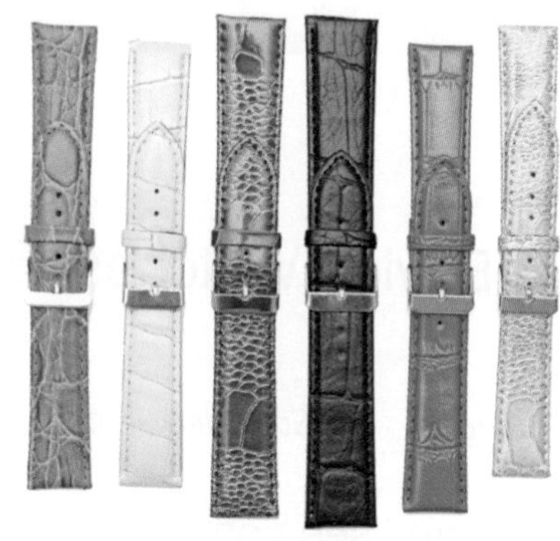

㉒ **watchband** 錶帶

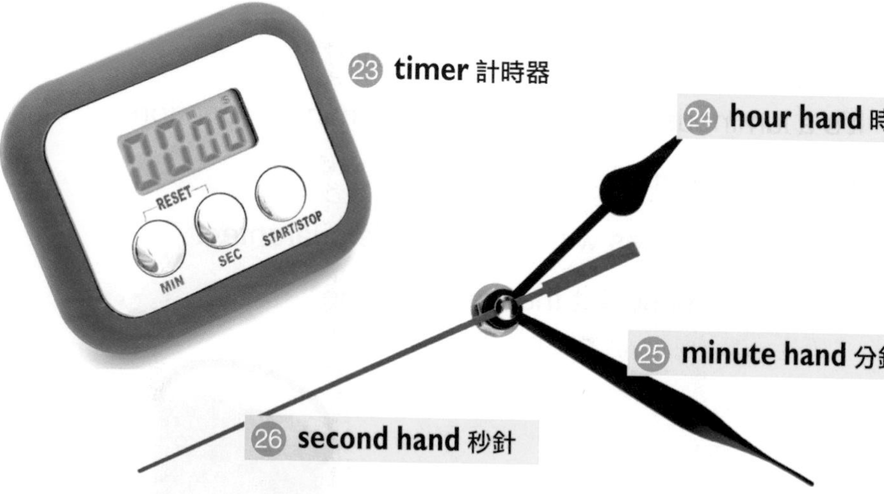

㉓ **timer** 計時器

㉔ **hour hand** 時針

㉕ **minute hand** 分針

㉖ **second hand** 秒針

㉗ **waterproof** 防水

㉘ **function** 功能

㉙ **anti-shock** 防震

㉚ **guarantee** 保固；保證書

㉛ **genuine** 真的；純的

㉜ **adjust** 調整

PART 2

Conversations

01 Buying Watches 買手錶 139

B *Bing* 賓 S *Salesclerk* 店員

B Can I see some men's watches?

S Of course. How about this one?

B What functions does this watch have?

S It's a luminous watch with a time-reminder function.

B Is it waterproof?

S Yes, and it comes with a worldwide guarantee.

B I'll take it. Please set the watch for me.

B 我可以看一下男錶嗎？

S 當然可以。這隻怎麼樣？

B 這隻有什麼功能？

S 它有夜光手錶，還有鬧鈴功能。

B 防水嗎？

S 防水，而且還有全球保固。

B 好，我要買。請幫我調好時間。

02 Buying Necklaces 買項鍊 (140)

W *Wendy* 温蒂　S *Salesclerk* 店員

W Would you please show me the necklace in the window?

S Is this the one you want?

W No, the one next to it.

S Here you are.

W Thanks. What kind of stone is this?

S It's a ruby. It is from South Africa. Would you like to try it on?

W Yes, please. How much is it?

S It costs $200.

W It looks good. OK. I'll take it.

W 可以讓我看看櫥窗裡的那條項鍊嗎？

S 您說這一條嗎？

W 不是，旁邊那條。

S 來，這裡。

W 謝謝。這是什麼寶石？

S 這是南非紅寶石。您要不要試戴看看？

W 好的，麻煩了。請問這條多少錢？

S 200美元。

W 很好看耶，好，那我就這買這條。

PART 3

Useful Expressions

01 Buying Jewelry 買珠寶首飾 141

請店員拿商品	1 May I see the necklace in the window? 我可以看一下櫥窗裡的項鍊嗎？
買珍珠項鍊	2 I'm looking for a pearl necklace. 我想看一下珍珠項鍊。 3 Is this pearl genuine? 這珍珠是真的還是人造的？
買寶石	4 What is this stone? 這是哪一種寶石？ 5 Where is this stone from? 這個寶石是哪裡產的？
買K金	6 A How many karat is this gold? 這是幾K金的？ B It's 18-karat gold. 這是18K金的。
買鑽石	7 Is this a real diamond? 這是真鑽嗎？
鑑定書	8 Does it come with an appraisal? 這有附品質鑑定書嗎？
量指圍	9 What size is this ring? 這個戒指是幾號的？ 10 Could you please measure my ring finger? 你能不能我量一下指圍？
要求試戴	11 May I try it on? 可以試戴嗎？
照鏡子	12 I'd like to look in a mirror. 我想照一下鏡子。
其他款式	13 Are there any other designs? 有別的款式嗎？

02 Buying Watches 買手錶 142

請店員拿手錶	14 May I see this? 我可以看看這隻嗎？（指著手錶說） 15 May I see the second watch from the left? 我可以看左邊數來第二隻手錶嗎？
想看女錶	16 Can I see some women's watches? 我可以看一下女錶嗎？
想看男錶	17 Can I see some men's watches? 我可以看一下男錶嗎？
買對錶	18 Do you carry pair watches? 你們有賣對錶嗎？
買勞力士	19 A Rolex for a man, please. 我要一隻男用的勞力士錶。
買防水錶	20 I'm looking for a waterproof watch. 我想買防水手錶。
詢問手錶功能	21 What functions does this watch have? 這隻錶有什麼功能？
有沒有防水	22 Is it waterproof? 這隻有防水嗎？
有沒有防震	23 Is it anti-shock? 這隻有防震嗎？
能不能計時	24 Does this watch have a timer function? 這隻錶有計時功能嗎？
調錶帶	25 Can the watchband be adjusted? 錶帶可以調嗎？
調時間	26 Set the watch, please. 請幫我調好時間。
有無保證書	27 Does it come with a guarantee? 有附保證書嗎？

Shopping for
Cosmetics

Chapter 17

購物：化妝保養品

PART 1

Key Terms

① **perfume** 香水

② **cologne** 古龍水

③ **cosmetics** 化妝品

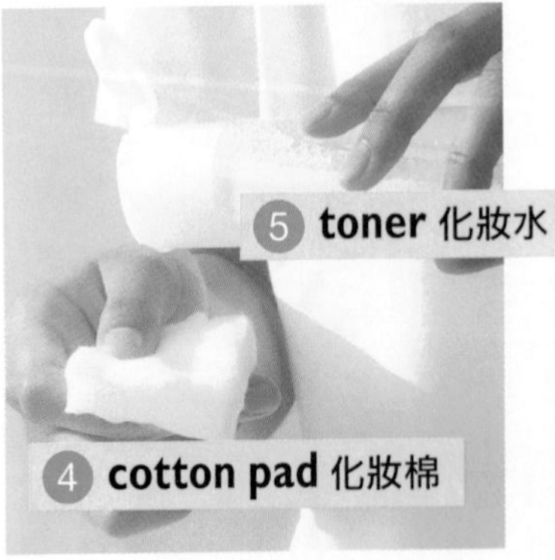

⑤ **toner** 化妝水

④ **cotton pad** 化妝棉

⑥ **makeup remover / makeup removing lotion** 卸妝乳

8 **pressed powder** 粉餅

7 **foundation** 粉底
- **BB cream (blemish balm cream)** BB 霜
- **CC cream (color correcting cream)** CC 霜

9 **puff** 粉撲

10 **eye shadow** 眼影

11 **eye shadow palette** 眼影盤

145

⑫ **eyebrow pencil** 眉筆

⑬ **eyeliner** 眼線筆

⑭ **mascara** 睫毛膏

⑮ **fake eyelashes** 假睫毛

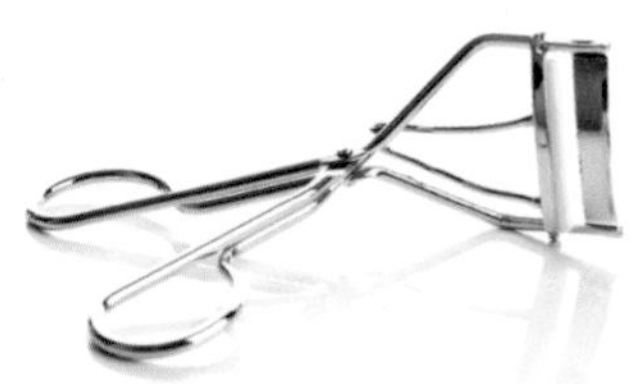

⑯ **lash curler** 睫毛夾

⑰ **lipstick** 口紅

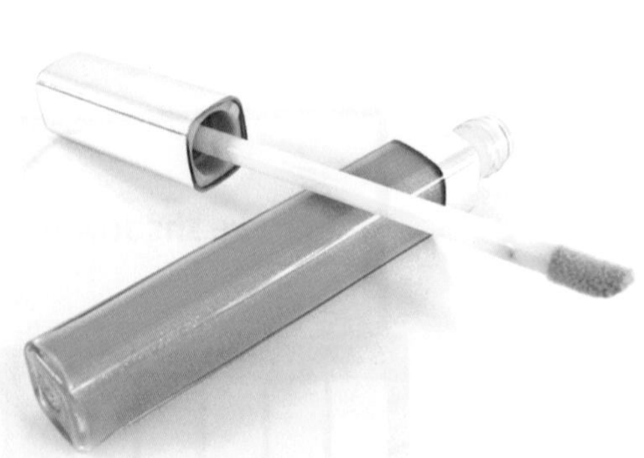

⑱ **lip gloss** 唇蜜

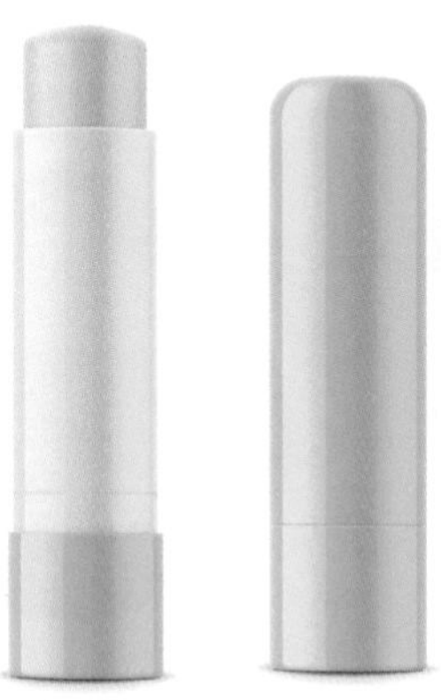

⑲ **lip balm** 護唇膏

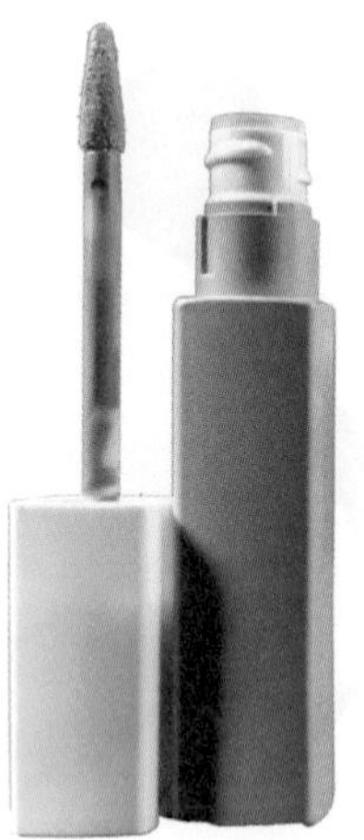

⑳ **lip stain/tint** 唇釉

㉑ **blush** 腮紅

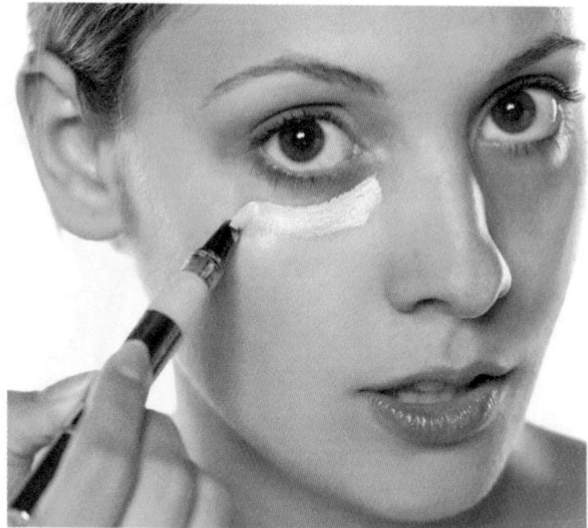

㉒ **concealer** 遮瑕膏

㉓ **loose powder** 鬆粉式蜜粉

147

㉔ **brush** 刷具

㉕ **lotion** 乳液

㉖ **cream** 乳霜

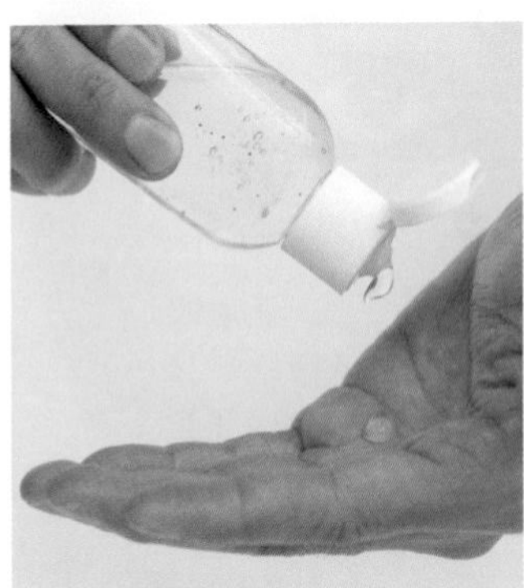

㉗ **gel** 凝膠

㉘ **facial mask** 面膜

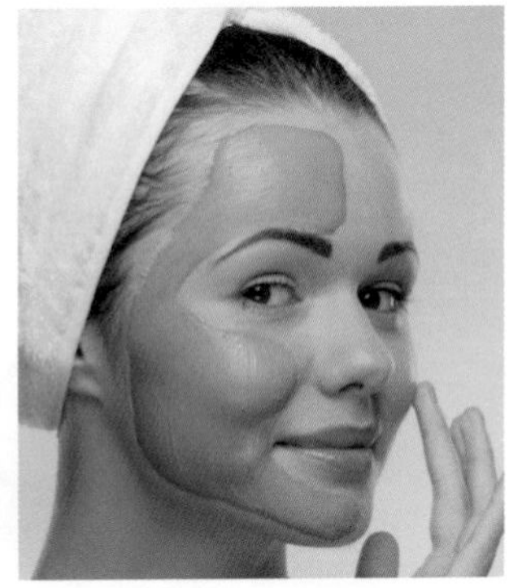

㉙ **mud mask** 泥膜

㉚ **nail polish** 指甲油

㉛ **nail clippers** 指甲剪

148

32 **moisturizer** 保溼用品；潤膚霜

33 **essence** 精華液

34 **oily skin** 油性皮膚

35 **dry skin** 乾性皮膚

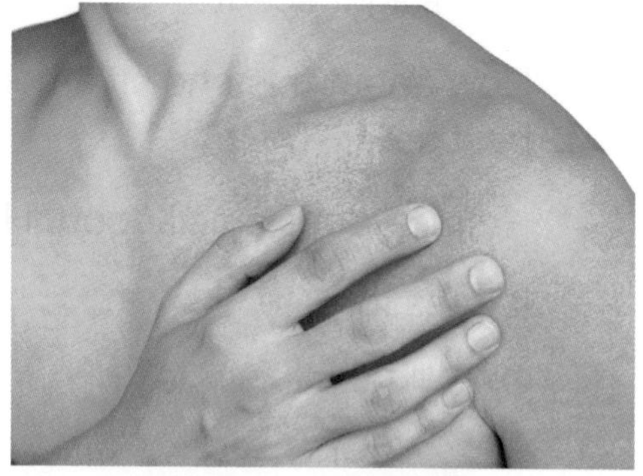

36 **sensitive skin** 敏感性肌膚

37 **acne** 粉刺；青春痘

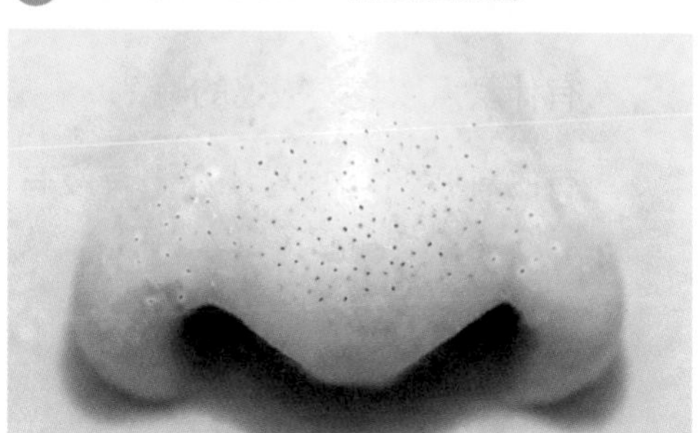

38 **blackhead** 黑頭粉刺

39 **scent** 香味
40 **light** 味道淡的
41 **strong** 味道濃的
42 **top note** 前味
43 **middle note** 中味
44 **base note** 後味
45 **floral scent** 花香調
46 **woody scent** 木質調
47 **citrus scent** 柑橘調

01 Buying Perfumes 買香水 149

S *Salesclerk* 店員 A *Amy* 艾美

S May I help you?

A Yes. I'm looking for some perfume. Do you have perfumes with a light scent?

S How about this one? It smells like green tea and is our best seller. Try it.

A Hmm, it does smell good. How much is it?

S It goes for $40.

A OK. I'll take this one.

S 有什麼可以為您服務的嗎？

A 有的，我想買香水，你們有沒有氣味清淡一點的？

S 這瓶怎麼樣？它是綠茶的味道，賣得非常好。您可以試聞看看。

A 嗯，真的不錯耶。這瓶多少錢？

S 40美元。

A 好，那我就買這一瓶。

02 Buying Lipsticks 買口紅 150

S *Salesclerk* 店員 A *Amy* 艾美

S May I help you?

A Do you have the latest lipstick from Christian Dior?

S Yes. What colors do you like?

A Any special colors?

S How about this one?

A Can I try it on and see how it looks?

S Of course. This product moisturizes at the same time.

A Looks good. I'll take it.

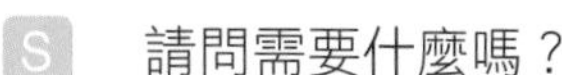

S 請問需要什麼嗎？

A 你們有賣迪奧最新出的口紅嗎？

S 有啊，您想要什麼顏色？

A 有沒有特別一點的顏色？

S 這隻如何呢？

A 我可以試擦看看嗎？

S 當然可以。這一款口紅的滋潤度很好。

A 看起來不錯，我就買這支。

PART 3

Useful Expressions

01 Buying Perfume 買香水 151

買香水	**1** I'm thinking of getting some perfume. 我想買香水。
指定品牌	**2** Do you carry the latest Chanel perfume? 你們有沒有賣香奈兒最新出的香水？
特定香味	**3** Which perfume has a rose scent? 哪一瓶香水有玫瑰的味道？
味道淡	**4** I'd like a little lighter scent of perfume. 我想要氣味清淡一點的香水。
詢問後味	**5** What is the base note on this perfume? 這瓶香水的後味是什麼？
試用品	**6** Do you have a sample of this? 這個有沒有試用品？
試聞香水	**7** Can I smell this bottle of perfume? 可以試聞這瓶香水嗎？
試噴香水	**8** Can I try this bottle of perfume? 可以試噴這瓶香水嗎？
暢銷品	**9** Which perfume is your best seller? 哪一瓶香水賣得最好？
詢問容量	**10** How many milliliters are there in this container? 這瓶香水的容量是多少毫升？

02 Buying Makeup and Skin Products
買化妝品或保養品 152

詢問膚質 ⓫ Ⓐ For oily skin, dry skin or sensitive skin?
請問是油性肌膚、乾性肌膚還是敏感性肌膚要用的？

油性皮膚 Ⓑ For oily skin, please. 油性肌膚用的。

Ⓑ My skin is oily. 我是油性肌膚。

詢問膚質 ⓬ Ⓐ What is your skin type? 請問您是什麼膚質？

乾性皮膚 Ⓑ My skin is dry. 我是乾性肌膚。

敏感性皮膚 Ⓑ My skin is sensitive. 我是敏感性肌膚。

問產品功能 ⓭ How does this product work? 這款產品有什麼功效？

問產品用法 ⓮ How do I use this lotion? 這款乳液要怎麼用？

買乳液 ⓯ I'd like two bottles of lotion. 我要買兩罐乳液。

買防曬粉底 ⓰ I am looking for a foundation with sun protection.
我想找有防曬的粉底。

彩妝顏色 ⓱ This color suits you. 這個顏色很適合您。

⓲ I'd like a brighter color. 我想要亮一點的顏色。

⓳ Do you have the latest lipstick from Christian Dior?
你們有沒有迪奧最新出的口紅？

試擦指甲油 ⓴ Can I try this nail polish? 我可以試擦這瓶指甲油嗎？

買睫毛膏 ㉑ Ⓐ What's the difference between these two mascaras?
這兩支睫毛膏有什麼不同？

Ⓑ This one makes your eyelashes look longer, and this one creates a curly effect. 這款是加長型，這款是捲翹型。

Shopping in
the Supermarket

Chapter 18

購物：逛超市

PART 1

Key Terms

1 **supermarket** 超市

2 **grocery store** 雜貨店

3 **shopping basket** 購物籃

4 **shopping cart** 購物推車

5 **aisle** 走道

6 **frozen food** 冷凍食品

⑦ **deli** 熟食

⑧ **dairy** 乳製品

⑨ **bakery** 烘焙食品

⑩ **beverage** 飲料

⑪ **checkout (counter)** 結帳櫃檯

⑫ **self-checkout** 自助結帳櫃檯

⑬ **express checkout** 快速結帳櫃檯

⑭ **cash-only checkout** 只收現金的結帳通道

155

15 **coupon** 折價券；優惠券

16 **voucher** 兌換券

18 **instant noodles** 泡麵

17 **potato chips** 洋芋片

19 **chocolate** 巧克力

20 **shampoo** 洗髮精

21 **hair conditioner** 護髮乳

(156)

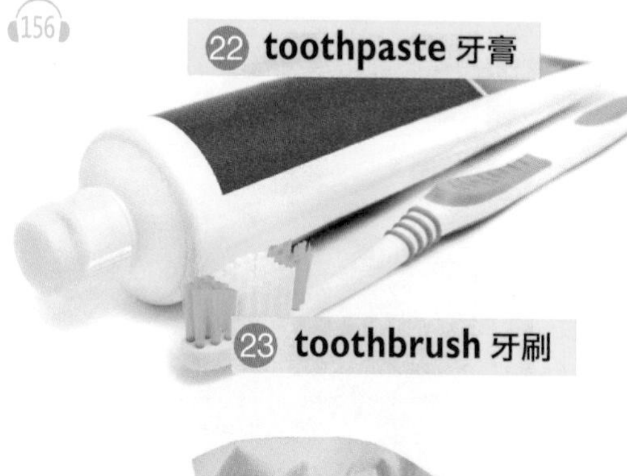

22 **toothpaste** 牙膏

23 **toothbrush** 牙刷

24 **sanitary/maxi pad** 衛生棉

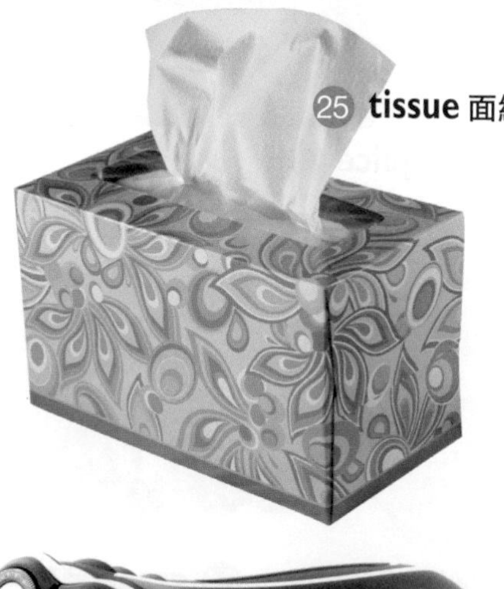

25 **tissue** 面紙

26 **deodorant** 止汗劑

27 **razor** 刮鬍刀

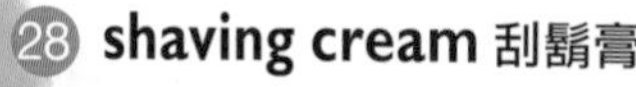

28 **shaving cream** 刮鬍膏

29 **sun protection** 防曬油

30 **mineral water** 礦泉水

31 **juice** 果汁

32 **apple** 蘋果

33 **orange** 柳橙

34 **grape** 葡萄

35 **kiwi fruit** 奇異果

36 **watermelon** 西瓜

37 **pineapple** 鳳梨

38 **banana** 香蕉

39 **strawberry** 草莓

40 **lemon** 檸檬

41 **cherry** 櫻桃

42 **coconut** 椰子

43 **melon** 甜瓜

44 **peach** 桃子

45 **tangerine** 橘子

46 **passion fruit** 百香果

47 **mango** 芒果

48 **pear** 西洋梨

49 **avocado** 酪梨

PART 2 Conversations

01 At a Grocery Store 在雜貨店 159

A *Amy* 艾美 S *Salesclerk* 店員

A Excuse me, do you sell apples?

S Yes. They are over there.

A Do you sell them individually or by weight?

S By weight. 60 cents per pound.

A Could you weigh these, please?

S $4.55, please. Anything else?

A A sack of cherries, please.

S Here you are.

A 不好意思，請問你們有賣蘋果嗎？

S 有，蘋果在那邊。

A 是論顆賣還是論斤賣？

S 論斤賣，每磅60分。

A 請幫我秤一下這些好嗎？

S 這樣是4.55美元。還需要什麼嗎？

A 請給我一袋櫻桃。

S 好的，這裡。

shopping list 購物清單

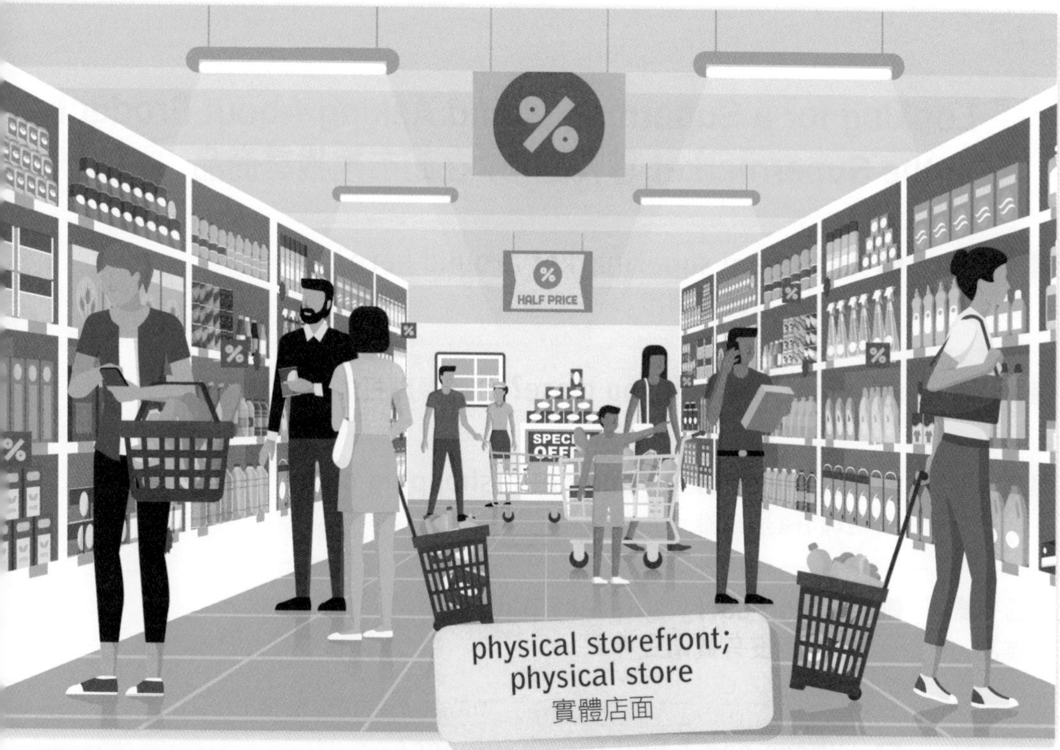

HALF PRICE

physical storefront; physical store
實體店面

online store
網路店面

Useful Expressions

01 Looking for a Supermarket and Asking About Products in the Supermarket 尋找超市／在超市裡找尋商品 160

尋找超市	1 Is there a supermarket around here? 這附近有沒有超市？
營業時間	2 What time do you close? 你們幾點打烊？
推車	3 We'd better go and get a shopping cart. 我們還是去推一台推車吧。
是否有賣某產品	4 Do you carry sanitary pads? 你們有沒有賣衛生棉？
詢問商品位置	5 Where can I find the shampoos? 請問洗髮精放在哪裡？ 6 Which aisle can I find the toothbrushes in? 請問牙刷在哪一條走道？
買整箱飲料	7 It's cheaper to buy beer by the case. 啤酒整箱買比較便宜。
按重量出售	8 This is sold by weight. 這個按重量計價出售。

按數量出售	9 This is sold by package. 這個是一包一包賣的。
買水果	10 What about some of these lemons? 買一點檸檬好嗎？
挑水果	11 Please help me pick out the best one. 請幫我挑個最好的。 12 Pick me out a good one, please. 請幫我挑個好一點的。 13 Pick out larger ones, please. 請挑大一點的。
買蛋	14 I'd like to get half a dozen eggs. 我要買半打雞蛋。
是否有打折	15 Is the toothpaste on sale today? 牙膏今天有打折嗎？ 16 Are these on sale only today? 這些只有今天特價嗎？
有效期限	17 What's the expiration date? 有效期限到什麼時候？

More Supermarket Vocabulary 更多超市單字

organic food 有機食品
litter 公升
gallon 加侖
shopping bag 購物袋
expire 過期
expiration date 有效期限

half a dozen eggs 半打雞蛋

a dozen eggs 一打雞蛋

one and a half dozen eggs 一打半雞蛋

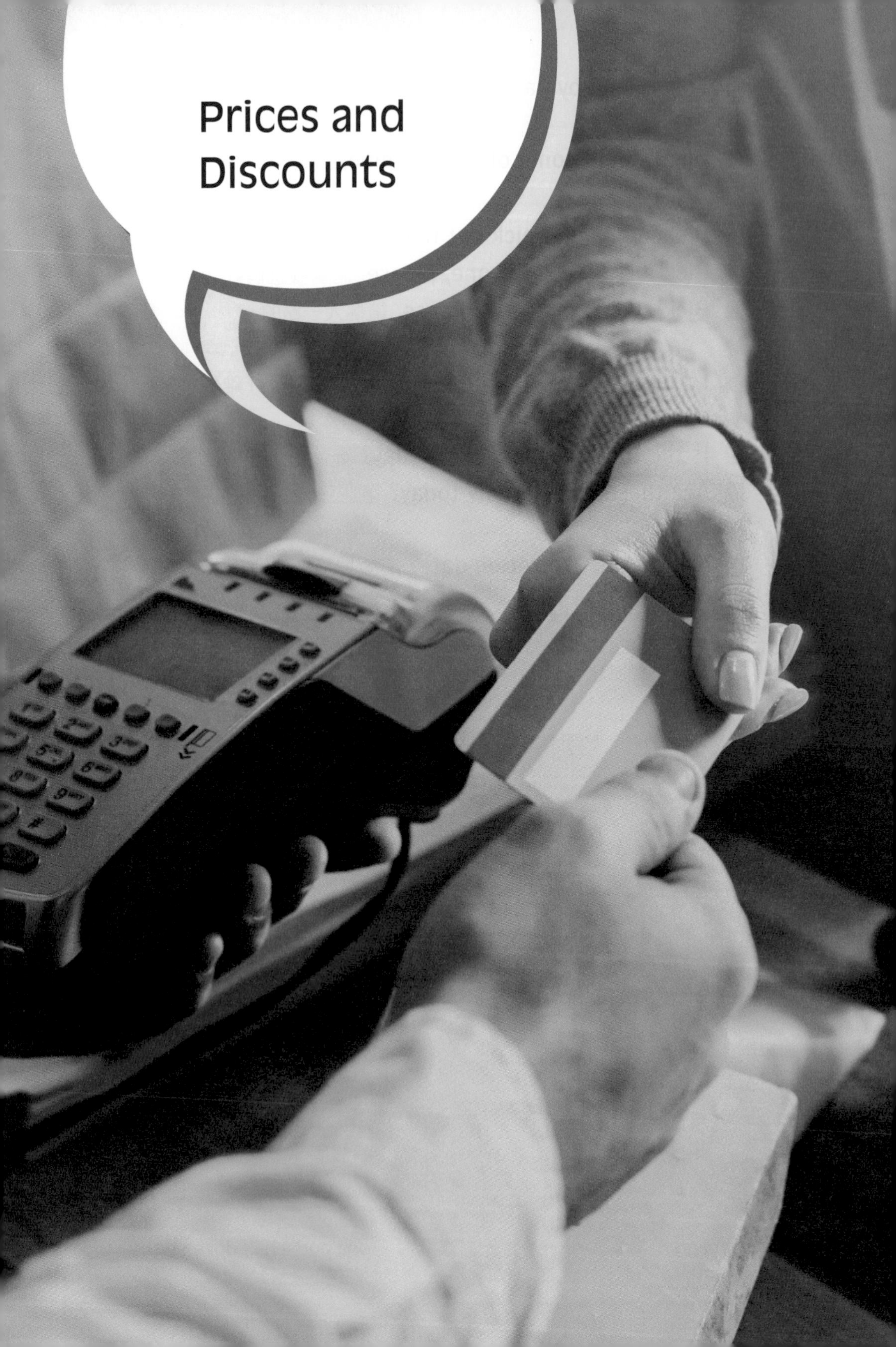
Prices and Discounts

Chapter 19

殺價與付款

PART 1

Key Terms

① **cash** 現金

② **cash register** 收銀機

③ **credit card** 信用卡

④ **credit card register** 刷卡機

⑤ **cashier** 收銀員

⑥ **bar code** 條碼

⑦ **QR code** QR 圖碼

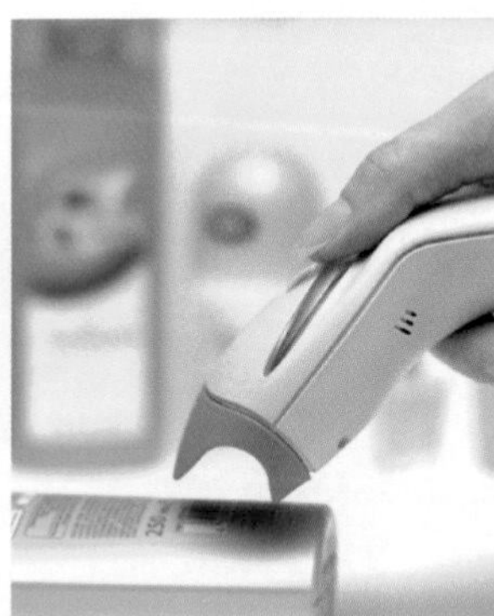

⑧ **bar code scanner** 條碼掃描器

⑨ **discount** 打折

⑩ **price tag** 價格標籤

⑪ **calculator** 計算機

⑫ **cheap** 便宜的

⑬ **expensive** 貴的

⑭ **margin** 利潤

⑮ **receipt** 收據

⑯ **plastic bag** 塑膠袋

⑰ **paper bag** 紙袋

⑱ **gift** 禮物

⑲ **afford** 買得起；付得起
⑳ **reasonable** 合理的；公道的
㉑ **price range** 價格幅度
㉒ **retail price** 零售價
㉓ **reduction** 減少；降低
㉔ **refund** 退款
㉕ **tax** 稅金
㉖ **shipping** 運送

PART 2

Conversations

01 Can You Make It Any Cheaper? 能不能算便宜一點？ 163

J *Jennifer* 珍妮佛 S *Salesclerk* 店員

J Could you show me the T-shirt on the model?

S Here you are. We have three different colors: white, blue, and pink.

J What's the price?

S $12.

J Can you make it any cheaper?

S It is cheap.

J I'll take it if you give me a discount.

S $10. That's the best I can do.

J OK. I'll take the blue one.

J 我能看一下模特兒身上那件Ｔ恤嗎？

S 來，請看。
一共有三種顏色：白色、藍色和粉紅色。

J 多少錢？

S 12塊美金。

J 能不能算便宜一點？

S 已經很便宜了。

J 你幫我打個折我就買。

S 最低就10塊了。

J 好吧，那我要藍色的。

02 How Much Is That One? 那一個多少錢？ 164

A *Andy* 安迪 S *Salesclerk* 店員

A I'm looking for a string of pearls for my wife.

S Yes, sir. What price range do you have in mind?

A I'm not sure. I don't know very much about the price of pearls.

S I see. Let me show you some samples of various qualities. This one is very nice. It's three hundred and fifty dollars.

A Is there a price reduction?

S We are having a sale now. The price has already gone down.

A How much is that one?

S It's two hundred and eighty dollars.

A OK. I'll take it. Thank you.

A 我想幫我太太買一串珍珠。

S 好的，先生。您的預算是多少？

A 我不確定，我不大清楚珍珠的行情。

S 這樣呀。那麼我給您看一些不同等級的樣品。這串很好看，價格是350美元。

A 有折扣嗎？

S 我們正在大特賣，價格已經降低了。

A 那條多少錢？

S 280美元。

A 好，我就買這串。謝謝妳。

PART 3

Useful Expressions

01 Asking About Product Prices 詢問產品價格 165

詢問價格

1. How much? 多少錢？
2. How much is this? 這個多少錢？
3. What about the prices? 價格多少？
4. How much do you say it is? 你說這個要多少錢？
5. What's the price of this? 這個定價多少？
6. How much for two? 買兩個多少錢？

說明價格

7. It would only cost you 10 dollars. 這個只要10美元。
8. It's one dollar only. 只要1美元。
9. It sells for eight dollars per pair. 這個每雙8美元。
10. The original price is 100 dollars and we take 10% off for the sale. 原價100美元，現在打九折。
11. The retail price of it is $9. 這個零售價是9美元。

價格在標籤上

12. The price of the shoes is marked on the price tag. 鞋子的價格在標籤上。

總計多少錢

13. Ⓐ How much all together? 總共多少錢？
Ⓐ How much does that come to? 總計多少？
Ⓑ It comes to ten pounds. 一共是10英鎊。
Ⓑ It adds up to 400 dollars. 共計400美元。

各種商品標籤 Different Kinds of Labels

環保商品 | 100%純有機 | 100%純天然

保證最低價 | 免運費 | 100%純棉

比較價錢

⓮ What's the difference in price between this and that?
這個和那個價錢有什麼差別？

⓯ The cheaper one is 30 dollars.
比較便宜的這個是30美元。

⓰ Is that the same price? 那件價格一樣嗎？

⓱ The price of these two is the same. 這兩個價格一樣。

優惠期限

⓲ The special price will be effective until June 20.
優惠價只到6月20日。

02 Complaining About the Price 覺得太貴 (166)

太貴

⓳ Too expensive! 太貴了啦！

⓴ I should call it rather expensive. 我覺得這個太貴了。

㉑ These prices are too high. 價格太高了。

國外觀光區的商品定價通常偏高，遊客向老闆殺價或討折扣，幾乎是不可避免的過程。但若是商家已在門口或牆壁貼上 **Fixed Price**（不二價），表示不願意降價，遊客就不應該再開口殺價，以免顯得不禮貌，成為不受歡迎的奧客。

產品不值這個錢

22 That seems a high price for the brooch.
胸針賣這個價格好像太貴了。

23 The price is not reasonable. 這價格不合理。

買不起

24 That's more than I can afford.
我出不起這個價錢。

03 Bargaining 討價還價 167

有沒有打折

25 Any discounts? 有打折嗎？

26 Are you having a sale on leather goods today?
你們今天皮件有在打折嗎？

打幾折

27 How much of a discount will you give?
你們打幾折？

特價後的價格

28 Is this the sale price?
這是特價後的價格嗎？

再算便宜一點

29 Could you cut the price a little, please?
可以再便宜一點嗎？

30 Can't you make it a little cheaper?
不能再算便宜一點嗎？

多買有沒有折扣

31 Ⓐ Is there a discount for two?
買兩個能不能算便宜一點？

Ⓑ We can offer you a better price if you buy more.
如果您多買一點，我們可以給您更優惠的價格。

比別家便宜才要買

32 If you can let us have a competitive quotation, we'll place our orders right now.
如果你給我的價錢比別家低，我們就馬上訂貨。

33 I should say our prices are generally lower when compared with others.
我必須說明，我們的價格跟別人相比，一般來說都比較便宜。

打折就買

34 I'll take it if you give me a discount.
你幫我打折我就買。

付現是否比較便宜

35 Could you give me a discount if I pay in cash?
付現有比較便宜嗎？

請顧客出價

36 How much are you willing to pay?
您願意出多少錢？

37 Is 20% off OK? 打八折好嗎？

38 How about 40 dollars? 您覺得40美元如何？

39 Can you sell it for 10 dollars? 這個可以賣我10美元嗎？

40 30 dollars, OK? 算30美元，好嗎？

41 My last price is 20 dollars. 我的底線是20美元。

在國外若是看到 20% OFF、30% OFF 這種標示，就代表商品正在打折。OFF 有「去掉」的意思，30% OFF 就代表拿掉原定價錢的 30%，還剩 70%，也就是打七折。

老闆的價格底線

42 Ⓐ Is that your best quote?
你最低只能賣這個價錢嗎？

Ⓑ That's the best I can do. 我不能再降了。

Ⓑ This is the lowest possible price.
這已經是可能的最低價格了。

Ⓑ I'm afraid these are the best terms we can offer.
恐怕這些已經是我們所能提供最優惠的條件了。

店家覺得價錢公道

43 It's cheap. 很便宜的。

44 The price is not bad. 價格不貴。

45 I think these prices are quite reasonable.
我覺得這些價格很公道。

46 Our prices are no more expensive than others.
我們的價錢不會比別人貴。

47 You'll find our prices are competitive.
您會發現我們的價格絕對不會比別家貴。

48 280 dollars. You can't be wrong on that, sir.
先生，280美元。這個價錢您絕對不吃虧。

折衷價格

49 Well, how about splitting the difference?
那麼，各讓一步怎麼樣？

一分錢一分貨

50 The price depends on the quality.
看品質，一分錢一分貨。

不二價

51 Our prices are fixed.
我們這裡是不二價的。

公定價

52 It's the standard price.
這是公定價格。

04 Paying 付款 168

決定要買

53 I'll take it. 我買了。

54 I'll take five of these. 我要買五個這個。

詢問付款地點

55 Where do I pay? 在哪裡結帳？

56 Where is the cashier? 請問收銀台在哪裡？

詢問付現或刷卡

57 A $70. Cash or credit card?
一共70美元。付現還是刷卡？
B Credit card, please. 刷卡。

是否能刷卡

58 Do you accept credit cards?
可以刷卡嗎？

還沒找錢

59 I haven't got the change yet. 你還沒找我錢。

找錯錢

60 You haven't given me the right change. 你找的錢不對。

61 I gave you a 100 dollar bill. 我給你的是一百元紙鈔。

索取收據

62 May I have a receipt? 請給我一張收據好嗎？

信用卡（credit card）

行動支付（mobile payment）

現金（cash）

各種支付方式
Different Kinds of Payment Methods

支票（paycheck）

05 Tax Refund 退稅 169

價錢是否含稅

63 Does the price include tax? 這個價錢含稅嗎？

64 Including tax? 含稅嗎？

產品是否退稅

65 Is this item tax free?
這個可以退稅嗎？

66 Can I get a tax refund for this?
這個可以退稅嗎？

退稅門檻

67 How much do I have to spend to get the tax refund?
我要買多少才能退稅？

退稅金額

68 How much refund will I get? 請問會退多少錢？

69 How much can I get refunded? 請問會退多少錢？

如何退稅

70 A What can I do to get the tax refund?
請問要如何辦理退稅？

索取退稅單

A May I have a tax refund form, please?
請給我一張退稅單好嗎？

要求出示護照

B Your passport, please.
請給我看一下您的護照。

詢問支付退款方式

71 A How would you like to receive this, by check or into your bank account? 你要我們寄支票或是轉帳給您？

B Into my bank account, please. 請轉帳給我。

收到退款時間

72 How long do I have to wait for the refund?
我要多久才能收到退款？

出國購物時，若是看到 Duty Free，代表該店家為免稅商店，在消費時通常需要滿一定金額並出示護照才能符合免稅資格；而若是看到 Tax Free 或 Tax Refund 的店家，則是代表可退稅，結算價格會是含稅價格，需自行至指定地點辦理退稅手續才能取得稅款，消費時記得要向店家索取退稅單，退稅方式有現金、支票、匯款及信用卡等，務必在退稅單上註明。（每國免稅與退稅方式不盡相同，宜在消費前先查明）

06 Packing of the Products After Purchase 商品包裝 170

bow 緞帶

不要盒子	73 I don't need the box. 我不要盒子。
索取塑膠袋	74 Can I have a plastic bag, please? 請給我一個塑膠袋好嗎？
分開包裝	75 Wrap them separately, please. 麻煩分開包。 76 Can I have separate bags for each item? 可以幫我每樣分開包嗎？
撕掉標籤	77 Take off the price tag, please. 請幫我把價格標籤撕掉。
禮品包裝	78 Can you wrap it as a gift? 可以幫我包成禮物嗎？
商品運送	79 Could you send it to Taiwan? 可以幫我寄到台灣嗎？
詢問運費	80 How much is the shipping cost? 運費要多少？
運送時間	81 How long does it take to ship this? 這個寄海運要多久？

gift box 禮物盒

wrap a gift 包裝禮物

wrapping paper 包裝紙

ribbon 緞帶

Taking Pictures and Buying Cameras

Chapter 20

拍照 & 買相機

PART 1

Key Terms

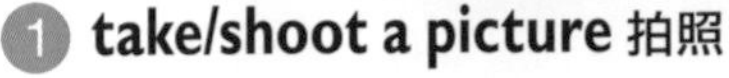
1 take/shoot a picture 拍照

2 photograph (photo) 照片

4 shutter 快門

3 digital camera 數位相機

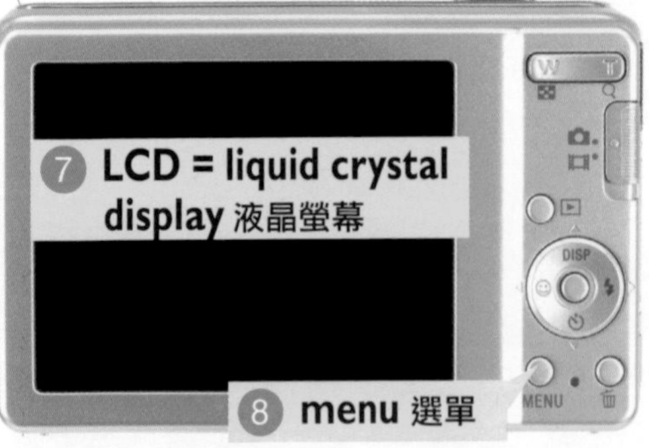

9 video camera 攝影機

⑩ **waterproof camera** 防水相機

⑪ **instant camera** 拍立得相機

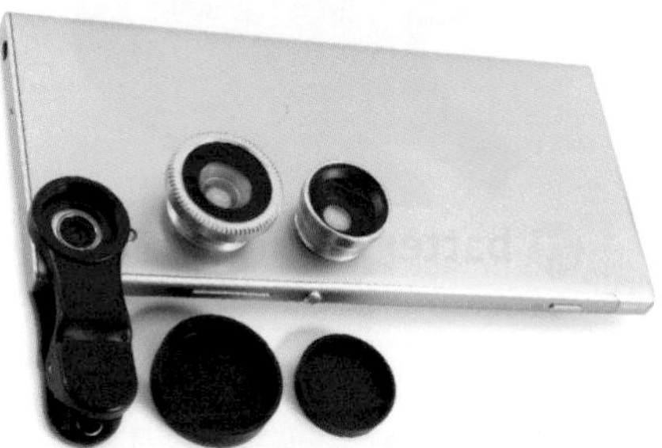

⑫ **mobile camera lens** 手機照相鏡頭

⑬ **memory card** 記憶卡

⑭ **film** 底片

⑮ **pixel** 像素

⑯ **zoom out** 使景物縮小

⑰ **zoom in** 使景物放大

173

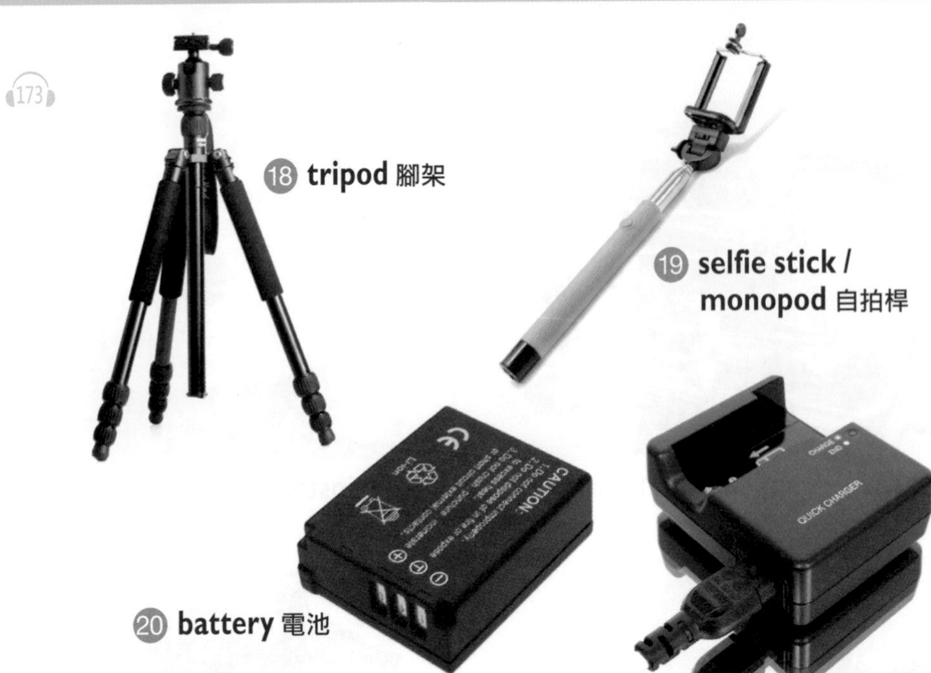

⑱ **tripod** 腳架

⑲ **selfie stick / monopod** 自拍桿

⑳ **battery** 電池

㉑ **battery charger** 充電器

cc by Andrey Zamoshnikov

㉒ **photo-printing kiosk** 相片列印機台

㉓ **print photos** 列印照片

㉔ **develop photos** 洗照片
㉕ **insert** 插入
㉖ **mode** 模式
㉗ **quality** 畫質
㉘ **self-timer** 定時自拍
㉙ **continuous shooting** 連拍
㉚ **vibration reduction** 防手震
㉛ **red-eye reduction** 防紅眼
㉜ **background** 背景
㉝ **durable** 耐用的
㉞ **capacity** 容量
㉟ **user-friendly** 方便使用的

01 Say "Cheese." 笑一個！ 174

J *Jenny* 珍妮　R *Rex* 雷克斯

J Excuse me, could you take a picture?

R No problem.

J Just press here. Give us the lake for the background, please.

R Say "cheese."

J Cheese.

R OK.

J Thank you.

J 不好意思，可以幫我們拍張照嗎？

R 沒問題。

J 按這裡就可以了（指著快門說）。我們要以湖為背景。

R 笑一個。

J （笑）

R 好了。

J 謝謝！

take/shoot a picture 拍照

02 Developing Film 洗照片 175

J *Jenny* 珍妮 C *Clerk* 店員

J Can I have this roll of film developed here?

C Sure. Let's see it.

J Here you are.

C What size of prints would you like to have?

J Regular will be fine. How long will it take?

C Only four hours.

J Good. I'll come back in the evening.

J 我可以在這裡沖洗底片嗎？

C 當然可以，我看看。

J 在這裡。

C 您要洗多大的尺寸？

J 一般的就好了。需要多久時間？

C 只要四個小時。

J 好，那我今天晚上來拿。

film 底片

03 Now Select the Photos You Want to Print.
接著，選擇妳要列印的照片。 176

M *Mike* 麥克 R *Rachel* 瑞秋

M We took some great photos today!

R Yeah. I'd love to print some out to put on my wall at home.

M I saw a photo-printing kiosk in that convenience store.

R Great! Let's go check it out.

[At the kiosk]

R It says first insert your USB drive or SD card into the slot.

M Now select the photos you want to print.

R Then insert the cash.

M Done. Now we just wait for your photos to print.

M 我們今天拍了一些不錯的照片！

R 是啊，我想要把一些照片印出來，貼在我家牆上。

M 我看到那家便利商店有相片列印機台。

R 太好了！我們去看看吧。

〔在相片列印機台〕

R 它這邊寫說，先插入你的USB硬碟或記憶卡。

M 接著，選擇妳要列印的照片。

R 然後放入現金。

M 完成了。現在只要等妳的照片列印就好了

PART 3

Useful Expressions

01 Taking Pictures 拍照 177

請人拍照	❶ Are you good at taking pictures? 你擅長拍照嗎？ ❷ Could you take a picture? 你能幫我拍張照嗎？
選擇背景	❸ Give me the landscape of the seashore for the background. 用海邊的景色幫我作背景。
告知快門按鈕位置	❹ Just press here, please. 按這裡就行了。
幫人拍照	❺ May I take a picture of you? 我可以拍一張你的照片嗎？
準備拍照	❻ Are you ready now? 你準備好了嗎？
笑一個	❼ Make a smiling face. 笑一個。 ❽ Say "Cheese." 笑一個。
請求合照	❾ Do you want to be in the picture with us? 可以一起照張相嗎？ ❿ Can I have a picture taken with you? 我可以和你合照嗎？
再拍一張	⓫ One more, please. 請再拍一張。
是否可拍照	⓬ May I take a picture here? 我可以在這裡拍照嗎？ ⓭ Is it allowed to take pictures here? 這裡可以拍照嗎？

no camera sign
「禁止拍照」標誌

selfie stick 自拍桿
selfie 自拍

是否可用閃光燈
⑭ May I use a flash?
可以用閃光燈嗎？

是否可錄影
⑮ May I videotape?
我可以錄影嗎？

02 Buying Film and Getting Negatives Developed
購買底片與沖洗底片 (178)

購買底片
⑯ I would like a roll of color film for 36 exposures.
我要一卷36張的彩色底片。

買電池
⑰ Do you have batteries? 你們有沒有賣電池？

⑱ I need batteries like this.
我要像這樣的電池。（拿電池給店家看）

沖洗底片
⑲ A Could you develop this roll of film?
你可以幫我沖洗這卷底片嗎？

A I'd like to have this film developed, please.
我要洗這卷底片。

沖洗尺寸
B What size of prints would you like to have?
您要洗什麼尺寸的？

A I want these pictures in size 5 by 7. 我要洗5乘7的。

A Regular will be fine. 一般的尺寸就好。

到沖洗店拿照片
⑳ When can I get my pictures?
我什麼時候可以來拿相片？

03 Buying Cameras and Having Them Repaired 買相機與修理相機 179

買照相機	21 A I'm looking for a camera. 我想買相機。
詢問相機種類	B What type of camera are you looking for? 您想買什麼樣的相機?
尋找數位相機	22 Is this a digital camera? 這台是數位相機嗎?
詢問相機功能	23 What functions does this model have? 這一款相機有什麼功能?
	24 Is there any difference between these two camera models? 這兩款相機有什麼不同?
相機像素	25 How many megapixels does this camera have? 這台相機有幾百萬像素?
自動對焦	26 Does this camera focus automatically? 這台相機有自動對焦嗎?
試用產品	27 Could I give them a try? 我可以試用一下嗎?
詢問按鈕功用	28 What is this button? 這個按鈕是作什麼用的?
相機好操作	29 It is very user-friendly. 這台非常好操作。
產品耐用	30 What kind is the most durable? 哪一種最耐用?

觸控式螢幕

31 This camera has a touchscreen interface.
這台相機有觸控式螢幕的操作介面。

32 To use the camera's functions, just touch the icons on the screen. 若要使用這台相機的功能，只要觸碰螢幕上的圖示就好。

33 You can adjust the settings by touching this icon here.
您可以觸控這裡的圖示來調整設定。

廣角功能

34 Can the lens take wide angle shots?
這個鏡頭有廣角功能嗎？

更換鏡頭

35 Can I change the lens? 可以換鏡頭嗎？

記憶卡容量

36 What is the capacity of the memory card?
記憶卡的容量是多少？

修理相機

37 Something is wrong with my camera.
我的相機有點問題。

38 I can't release the shutter.
快門按不下去。

39 How much do I have to pay for the repair?
修理這個要多少錢？

touchscreen 觸控式螢幕

相機術語 Camera Terms

release the shutter
釋放快門

insert SD card 插入記憶卡

point-and-shoot camera; compact camera
全自動相機；傻瓜相機

single-lens reflex camera
(SLR camera) 單眼相機

waterproof camera
防水相機

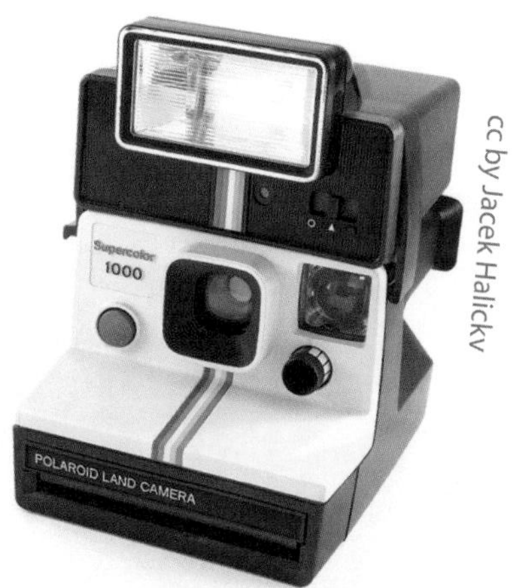

cc by Jacek Halickv

instant camera 拍立得相機

digital single-lens reflex camera
(DSLR camera) 數位單眼相機

zoom lens 變焦鏡頭

mirrorless interchangeable camera (MICL)
微單眼（無反光鏡可換鏡頭相機）

SLR-like camera 類單眼

At the Post Office

Chapter 21

在郵局

Key Terms

① **post office** 郵局

② **stamp** 郵票

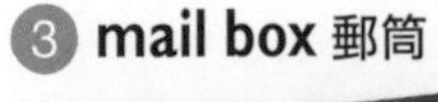

③ **mail box** 郵筒

④ **postcard** 明信片

181

5 **envelope** 信封

John Smith
123 Long Street
Radstock, FL 32178

6 **sender** 寄件人

8 **return address** 寄件地址

7 **postmark** 郵戳

Ellen Lin

9 **recipient** 收件人

7F.-3, No.88, Sec. 3, Hsin Sheng S. Rd.,
Da'an Dist., Taipei City 106, Taiwan,
R.O.C

10 **mailing address** 收件地址

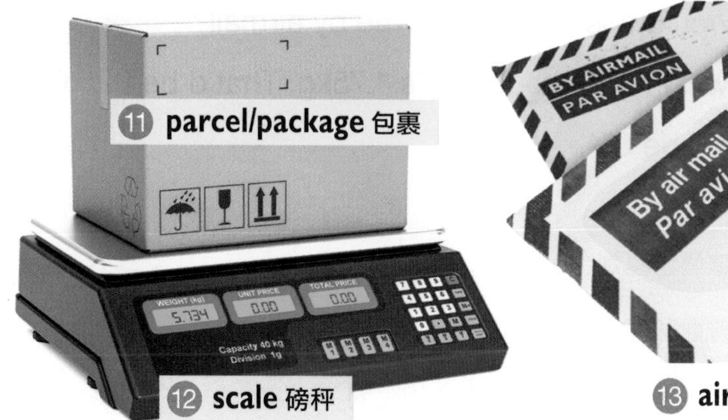

11 **parcel/package** 包裹

12 **scale** 磅秤

13 **airmail** 航空郵件

14 **surface mail** 普通郵件
15 **express mail** 快遞
16 **registered mail** 掛號
17 **special delivery** 限時專送
18 **postage** 郵資
19 **commemorative stamp** 紀念郵票
20 **overweight** 超重的
21 **fragile** 易碎的
22 **insurance** 保險
23 **printed matter** 印刷品

PART 2

Conversations

01 Sending a Parcel to Taiwan From Britain 從英國寄包裏到台灣 182

T *Tim* 提姆　P *Post Officer* 郵局人員

T Good morning, I want to send this parcel to Taiwan.

P Airmail or surface mail?

T How long would surface mail take, compared with airmail?

P Oh, anything up to 2 or 3 months for surface mail. It depends on the sailing of the ships. Airmail would only take 1 to 2 weeks.

T How much would this parcel cost me by airmail?

P Just let me weigh it for you. That's 1.75kg. That'd be £20.6.

T Thanks. That'll be OK.

T 早安，我想寄這個包裹到台灣。

P 航空郵件還是普通郵件？

T 和航空郵件相比，普通郵件需要花多久的時間？

P 嗯，普通郵件需要兩到三個月，視船的航行情況而定。航空郵件只要花一到兩星期。

T 這個包裹的航空郵費是多少？

P 我來幫你秤一下重量，1.75公斤，這樣是20.6英鎊。

T 謝謝，沒問題。

01 Buying Postal Products and Sending Mail
購買郵政產品與寄信 183

尋找郵票販售窗口

1 Ⓐ Excuse me. Where can I buy stamps?
不好意思，請問我要在哪裡買郵票？

Ⓐ At which window do they sell stamps?
哪一個窗口有賣郵票？

Ⓑ Third on the right is the counter.
右邊第三個櫃檯就是。

購買郵票

2 Ⓐ What kind of stamp do you need?
您要什麼郵票？

Ⓑ Please give me nine five-cent stamps.
請給我九張五分的郵票。

3 Here's three dollars and fifty cents in stamps.
這些郵票一共是美金三元五角。

4 I'd like to have some commemorative stamps.
我想買幾張紀念郵票。

買信封

5 Do you sell envelopes here?
這裡有賣信封嗎？

買明信片

6 Ⓐ I'd like to buy some postcards.
我想買幾張明信片。

Ⓑ How many postcards do you want?
您要幾張明信片？

尋找寄包裹櫃檯

7 Where's the parcel post counter, please?
寄包裹的櫃檯在哪裡？

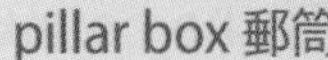
pillar box 郵筒

post box 郵箱

寄包裹

8 I'd like to mail this package to Taiwan.
我想寄這個包裹到台灣。

9 What's the size and weight limit for mailing a package?
郵寄包裹的大小和限重是多少？

郵件秤重

10 Would you please weigh this letter for me?
請幫我秤一下這封信好嗎？

11 Put the parcel on the scale, please.
請把包裹放在秤上。

郵件限重

12 Ⓐ What's the maximum weight allowed?
最高限重是多少？

Ⓑ The limit is 15 pounds per package.
每包限重15磅。

郵件超重

13 Your letter is 10 grams overweight.
您的信超重10公克。

14 You'll have to pay 30 cents extra because it's overweight.
您必須另外付30分的超重費。

letter box 信箱

Post-Office Box; PO Box;
Postal Box 郵政信箱

Postman;
mailman 郵差

貴重物品

15 Does the letter have anything valuable in it?
信裡面有貴重物品嗎？

是否有易碎品

16 Are the contents fragile?
裡面有易碎品嗎？

郵件寄出時間

17 Ⓐ Will I be able to catch the last mail pick-up today?
請問我來得及寄今天的末班郵件嗎？

Ⓑ I'm afraid the last mail has been dispatched.
最後一批郵件恐怕已經發出了。

若有從國外寄明信片或包裹回台灣的需要，建議在出國前，先到中華郵政的網站（http://www.post.gov.tw）查詢自己家裡的英文地址。如果忘了查，也不知道該怎麼寫，可以用中文寫地址，最後再加上 Taiwan, R.O.C.。

02 Choosing Mailing Service Options 選擇郵寄方式 184

郵寄方式

18 How do you want to send it? 您想怎麼寄？

19 By regular mail? 寄普通郵件？

20 Do you wish to send it by airmail? 您要寄航空郵件嗎？

郵寄地址

21 Where would you like to send it? 您要寄到哪裡？

22 Be sure to put down the address of the receiver clearly.
務必把收信人地址寫清楚。

限時專送

23 I want to send this letter special delivery.
這封信我想寄限時專送。

航空郵件

24 I want to send this by registered airmail.
這封信要寄航空掛號。

25 It's much better to use airmail. Sea mail takes too much time. 最好寄航空郵件，海運太慢了。

掛號

26 A Please register this letter. I'd like a receipt.
這封信請寄掛號，我要收據。

B You'll have to take your letter to the registered mail section which is the next window.
您必須把信拿到隔壁的掛號信窗口辦理。

詢問郵遞時間

27 A How long does it take by regular mail?
普通郵件要多久時間？

B It may take about a week at the most.
最久可能要一星期。

28 It usually takes about 7 days by airmail.
航空郵件通常要七天。

最快寄達的方式

29 Ⓐ What's the fastest way to send this package?
寄這個包裹最快的方式是什麼？

Ⓑ Airmail special is the fastest way, but it's expensive.
航空快遞最快，不過很貴。

保險

30 Do you want it insured? 您的郵件要保險嗎？

31 You should insure your packages against loss and damage. 您的包裹應該要保險，以免遺失損壞。

32 Ⓐ What are the insurance rates? 保險費率是多少？

Ⓑ That all depends on the value. 那得視價值而定。

Ⓑ The insurance is 50 cents. 保險費50分。

詢問郵資

33 Ⓐ How much do I need for these letters?
寄這些信要多少錢？

Ⓑ That comes to 15 dollars, please. 一共是15元。

34 You should buy a 20-cent stamp.
您應該買一張20分的郵票。

印刷品

35 Can I send these books as printed matter?
這些書我可以用印刷品寄嗎？

36 It's printed matter. 這是印刷品。

37 The rate for printed matter is cheaper.
印刷品的郵資比較便宜。

Making
Telephone Calls

Chapter 22

打電話

PART 1

Key Terms

1 **pay/public phone** 公共電話

2 **telephone booth** 電話亭

3 **coin** 硬幣

4 **phone card** 電話卡

5 **dial** 撥號

6 **dial tone** 撥號音

7 **operator** 接線生

⑧ **push-button landline telephone**
按鍵式有線電話

⑨ **cordless phone** 無線電話

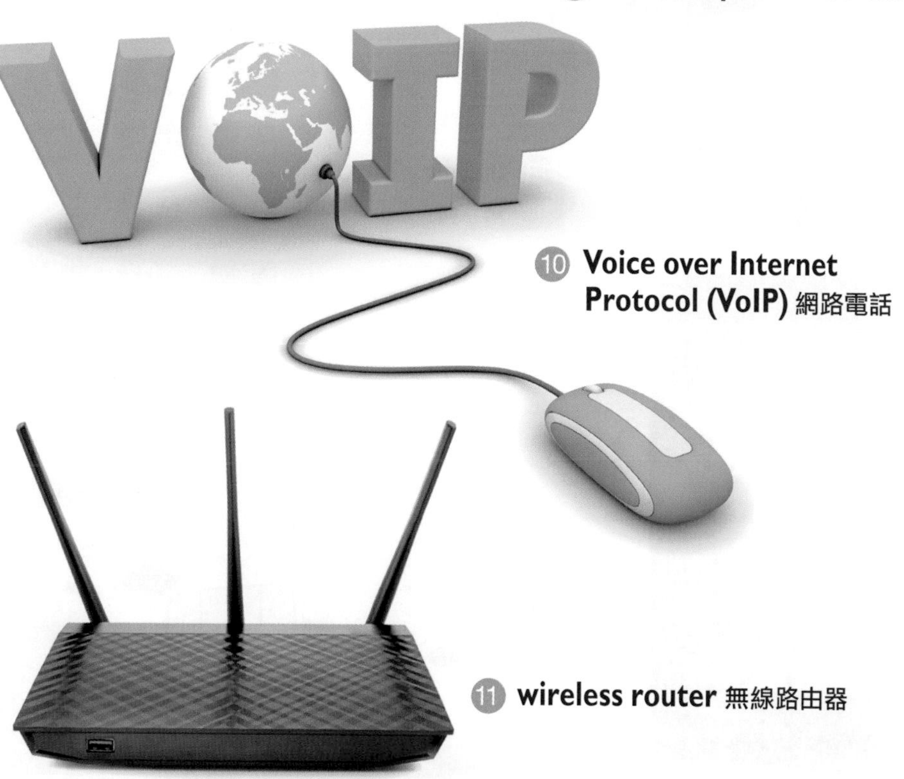

⑩ **Voice over Internet Protocol (VoIP)** 網路電話

⑪ **wireless router** 無線路由器

⑫ **handset** 電話聽筒

⑭ **display screen** 畫面顯示

⑬ **dial pad** 按鍵鍵盤

⑮ **redial key** 重撥鍵

⑯ **hold key** 保留鍵

⑰ **volume keys** 音量調整鍵

⑱ **star key/button** 米字鍵

⑲ **pound key/button** 井字鍵

⑳ **cellphone** 手機

㉑ **SIM card (subscriber identification module card)** SIM 卡

22 **power bank / portable battery charger**
行動電源

23 **portable Wi-Fi router / pocket Wi-Fi** 隨身 Wi-Fi 路由器

24 **AC adaptor** 電源供應器／變壓器

25 **adaptor plug** 轉接頭

26 **phone charger / charge and sync cable** 充電線

27 **telecommunications company**
電信公司

28 **beep** 嘟聲

29 **leave a message** 留言

30 **put A through B** 將 A 轉接給 B

31 **be put on hold**
保持通話，等待轉接

32 **answering machine**
電話答錄機

33 **voicemail** 語音信箱

34 **extension** 分機

35 **hang up** 掛斷（電話）

36 **area code** 區域電話號碼；區碼

37 **toll-free number** 免付費電話號碼

01 Making a Collect Call 打對方付費電話 189

T *Tim* 提姆 O *Operator* 接線生

T Overseas operator? I would like to make a collect call to Taipei, Taiwan, please.

O Your name, please?

T Tim Chen.

O What's the number, please?

T The area code is 2, and the number is 2367-9960.

O The line is connected. Please go ahead.

T 接線生嗎？我想打一通對方付費電話回台灣台北。

O 貴姓大名？

T 提姆・陳。

O 電話號碼是？

T 區碼是2，電話號碼是2367-9960。

O 已經接通了，請說。

從國外打電話回台灣的方法

❶ 打市內電話

所在國之國際冠碼＋
台灣國碼 886＋
區域號碼（去掉 0）＋
市內電話號碼

【例】從美國打回台北
001 + 886 + 2 + 2821345

02 Finding a Pay Phone 尋找公共電話 190

S *Sandy* 珊蒂 T *Tommy* 湯米

S Excuse me. Do you know where I can find a pay phone?

T There is one around the corner.

S Can I make an international call from that pay phone?

T Yes, but you have to get a phone card first.

S Where can I get a phone card?

T You can get one in the grocery store over there.

S Oh, I see it. Thank you.

S 不好意思，請問哪裡有公共電話？

T 轉角就有一個。

S 那個公共電話可以打國際電話嗎？

T 可以，不過妳要先買電話卡。

S 電話卡要去哪裡買？

T 那邊那家雜貨店有賣。

S 喔，我看到了，謝謝你！

❷ 打手機

所在國之國際冠碼 +
台灣國碼 886 +
手機號碼
（去掉最前面的 0）

【例】從美國打回台北
001 + 886 + 922835616

Useful Expressions

01 Looking for a Pay Phone and Making a Call 尋找公共電話與打電話 191

買電話卡

1 Where can I get a phone card? 請問哪裡有賣電話卡？

2 I would like an international phone card, please. 我要買一張國際電話卡。

電話卡費率

3 Which card has the cheapest rate to Taiwan? 哪一種電話卡打去台灣費率最低？

4 What is the rate? 請問打電話如何計費？

換零錢

5 May I get some change? I need to make a phone call. 我可以跟你換零錢嗎？我想打電話。

詢問國際冠碼

6 What is the international code here? 請問這裡的國際冠碼是多少？

尋找公共電話

7 Where is a pay phone? 請問哪裡有公共電話？

8 Where can I find a pay phone near here? 這附近哪裡有公共電話？

問公共電話的用法

9 Excuse me. Can you tell me how to use the phone? 不好意思，請問這個電話要怎麼用？

能否打國際電話

10 Can I make an international call from this public phone? 這部公共電話可以打國際電話嗎？

該投多少錢

11 How much should I put in? 我該投多少錢？

12 Which coin can I use? 我該投哪一種硬幣？

請接線生轉接

13 I want to make an overseas call to Taiwan. The number is 2367-9960. 我要打一通越洋電話回台灣，號碼是2367-9960。

02 Telephone Phrases 電話用語 

打電話給國外友人	14 A May I speak to Debbie, please? 請問黛比在嗎? B Speaking. 我就是。
詢問來電者身分	15 A May I ask who is calling, please? 請問您是哪位?
表明自己的身分	B This is Peggy from Classic Books. 我是古典出版社的佩琪。 B It's James here. 我是詹姆斯。
請稍候	16 Just a moment, please. 請稍等。 17 Hold on. 稍等。 18 Hang on. 稍等。
要找的人不在	19 I am afraid he is not in right now. 很抱歉,他現在不在。 20 He's just gone out. Would you like to call him back later? 他剛出去。你可不可以待會再打來?
留言	21 Would you like to leave a message? 你要留言嗎? 22 May I leave a message? 我可以留話嗎?
詢問何時可聯絡到對方	23 Will he be in the office tomorrow morning? 他明天上午會在辦公室嗎? 24 What time could I reach him? 我什麼時候才可以聯絡上他呢?
打對方手機	25 I'll try and get him on his cellphone. 我會用手機和他聯絡看看。
打錯電話	26 I must have the wrong number, sorry for bothering you. 我一定是打錯電話了,對不起打擾您了。 27 I'm afraid you've got the wrong number. 你可能打錯了。
確認電話號碼	28 Could I check the number? Isn't it 6548-4290? 我可以確定一下號碼嗎?這裡是6548-4290嗎?

At the Hospital

Chapter

23

在醫院或藥房

PART 1

Key Terms

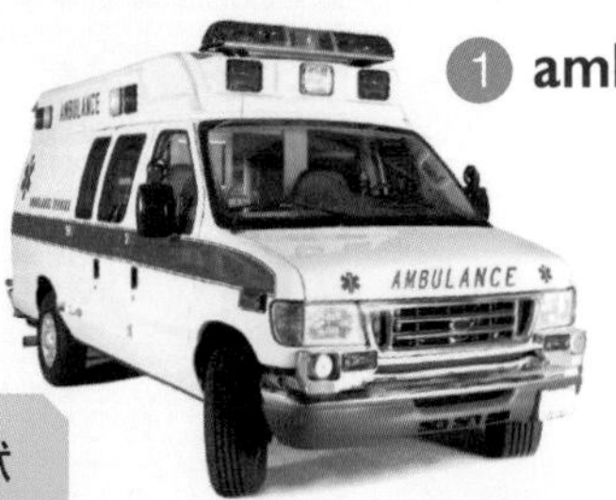

1 **ambulance** 救護車

2 **doctor** 醫生

3 **symptom** 症狀

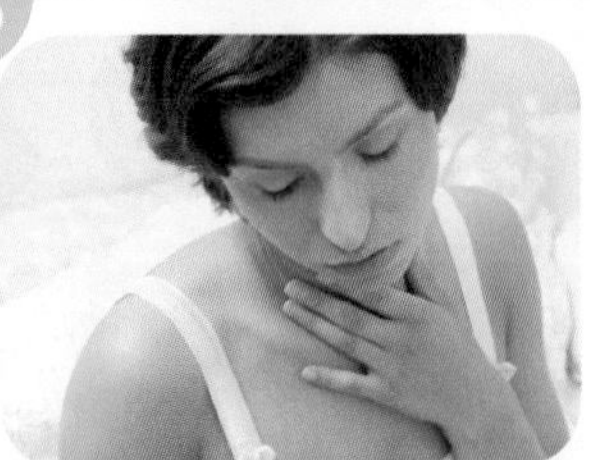

4 **sore throat** 喉嚨痛

5 **cough** 咳嗽

6 **runny nose** 流鼻水

7 **sneeze** 打噴嚏

8 **stuffy nose** 鼻塞

9 **dizzy** 頭暈

10 **vomit / throw up** 嘔吐

11 **headache** 頭痛

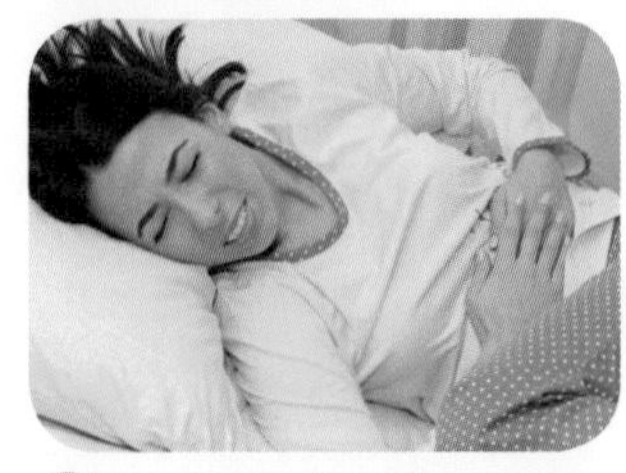

12 **stomachache** 胃痛

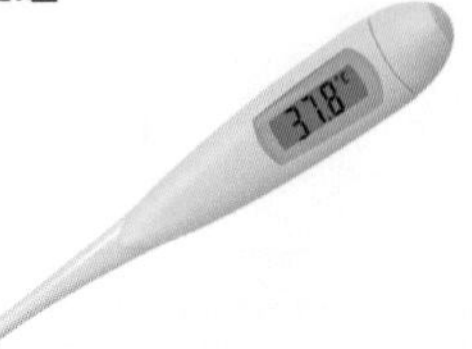

13 **fever** 發燒

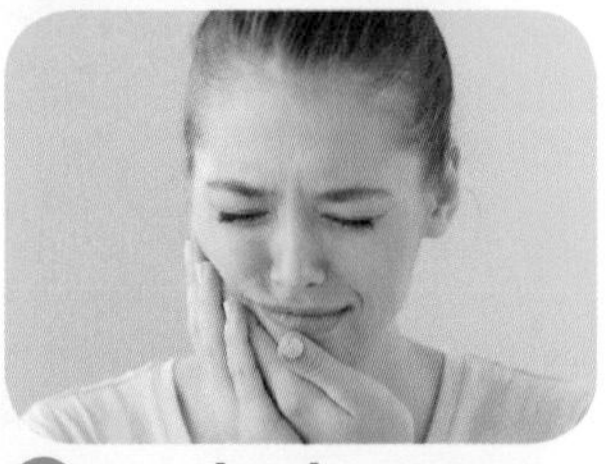

14 **toothache** 牙齒痛

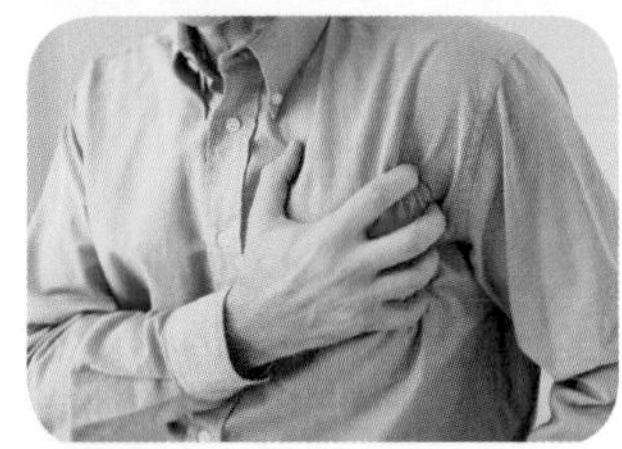

15 **heart attack** 心臟病發作

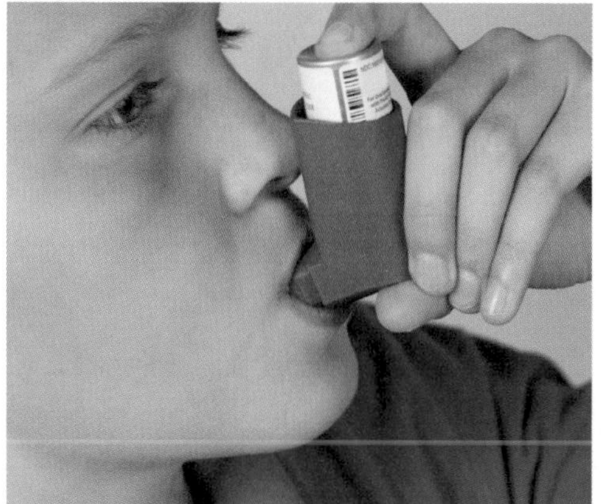

⑯ **asthma** 氣喘

⑰ **sprain** 扭傷

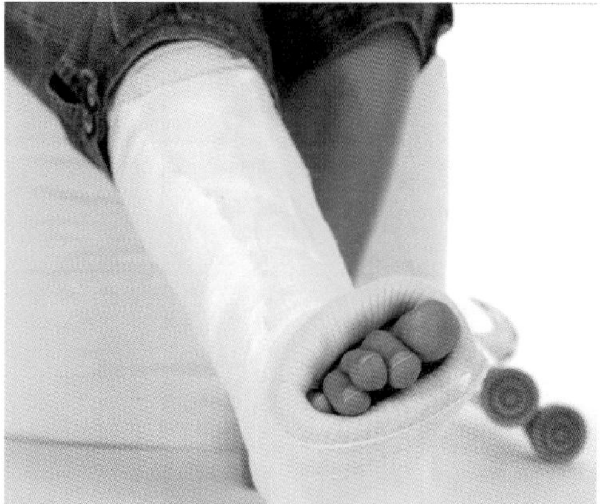

⑱ **fracture** 骨折

⑲ **allergy** 過敏

⑳ **food poisoning** 食物中毒

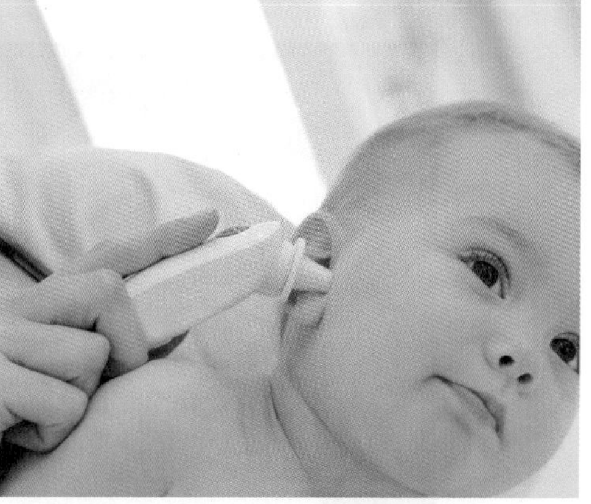

㉑ **take someone's temperature** 量體溫

195

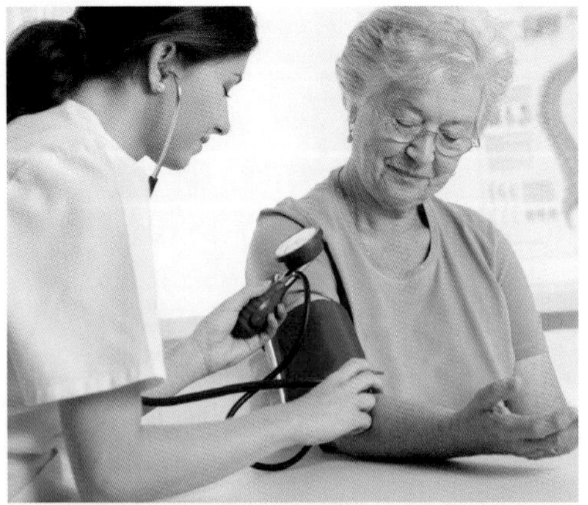

㉒ **take someone's blood pressure** 量血壓

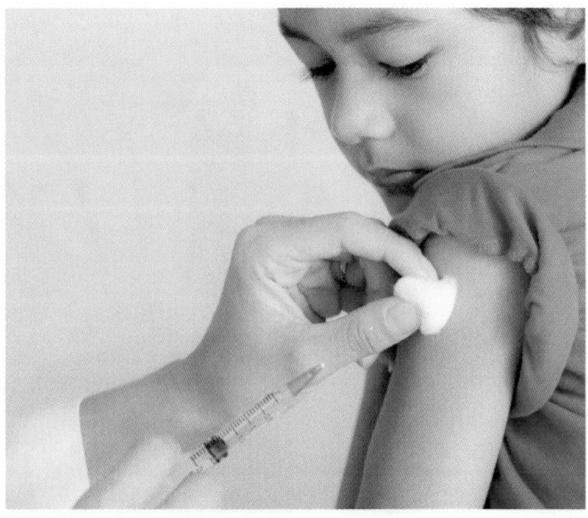

㉓ **injection** 打針

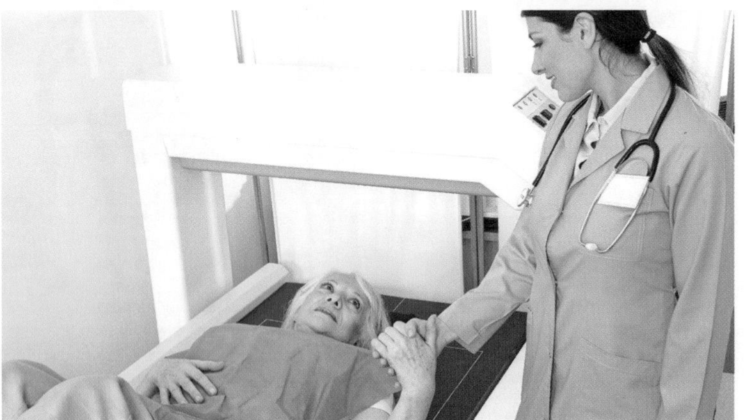

㉔ **check-up** 檢查

㉕ **prescription** 處方箋

㉖ **pharmacy / drug store** 藥局

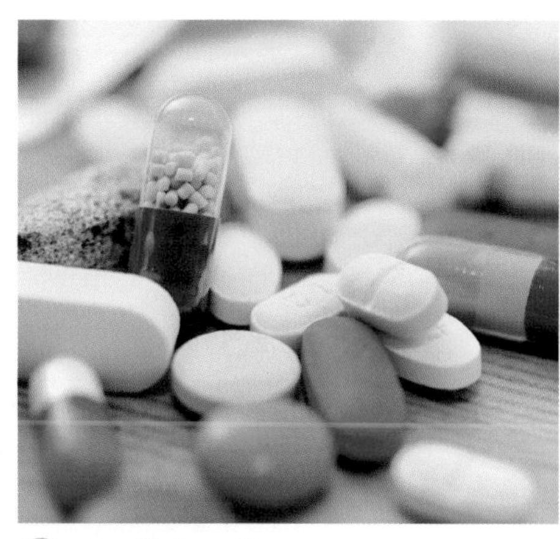

㉗ **medicine** 藥

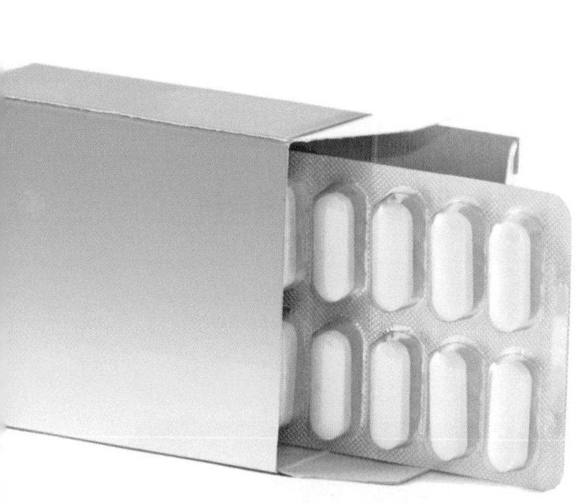

㉘ **painkiller** 止痛藥

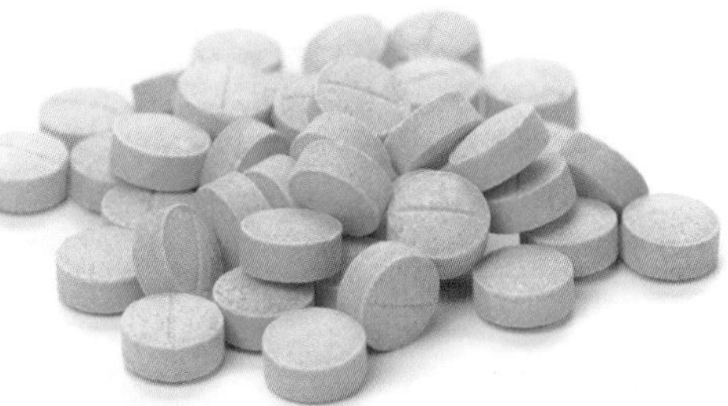

㉙ **pill/tablet** 藥丸

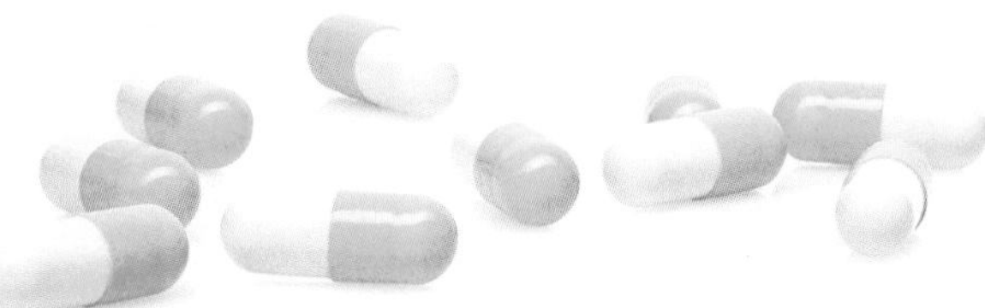

㉚ **capsule** 膠囊

31 **powder** 藥粉

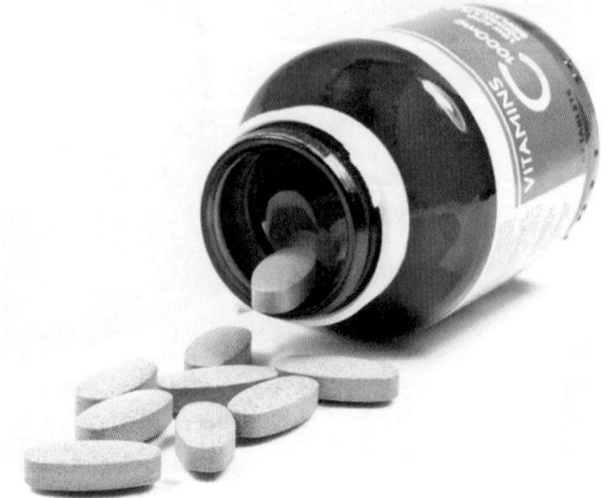

32 **vitamin** 維他命

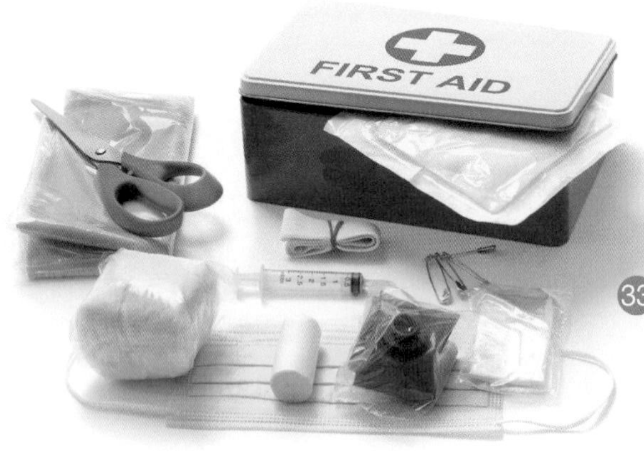

33 **first-aid kit** 急救箱

34 **cotton swab / Q-tip** 棉花棒

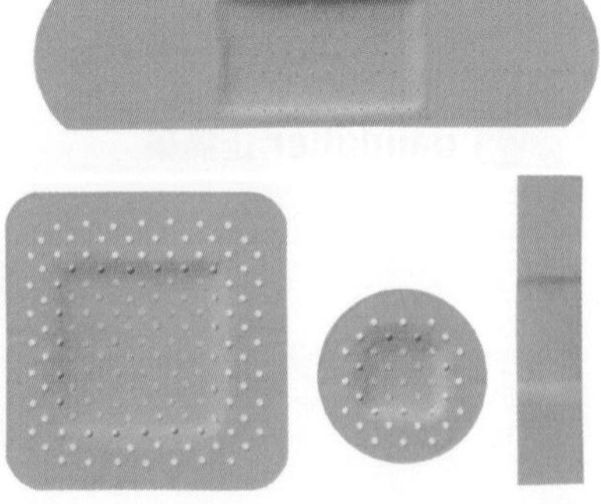

35 **Band-Aid** OK 繃（英文採用商標名稱）

198

36 **bandage** 繃帶

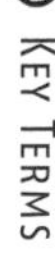

37 **gauze** 紗布

38 **eye drops** 眼藥水

39 **make an appointment** 預約門診

40 **flu** 流行性感冒

41 **cold** 感冒

42 **jet lag** 時差反應

43 **ache** 疼痛

44 **bruise** 瘀傷；擦傷

45 **cramp** 抽筋；痙攣

46 **hiccup/burp** 打嗝

47 **fart** 放屁

48 **cavity**（牙齒）蛀洞

49 **diarrhea** 拉肚子

50 **constipation** 便秘

51 **high blood pressure** 高血壓

52 **faint** 昏倒

53 **diabetes** 糖尿病

54 **insulin** 胰島素

01 I've Got a . . . 我患了…… 199

P *Peggy* 佩琪　D *Doctor* 醫生

P I've got a headache and a sore throat.

D How long have you had it?

P It all started the day before yesterday.

D I think you've got the flu. There's a lot of it about.

P What should I do?

D Take some medicine and stay in bed for a day or two.

P 我頭痛，還有喉嚨痛。

D 症狀持續多久了？

P 前天開始的。

D 我想妳是得了流行性感冒，最近正在流行。

P 那該怎麼辦？

D 吃些藥，躺著休息一兩天。

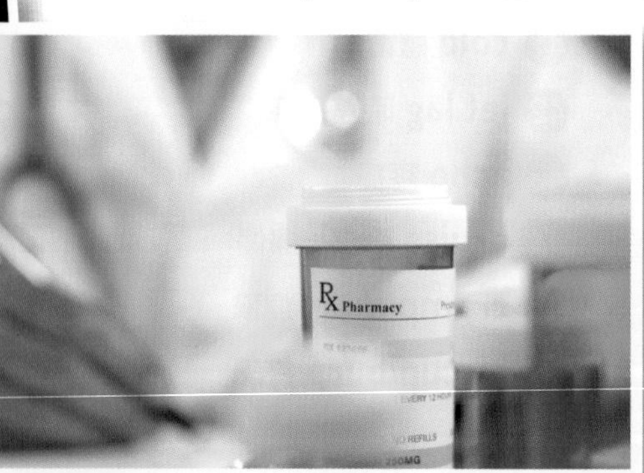

Doctor with RX prescription 醫生寫處方箋

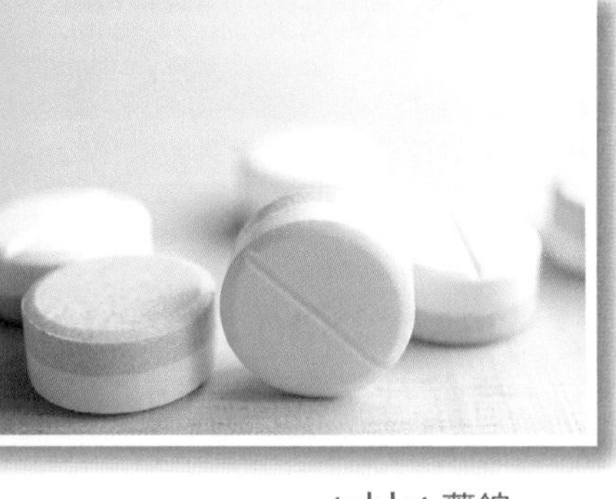

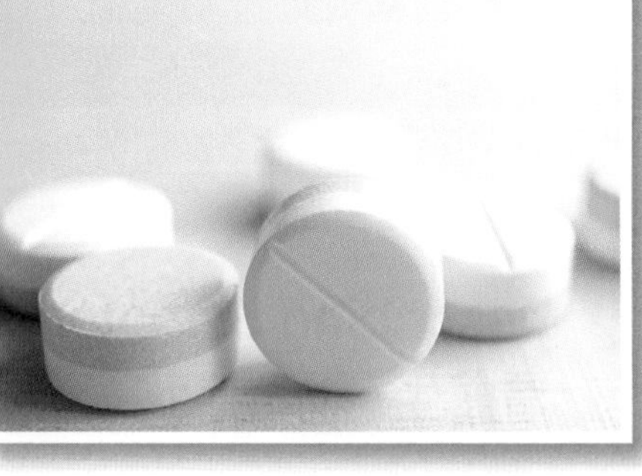

tablet 藥錠

02 At a Drugstore 到藥房買藥

V *Vincent* 文森 P *Pharmacist* 藥師

V Have you got anything for diarrhea?

P Yes, here you are. These tablets are very effective.

V How should I take this medicine?

P Take two tablets every six hours.

V I see. I'll follow your instructions.

P And take a good rest for a few days.

V Thank you.

V 你們有止瀉藥嗎？

P 有，這裡。這種藥還滿有效的。

V 這藥該怎麼吃？

P 每六小時吃兩顆。

V 我知道了，我會照指示吃。

P 記得好好休息。

V 謝謝。

Rx [ˋarˋɛks]

指醫生開的處方箋，原符號見下圖，出自拉丁字 recipe 的縮寫。

PART 3

Useful Expressions

01 Describing Symptoms to the Doctor
看醫生（說明症狀）201

詢問症狀	1 What's the trouble? 什麼地方不舒服？ 2 What seems to be the problem? 你覺得哪裡不舒服？ 3 Do you have any symptoms? 有什麼症狀嗎？ 4 Any other symptoms? 還有其他症狀嗎？
發燒	5 I have a fever. 我發高燒。 6 I'm running a temperature. 我正在發燒。 7 The fever won't go away. 發燒不退。
頭痛	8 I have a terrible headache. 我的頭很痛。
頭暈	9 I keep feeling dizzy. 我一直覺得頭暈。
感冒	10 I think I have a cold. 我好像感冒了。
喉嚨痛	11 I have a sore throat. 我喉嚨痛。
咳嗽	12 I keep coughing. 我一直咳嗽。
鼻塞	13 My nose is stuffy. 我鼻塞。
流鼻水	14 I have a runny nose. 我流鼻水。

嘔吐	15 I feel like throwing up. 我想吐。 16 What I eat won't stay down. 我一吃就會吐。
胃痛	17 I have a stomachache. 我胃痛。
拉肚子	18 I have diarrhea. 我拉肚子了。
便秘	19 I have constipation. 我便秘了。
氣喘	20 I have asthma. 我會氣喘。
食物過敏	21 I have a food allergy. 我食物過敏了。
症狀何時開始	22 A How long have you had it? 你這個症狀多久了？ A When did the symptoms start? 症狀什麼時候開始的？ B It all started yesterday. 昨天開始的。

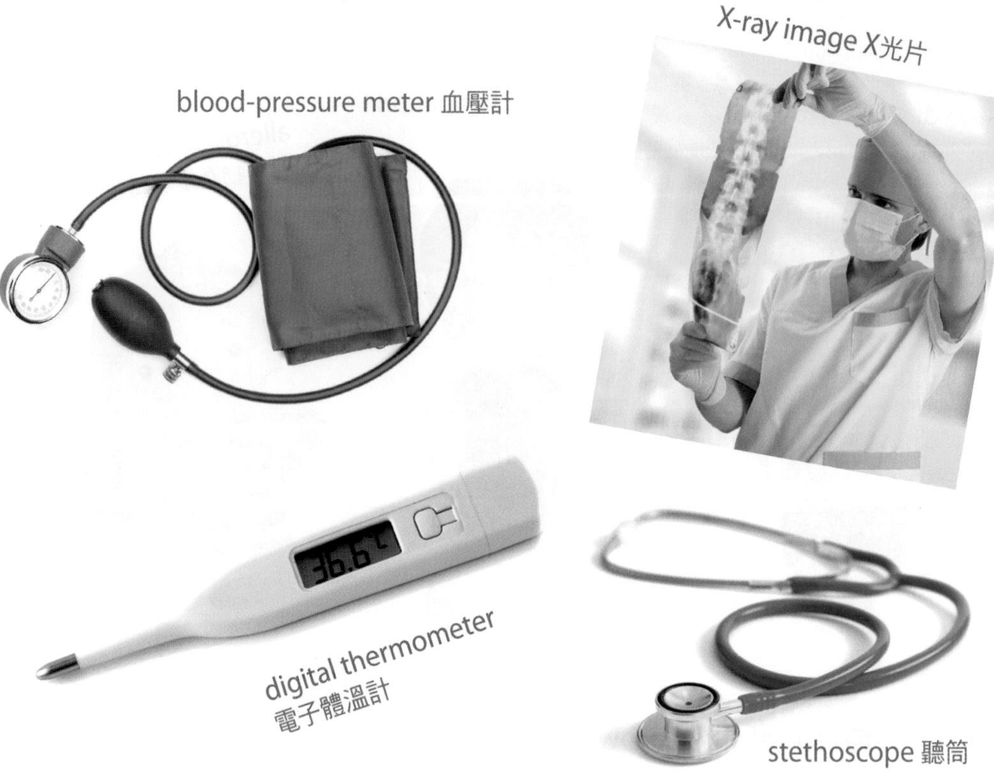

症狀持續多久

23 I've been sick for ten days. 我已經病了十天了。

24 I've had a bad headache for three days.
我的頭已經痛了三天。

流行感冒

25 Colds are going around these days. 最近感冒正在流行。

26 The flu is going around. Do you have a fever and nausea, too? 感冒正在流行。你有發燒及噁心的症狀嗎？

02 Given a Diagnosis and Prescription from the Doctor 醫生檢查及開藥 202

看舌頭

27 Now show me your tongue and say "Ah."
讓我看看你的舌頭，說「啊」。

量脈搏

28 Let me feel your pulse. 我來量一下你的脈搏。

量血壓

29 The nurse will take your blood pressure.
護士會幫你量血壓。

量體溫

30 I need to take your temperature. 我幫你量個體溫。

身體檢查

31 Lie down and I'll give you a thorough examination.
躺下來，我幫你做全身檢查。

照X光

32 You'd better take an X-ray and find out what's wrong.
你最好照張X光片，看看是哪裡有問題。

驗血

33 You'll take a blood test. 你要去驗血。

打針

34 I'll give you an injection. 我會幫你打一針。

扭傷

35 A I have sprained my ankle. 我扭傷腳踝。

會不會痛

B Does it hurt? 會痛嗎？

會不會過敏

36 Do you have any allergies? 你會過敏嗎？

37 Are you allergic to any drugs?
你有沒有對什麼藥物過敏？

不嚴重

38 It's nothing serious. 不嚴重。

多休息

39 All you need is a few days in bed.
你需要的是臥床休息幾天。

醫生開處方

40 I'll give you a prescription. 我幫你開個處方。

41 Take this prescription to a pharmacy and buy some medicine. 拿這張處方箋到藥局買藥。

索取診斷書

42 Please write a medical report for my insurance company.
請幫我開一張診斷證明，我要申請保險用的。

03 At a Pharmacy 藥房買藥 203

拿處方箋到藥局

43 Can I get my prescription filled here?
我可以在這裡拿處方箋上的藥嗎？

沒有處方箋

44 Can I get the medicine without a prescription?
沒有處方箋可以買藥嗎？

買止痛藥	45 I would like some painkillers. 我想買止痛藥。
買頭痛藥	46 Do you have anything for a headache? 有沒有頭痛藥？
買止瀉藥	47 Do you have anything for diarrhea? 有沒有止瀉藥？
買感冒藥	48 Can you give me something for a cold? 有沒有感冒藥？
買咳嗽藥	49 I'd like to have some cough medicine. 我想買咳嗽藥。
詢問藥物療效	50 What is this capsule for? 這顆膠囊是吃什麼的？
服藥方式 服藥時間	51 Ⓐ How should I take this medicine? 這種藥要怎麼吃？ Ⓐ When do I take this medicine? 這種藥是什麼時候吃？ Ⓑ Take two tablets after each meal. 每餐飯後兩顆。 Ⓑ Take one pill every six hours. 每六小時服一粒。 Ⓑ Take one tablet when you have pain. 覺得痛就吃一顆。
副作用	52 Are there any side effects? 有沒有副作用？
皮膚乾裂	53 Do you have anything for chapped skin? 有沒有擦皮膚乾裂的藥？
買OK繃	54 Do you have a Band-Aid? 你們有沒有賣OK繃？
買繃帶	55 I'd like some bandages. 我要買繃帶。
買急救箱	56 I want a small first-aid kit. 我要買一個小的急救箱。

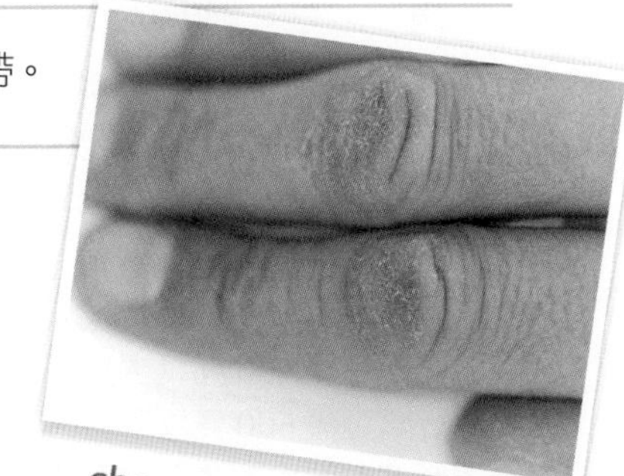
chapped skin 皮膚乾裂

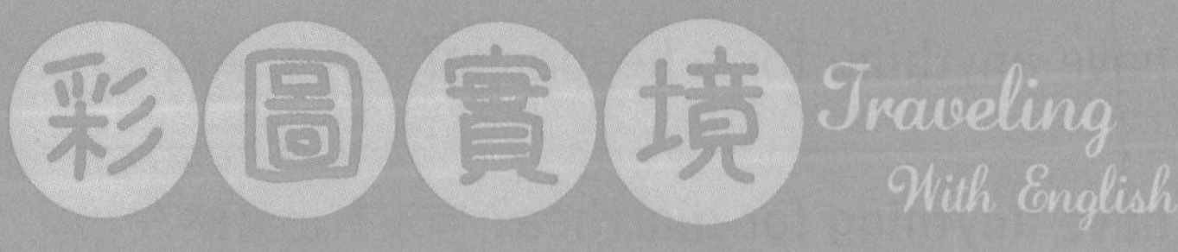

暢銷彩圖三版

熱銷兩萬本，
學校熱門指定用書

旅遊英語

P. Walsh ◎著

丁宥榆／賴祖兒◎譯

Helen Yeh ◎審訂

編　　輯　賴祖兒／丁宥榆
主　　編　丁宥暄
內文排版　劉秋筑
封面設計　林書玉
製程管理　洪巧玲
發 行 人　黃朝萍
出 版 者　寂天文化事業股份有限公司
電　　話　+886-(0)2-2365-9739
傳　　真　+886-(0)2-2365-9835
網　　址　www.icosmos.com.tw
讀者服務　onlineservice@icosmos.com.tw
出版日期　2021 年 9 月 三版三刷

郵撥帳號 1998620-0 寂天文化事業股份有限公司
劃撥金額 600 元（含）以上者，郵資免費。
訂購金額 600 元以下者，請外加郵資 65 元。
〔若有破損，請寄回更換，謝謝。〕

國家圖書館出版品預行編目 (CIP) 資料

彩圖實境旅遊英語 (寂天雲隨身聽 APP 版)= Traveling with English/ P. Walsh 著 . -- 三版 . -- [臺北市] : 寂天文化 , 2021.09 印刷
面；　公分
ISBN 978-626-300-019-3 (20K 平裝)
1. 英語 2. 旅遊 3. 會話
805.188　　110008444